BLOOD BATTLE

I managed to avoid another attack from a curved blade and turned just in time to see one of the vamps who'd held back come charging in. I raised my hand to fire, but the vamp I dodged came at me and hit the top of the gun with the hilt of his blade, knocking it from my hand.

I didn't have time to draw another weapon. I dropped low and swung my leg out, catching the vamp who'd knocked [illegible] s balance, [illegible] t out from [illegible] e vamp fe[illegible]

The o[illegible]

Rooki[illegible]

I braced myse[illegible] point would meet him or [illegible] eyes widened and he tried to twist [illegible] stead impaled himsel[illegible]

slid[illegible]

H[illegible]

Books by E.S. Moore

TO WALK THE NIGHT

TAINTED NIGHT, TAINTED BLOOD

BLESSED BY A DEMON'S MARK

Published by Kensington Publishing Corporation

Blessed by a Demon's Mark

E.S. MOORE

KENSINGTON PUBLISHING CORP.
http://www.kensingtonbooks.com

2/13
7⁹⁹

KENSINGTON BOOKS are published by

Kensington Publishing Corp.
119 West 40th Street
New York, NY 10018

All Kensington Titles, Imprints, and Distributed Lines are available at special quantity discounts for bulk purchases for sales promotions, premiums, fund-raising, and educational or institutional use.

Special book excerpts or customized printings can also be created to fit specific needs. For details, write or phone the office of the Kensington special sales manager: Kensington Publishing Corp., 119 West 40th Street, New York, NY 10018, attn: Special Sales Department, Phone: 1-800-221-2647.

ISBN-13: 978-0-7582-6874-7
ISBN-10: 0-7582-6874-2

First Mass Market Printing: January 2013

10 9 8 7 6 5 4 3 2 1

Printed in the United States of America

For my dad, Steve Moore. I'll miss you, always.

1

A shudder ran through me as I huddled on the bed. My fingers squeezed into the mattress in a vain attempt to stop my hands from shaking. My throat was dry, constricted. Every breath burned. Every attempt to swallow ended with me just about choking on my tongue. Every fiber of my being screamed at me to feed, to leap across the room and tear apart the two men sitting across from me.

"You're doing fine, Kat," Levi said. His voice was a calming balm to my screaming mind. "Just relax. Breathe in slowly and let it out nice and easy. It will be over soon, I promise."

I bared my fangs at him. Blood dripped down my chin from where they'd ripped through my gums. I was breathing fast, hard, still too wired to relax. I felt like a junkie who'd been denied her fix. It was all I could do to keep from breaking something.

Or someone.

I closed my eyes and swallowed, shutting out anything and everything I could. I could do this. This was the last night of the full moon and if I made it through the torture, I could relax for another month before it would start all over again.

My breathing slowed now that I wasn't looking at anyone. I could still feel them there, watching me, but since I couldn't see the pulse in their necks, see the warmth radiating off them, I was able to get myself under some semblance of control.

"Good," Levi urged. "You're doing great. Don't you think she's doing great, Ronnie?"

I refused to open my eyes but could almost feel the slight dip of Ronnie's head as he gave his assent. It was the only kind of response I ever saw him give.

An image of Ronnie sprung to mind. He was staring blankly at me, waiting, neck exposed. I could feel his slow, easy breath, could almost taste his skin between my teeth. All I'd have to do was bite down and my mouth would fill with the sweet nectar of life. His blood would revitalize me, would make me strong, powerful.

A growl rumbled in my chest. My eyes opened and settled on Ronnie where he sat, looking just like I'd seen him in my head. I started to slip from the bed. One foot hit the floor. It would be so easy to propel myself off the bed and end the pain. I fought hard against myself, but it was a losing battle. My other foot touched the floor.

"Easy," Levi said. "You've controlled yourself spectacularly. Don't ruin it now by giving in to your baser instincts. Fight it. You don't have to give in to the hunger. You can do this."

A soothing warmth spread over me as he spoke. I relaxed and slid back onto the bed, easing my back against the headboard. I needed its firmness for support. I focused on breathing nice and easy, letting all violent thoughts flow from me like Levi had taught me to do in our previous sessions. I licked my lips clean of blood and settled my gaze onto Levi's own.

He was smiling at me. He sat with his legs crossed as if he knew I wouldn't attack; not this time anyway. He hadn't been so confident a month ago. I took that as a sign I was making progress.

Ronnie was in the chair beside him, seemingly oblivious to everything that was going on in the room. He was central to my training, though he probably didn't know it. I sometimes wondered if anyone was really in there. To look into his eyes was to see emptiness.

We started my training almost as soon as I'd moved in a few months back. Levi had promised he could teach me to control my inner hunger, that even during the full moon when the Madness took over, I'd be able to keep from feeding, from killing.

The first month had been an utter disaster. The moment the moon had risen, I was up and off the bed, trying to tear at him. He'd been forced to lock me in the room. Even then, it took me a good hour before I calmed down. After that, I was okay as long as no one bothered me; but the moment anyone came near me, all I wanted to do was feed.

But a mere three months later, I was able to sit here, albeit with much difficulty, with two men in the room, without killing either. Despite the hunger, despite the desire to tear them both to shreds, I felt good about what I'd accomplished thus far.

"Good." Levi's grin widened.

All of the tension eased out of my shoulders and I managed a smile of my own. I could still feel the Madness wanting to take hold, but I was able to keep it at bay. I hadn't had blood in five nights and was still able to hold on, which was a miracle in itself.

I took a deep breath and let it out slowly. A faint thump upstairs reminded me that Eilene and Sienna were in the house. They didn't know exactly what went on in my room during these full moon nights, though I suspected they had an idea. What else could we possibly be doing?

Knowing they were there sometimes helped. Other

times, it made the hunger worse. Part of me wished Levi would make them leave the house so I wouldn't be tempted. Just because I was doing good now, didn't mean I'd be so lucky the next time.

I glanced toward the wall, wishing there was a window in the room so I could look out at the sky. While there was a light dusting of snow and the cloud cover would hide the moon, it did little to abate the onset of the Full Moon Madness. Even the thick walls couldn't stop its effect on me. I'm not sure if seeing it would hinder my progress or help.

I felt myself calming even more as the seconds ticked by. Levi had done a good job teaching me how to control my inner beast. He'd done far more than I'd ever managed to do on my own. He kept a supply of blood bags in the fridge to drink from when the urge to feed was too great. It had been months since I'd fed on an actual living person.

The blood bags didn't completely erase the hunger, but they eased it enough so I wasn't constantly thinking about feeding. They tasted like shit, but it was a small price to pay for being free of the need to feed and kill for survival.

"I think we should up the stakes a bit," Levi said, sitting forward. The chair creaked with the movement and my anxiety level went through the roof.

My hands balled into the sheet again. I was terrified at what he might be planning to do. I mean, what else could he do to me that he hadn't already done? There was only so much I could take. I'd hate myself if I ended up killing him because he pushed me too far.

Levi studied me as if waiting for some sign that I was ready. He didn't look scared. In fact, he looked so calm you would have thought he was relaxing in his own room with a cup of tea and a good book instead of sitting in a room with a half-starved vampire.

I sat there, tense, afraid to move; but after a few seconds of his steadfast gaze, I found myself relaxing. My hands unclenched and I sat back, doing my best to appear calm and collected, though I felt anything but calm inside.

"Good," he said with a nod. "That's very good. You can control it whenever you want. Before long you'll fit right in. The desire for blood will no longer control you. No one would know you to be anything but human."

He reached into his pocket and removed a small penknife. He opened it and turned it so the light would catch the blade. It looked extremely sharp.

I tensed, unsure what he planned on doing with the knife. If he came anywhere near me with it, he wouldn't just lose the blade, but his arm as well. I was okay as long as everyone was just sitting there. If he were to intentionally antagonize me, I had serious doubts I could control myself.

"There is just one more test I need to run." He turned the knife over slowly in his hand. "If you can make it through this . . ." He left the rest unsaid.

Levi's grip on the knife firmed and he reached out, causing me to jerk back. But it wasn't me he reached for.

He went for Ronnie.

The other man didn't even flinch as Levi took his arm. Nothing on his face gave any indication he knew what was happening or cared one way or the other what was being done to him. He was like a living puppet, only moving when his master pulled his strings.

"No," I said, pushing back hard against the headboard. I didn't want to see him hurt Ronnie, even to test me. I had an idea I knew what was coming, and I wasn't so sure I could keep from losing it. "Please."

Levi's eyes locked on mine. "This is a necessary step

to your recovery. I can't help you if you don't let me do this. You'll be fine."

Warmth flooded over me and I nodded. I sucked back the blood that was still dribbling from my gums, used it to temper the hunger raging inside of me.

My head felt cloudy, as if it were full of thick smoke. It made it hard to think clearly, made it hard to order my thoughts. I knew if I were to really think about it, I would never hurt Ronnie or Levi or the girls upstairs, but the Madness had a way of fogging my mind. All it would take is one moment of confusion and one of them would be dead.

But here in Levi's presence, I did better. Something about him allowed me to take control of my own brain, forced me to see through the cloud and understand that the moon didn't have complete control over me. Only I did. Once I realized that, the rest would be easy.

Levi studied me a moment more before pressing the knife into Ronnie's palm.

Blood immediately welled in the wound, filling his hand. It pattered on the thin plastic sheeting Levi had spread on the floor before we started.

My throat closed up as soon as the smell of blood hit me. I couldn't look away from it even though I knew I would have to soon or I wouldn't be able to stop myself from flying off the bed. The urge was too powerful. There was no way I was going to be able to control my hunger.

Levi tipped Ronnie's hand so the blood pooling in his palm dripped onto the plastic. Each drop sounded like a gong to my ears as it hit the floor.

I started panting. My every muscle tensed as if I was going to spring, but yet I stayed put. I could almost taste the blood, could almost feel it on my tongue. The scent was overpowering; it filled my senses until it was the only thing I knew.

And still, I held back. As much as I wanted to feed, I

knew I couldn't. I could hold on; I could wait it out. Levi would eventually leave me alone in the room and I could relax. I just needed to hold on for a few minutes more and it would all be over.

I forced my gaze from Ronnie's bloody palm. His arm was littered with tiny scars, as if this wasn't the first time this had happened. It was easy to imagine him sitting there, letting Levi cut him night after night, just so the bigger man could save someone just like me.

My hands dug into the mattress so hard it was a wonder my fingers didn't pop through. I forced myself to ease my grip even though I was half afraid to do so would be to ease the tentative grip I had on my control. Each finger unclenched slowly, the ligaments and joints popping as I straightened them. It hurt like hell.

"Get him the fuck out of here," I growled. I was shaking violently now. As much as I wanted to keep control of my hunger, it just wasn't happening. I was trying hard to breathe through my nose because I could taste the blood on my tongue every time I opened my mouth.

I felt myself moving forward and stopped just before I leaped from the bed. Ronnie was too close. I could be on him in half a second, could have my mouth on his hand, teeth tearing at the flesh, long before Levi could even think to pull him away. I could suck on the wound until the flow slowed and then finally stopped. It wouldn't kill him.

Not right away anyway. If I were to move my mouth a mere two to three inches up to his wrist, I could feed until completely sated.

I think the fear of not being able to stop was what kept me in place when Levi shook his head. If I moved, I would kill Ronnie, maybe Levi as well. Nothing could stop me. They were unarmed, aside from Levi's tiny knife. I could kill them both before the girls upstairs heard the first scream.

A sudden wash of warmth flowed over me and I blinked, head suddenly clear. I was sitting on the very edge of the bed, almost all the way onto the floor. I hadn't even realized I'd been moving until that very moment.

I scooted back, dropping my head so I wouldn't have to look at the two men, at the blood still dripping onto the plastic. Even though I knew Levi was trying to help, part of me wanted to kill him for torturing me like this.

"I think we can call our little test a success," Levi said. The self-satisfaction was clear in his voice, as if *he* had been the one to have overcome the Madness and hunger. "You don't have complete control yet, but I'm sure you will soon enough."

I growled, letting him know how unlikely I thought that prospect to be.

Levi chuckled as he stood. "We'll leave you be. You've had a rough night and deserve a little respite from what I've put you through. I completely understand if you hate me." He winked. "And I'll be sure to lock the door for your peace of mind."

A simple door and lock wouldn't stop me if I really wanted to get out, but he was right, the idea of a locked door between me and the Purebloods did make me feel better.

"You did good," Levi said. "Tomorrow night we'll have dinner and toast your success."

My stomach clenched as Ronnie stood at a motion from Levi. His blood pumped just a little faster, making another small drop ooze from his palm. It was all I could do to keep from reaching out and grabbing his hand just so I could have a taste.

Levi opened the door and held it out for Ronnie, who walked past him without a word. Levi hesitated a moment, like he was going to say something else, but instead, he turned and walked out, closing the door behind him.

I waited until the lock clicked before leaping from the bed onto the plastic. My fingers tore into it as I pulled it up to my face. I lapped at the blood, sucked at the plastic to get every single drop.

I wanted more. The tiny amount of blood that had spilled from Ronnie's palm was far from enough to sate my hunger. A big part of me wanted to give in to the beast, to break through the door and find someone to feed upon. I could drain them, could keep the hunger at bay for a week more. I could end the pain.

I rose from the floor, blood on my chin, and started stalking around the room. I felt like a caged animal despite the fact I knew I could break free anytime I wanted. I was making strange growling sounds deep in my chest as I breathed in and out, like a beast that knew its food was sitting just out of reach.

I bit my lip, drawing blood. I refused to give in. I dug my fingers into my temples, closed my eyes, and tried to push away all thoughts of blood and food. I kept seeing the blood dripping from Ronnie's hand and was forced to open my eyes lest it took hold of my mind for good.

Another growl bubbled up from somewhere deep inside, but somehow my head cleared just a little bit. I might still be in near full-fledged bloodlust, but at least now I was able to think through it.

I sat heavily on the bed. The sun would be up soon, dampening the effects of the full moon, and from there, everything would be easy. I knew my control was shot because of the Madness. A few more hours and I'd be in full control of myself once more.

The urge to feed started to subside and I slumped down onto the bed. A tear fell from the corner of my eye. I wiped it angrily away.

Why was he doing this to me? Deep down I knew Levi was trying to help, but it was hard to see it through the hunger and fog in my head. It felt less like he was helping and more like he was torturing me for his own amusement.

And that's exactly what it was: torture. I'd seen vampire Counts do the same thing to their prisoners. They'd tempt them with blood kept just out of their reach until it drove them insane.

I found myself standing and heading toward the door. I didn't need Ronnie's blood or anyone else's as long as I got Levi's. He deserved to be punished for what he was doing to me. The bigger man would fill me up so much more than the smaller Ronnie or either of the girls upstairs.

The thought of Eilene and Sienna brought some sense back and I backed away from the door. My legs bumped against the edge of the bed and I sat down hard. I took a deep breath, let it out through my teeth, and found a smile spreading across my lips.

I'd done it. I'd controlled my hunger, controlled the Madness.

My fangs retracted; my head cleared a little more. I wiped away the last of the blood that had fallen from my gums and managed not to lick my hand clean.

I was doing better. I'd made it. I could defeat this thing, could do exactly what Levi said I could do.

I started to laugh, to exalt in my success, but that was when the pain hit.

It came from directly behind my left ear. It seared into my brain and I screamed. I clutched at my head like it might explode, and right then, it sure as hell felt like it was going to.

I fell back and immediately rolled off the bed. I hit the floor with a thump, and another jolt of pure agony caused me to scream again. My feet kicked out so hard I knocked over the chair Levi had been sitting in. It slammed against the wall with a crash, punching a small hole into the plaster.

My fangs were out again, but instead of hunger, all I could feel was the pain. It shot through me again, bowed my back off the floor. My eyeballs felt like they were about to pop from my skull from the building pressure.

The pain came again; this time it was so bad I couldn't even scream. My breath cut off and everything went black for an instant before my vision cleared. I gagged as my stomach heaved and the remnants of my last meal came shooting out of my mouth, drenching me in my own vomit.

I shuddered uncontrollably on the floor, gagging and spitting. The pain sliced through my head once more, but this time I barely felt it. A steady stream of drool fell from my lips onto the plastic, pooling beneath my face.

And then it was over.

Just like that, the pain stopped. I threw up again, but this time little more than bile came up.

I scooted across the floor until my back bumped up against the bed. I brought both my legs up and curled into a little ball, terrified the pain would come again.

2

I was still shaky the following night. I got up and hurried to the shower upstairs, doing my best to avoid everyone. I didn't want to have to try to explain myself to Levi or one of the girls if I didn't have to.

Levi was talking to someone in the kitchen and I scrambled past, hoping it was his wife and adopted daughter. I made it all the way upstairs and into the bathroom without seeing anyone. I closed the door behind me with a sigh of relief.

The shower helped rid me of most of the shakes, and I was feeling mostly normal by the time I was dried off and dressed. Something about slipping into the warm clothes soothed my mind. Sienna had picked out both the black sweater and the blue jeans for me. It wasn't something I'd normally wear, but somehow it felt right. I think it was because Sienna had chosen them for me specifically that made the clothing feel perfect.

The steam was still heavy on the mirror as I began to brush out my hair. I was afraid to leave the bathroom, knowing I'd have to face the family when I did. I took my time to work out the tangles, inch by painful inch. Water droplets ran down the mirror, giving me a fractured look at myself in the trails they left behind.

From what I could see of my face, I looked haggard. The Madness hadn't been that bad for a long time, and what had come after had only made it worse. I wished I didn't know what the pain meant, but I knew. It was hard not to.

My fingers found the raised bumps behind my ear. Ethan's demon, Beligral, had marked me before I'd fled to Delai. I'd made a pact that I would return to see him. I'd almost forgotten about his mark, and I supposed the agonizing pain had been his way to remind me.

My gut churned at the thought of the demon, of Ethan. And of home.

I sat on the toilet as the strength went out of my legs. I'd tried really hard to push thoughts of home out of my head. I'd killed my brother there, shot him just as he'd opened his mouth to speak. I didn't know if he was going to say my name or just snarl something inarticulate at me, but in the end, it really didn't matter what he might have said.

I killed him.

He will never speak again.

I stood in a rush and slammed the brush back into its drawer so hard I nearly tore it out of its tracks. I leaned on the sink and tried to control the anger that bubbled deep inside my chest.

I knew I was going to have to go home to confront Beligral. I was pretty sure if I didn't act soon, he would send more pain. The first time was bad enough, but what if he did it while I was talking to Levi or Eilene. I didn't even want to consider how Sienna would react.

It felt like I was being forced to choose between two homes. A big part of me just wanted to leave my past in the past and forget about everything I'd left behind. There was so much loss, so much pain in my old life, I really wasn't sure I wanted to go back to it.

Delai had become my home, a place I could live without fearing for my life every damn second of the night. Here, I didn't have to be Lady Death. I could simply be Kat Redding, vampire on the mend.

I smiled bitterly. When Levi told me he could help with my hunger, I'd thought he'd gone crazy. I figured at most he might be able to keep me from blindly killing someone, which was something I was already good at, but he'd gone so much further. While I'd never known a vampire who could completely control their hunger without going insane or becoming so emaciated they might as well have been dead, it wasn't out of the realm of possibility.

At least not now. I would never have been able to do this on my own. Something about Levi calmed me, helped me sort through the tangle of emotions that flooded my head every time I got hungry for blood. The blood bags he kept for me helped curb the need to feed on a living person. How much longer until I didn't need them at all?

"Kat?" Sienna's tentative voice drifted up the stairs. By the sound of it, I knew she'd heard me thrashing around last night.

I took one last look at myself in the mirror and tried to put on a face that didn't look so exhausted. It wasn't easy, but I managed.

"I'm coming," I called as I left the bathroom. I tried to sound cheerful, but it came out sounding strained.

Sienna was waiting at the bottom of the stairs, her blond hair pulled back out of her face. The concern was clear in her eyes as she watched me descend. While I was sure she'd heard me screaming the night before, I hoped she hadn't gone into the room to check on me while I was lying on the floor comatose.

"Dinner's ready." She gave me a weak smile that made her look even younger than her nineteen years. On a good day, she looked at most sixteen. She had one of those faces that would be eternally young, which was both a curse and a blessing. Any vamp who saw her would want to capture her young beauty for his own enjoyment.

I pushed the thought out of my mind and smiled at her. I rested my hand on her wrist, squeezing gently as I passed. My touch seemed to dispel any trepidation she might have had about my well-being. Her smile widened and she followed me out into the dining room.

Sienna's adopting mom, Eilene, was sitting at the table, hands resting in her lap. She'd been sick when I'd first moved in months ago, and she hadn't improved since then. I wasn't sure what was wrong with her, but whatever it was, it left her weak and tired nearly all the time. Her features were wan and thin, her skin pulled tight over her cheekbones, while it sagged everywhere else. She couldn't weigh any more than eighty pounds.

She glanced up as we entered. She settled her tired eyes on me for only half a second before looking away.

"Levi will be in in a minute," she said, voice soft as if it hurt to speak.

Sienna took her place at the table, keeping her head low. She was always shy around her parents. I'd only ever seen her open up when neither of them were around, and that wasn't too often. One of them always seemed to be hovering around, though the young girl was worse when it was Levi who was in the room.

I studied Eilene for a few moments before sitting. The chair creaked as I sat down. It sounded loud in the hushed silence of the dining room.

Sienna glanced up at me and her mouth quirked in a small smile before she resumed looking at the top of the table. She brushed a stray strand of hair out of her face before dropping both her hands into her lap.

I felt bad for the girl. As much as I liked Levi, he did have a strong hand when it concerned his adopted daughter. She was never allowed to leave the house and had no friends I knew of. She spent most of her time in her room, where I could only assume she read. There were no televisions in the house; no music ever drifted through the walls. It felt like we were living in a monastery sometimes.

Levi came in, drawing my attention away from the girl. His arms were laden with food. He always liked to feast after the full moon, and tonight was no different.

"Dig in," he said, a wide smile on his face. He unloaded the plates on the table. "Tonight we will celebrate the accomplishments of our guest. She did wonderfully last night." He gave a little golf clap, though no one else at the table joined in.

He didn't seem to mind. Without missing a beat, Levi swept up his plate and began loading it with the food he must have spent hours cooking.

"Where's Ronnie?" I asked, picking up my own plate. The quiet man always ate dinner with us.

I picked at the food, choosing only small portions to be polite. I really wasn't hungry, but I didn't want to be rude either. Besides, I had to eat real food too. No sense starving myself over a rough night. I'd probably need my strength when I faced Beligral next.

A cold chill ran up my spine at the thought of the demon. I suppressed a shudder as I set my plate down in front of me.

"He's got things to do." Levi didn't look my way as he spoke, but it was clear he didn't want to discuss it.

I didn't press him, though I did wonder where Ronnie was. He didn't seem the type who could do much of anything on his own, and he almost never missed a meal.

Levi gave a brief nod at the table at large and we began to eat.

Sienna and Eilene didn't say a word throughout the meal. Levi chatted amiably, not really talking to anyone in particular. I barely listened to him and I doubted the other women did either. About halfway through the meal he started talking about how I handled the night before, though he left out the bit about what he'd done to Ronnie. I was pretty sure he didn't want them to know he was cutting up the poor man just to see if I would eat him.

The spot behind my ear began to throb, as if the memory of my bad night was going to bring back the pain. I was trying hard to forget about it, to just get through the meal so I could make a decision as to what to do about the demon. I didn't want anyone else to know about it if I could help it.

I found myself rubbing absently behind my ear and I jerked my hand away, but I was too late.

"Is everything okay?" Levi asked, giving me a concerned look.

I nodded and pretended nothing had happened.

"You don't look okay."

"I'm fine."

He frowned and crossed his thick, hairy arms in front of him. "I don't think so."

Sienna shifted uncomfortably in her seat. Eilene was watching the exchange with a faint frown. Neither woman would speak up, knowing Levi wouldn't like them butting in to the conversation without his leave.

"It was a rough night," I said. "I have a headache."

"A headache?" He shook his head. "I doubt that. There's something else going on."

"Is there?"

He stared at me and I stared right back. I didn't care how much he might have helped me; Levi didn't need to know every damn thought that went through my head.

Levi took a deep breath and a smile split his face. "Well, then," he said, his voice booming in the room. "I guess that's that." He leaned forward and started eating again. He took a bite, glanced at me, and winked as if we were sharing a secret.

Sienna was staring at me and I could see the question in her eyes. I seriously doubted Levi would give up that easily, and it was obvious I was going to have to tell Sienna something. If I wanted the girl to trust me, I couldn't hold back on her.

It was strange having those sorts of feelings for the girl. I didn't know why, but I'd grown attached to her over the last few months. Was it her innocence? The way she never flinched when I moved in. She treated me more like a person than most anyone I knew.

In a way, she reminded me of Ethan.

The rest of the meal passed without further incident. As soon as I was done, I excused myself and went back to my room. I didn't want to face any of the questions I knew were to come just yet. I hoped they'd be content to spend some family time together and let me sulk a while before bombarding me.

The plastic had been removed from my room, so someone had come down and seen the mess I'd left. Part of me hoped Eilene had done it. She was the only member of the family who wouldn't ask questions.

I started pacing the moment the door was closed. I kept looking at the closet, knowing my old clothes were in there. I hadn't worn them since the day I'd arrived. Eilene had washed them by hand before I'd shoved them as far back into the closet as I could get them.

I probably should have thrown them out. There were too many bad memories associated to those few articles of clothing.

But I hadn't. I needed the reminder of my old life so I

didn't turn back into the person I had started to become before the day I'd ended my brother's life.

A part of me knew I'd come to Delai to die. It was the only place I knew where I could be left alone to fade away into nothing. I could die in peace here, could forget about everything I'd done, all the people I'd killed. It was supposed to be my final sanctuary.

But at some point, things changed. I'd gotten to know the family, had come to like them. They'd somehow *become* my family. While the peace might have been broken because of the demon mark, I still thought of Levi's house as home.

But thoughts of the demon made me think of Ethan. Tears sprang to my eyes and I sank down onto the bed. How could I have left him to fend for himself like this? The world was dangerous and he wasn't nearly as resilient as I was. I wasn't so sure he could survive in the harsh world without me.

Of course that wasn't true. Ethan was resourceful. He always found a way to conquer his fears. He'd even managed to leave the house, despite his fear of the outdoors, so he could save Jonathan.

I wondered if he'd managed to get the Luna Cult Denmaster somewhere safe all those months ago. The last I'd seen of both men, Ethan was helping the paralyzed wolf up the stairs after Jonathan's fight with my brother ended with him meeting the sharp end of one of my silver swords.

My hands clenched into fists and I just about punched the wall. I didn't know which way was up anymore. I thought I'd found a home here, a place away from the nightmares of my life, but I hadn't gone anywhere, really. I was still the same person.

I was still a killer.

A knock at the door had me wiping away angry tears.

"What?" I snapped, expecting it to be Levi. I so didn't want to be disturbed right then.

"I'll come back later." Sienna's small voice came from the other side of the door.

I groaned. I refused to turn her away of all people. "No, wait," I said, sighing. I rose and opened the door before she could walk away. "I'm sorry. I didn't mean to snap at you."

Sienna turned back to face me. She hadn't moved from in front of the door, as if she knew I'd answer for her. "I just wanted to make sure you were okay."

"I'm fine," I said, trying my damnedest to smile. It didn't quite work, but at least I didn't grimace. "Where's your dad?"

"He's not here right now," Sienna said, and the relief was clear in her voice. "He went out after Ronnie or something."

"Do you know where he went?"

She shrugged. "He does that sometimes. Dad always tries to say he is doing something important, but I think Ronnie just gets it in his head to take a walk and forgets to stop. Usually he comes home before anyone knows he's gone. Last night must have been pretty bad for him not to have come back right away."

She didn't know the half of it.

"What was it you wanted?" I asked, leaning against the door frame. Talking to Sienna always seemed to calm me a little. I really did like the young girl, even if she was far too timid for her own good. She would never survive outside Delai, I was sure.

Sienna licked her lips and looked shyly away. I found the insecure gesture endearing. "I was just wondering why you were so upset today. I could tell something was bothering you."

I paused to try to come up with an answer that wouldn't scare the girl. I mean, she knew I was a vampire, but I'd never gone full-on vamp around her. She might not know how bad I got, and I never wanted her to see it either.

Before I could come up with something to say, Eilene came down the stairs behind her.

"Sienna, go upstairs and clean your room."

The girl didn't hesitate. The moment her mom spoke, Sienna turned and hurried up the stairs. The sound of her footsteps receded and her bedroom door slammed closed a few seconds later.

"You've got to leave." Eilene spoke before I could ask her why she'd sent the girl away. She leaned against the wall and closed her eyes like the effort to stand was too much for her.

I frowned. "Leave?" I said. "Why?"

"Because you have to." Eilene opened her eyes and looked up at me. She looked exhausted, like she'd been the one who stayed up all night fighting the urge to feed. "Something is forcing you away. I can feel it in the air, can see it when I look at you."

My hand went reflexively up and I touched the mark behind my ear. Other than the raised skin, I couldn't tell it was there. I wondered if she'd seen the mark and put two and two together somehow.

"I don't know," I said. "I don't want to go."

"That doesn't matter," she said with a sigh. "You need to leave."

"But Sienna—"

Eilene cut me off. "She'll get over it. I don't think you should tell her you're leaving. And you definitely don't want to tell Levi." She spoke her husband's name with such bitterness it took me aback.

I knew things were strained between the couple, but listening to her now, it appeared it was far worse than I'd thought. At first, I'd assumed she just didn't like how Levi was spending so much time with me, that she was jealous, but I quickly realized that wasn't the case. Levi had helped others before me. My time with him didn't seem to bother her in the slightest.

But there was definitely something else going on between them. The bitterness was there on a nightly basis. He pretended not to notice, but I sure as hell did.

"I'm not sure I want to go," I said. The thought of going home again made me sick.

"But you have to." Her gaze flickered to the side of my head, confirming my suspicion that she knew about the mark. "You have no choice."

She glanced up the stairs and forced herself erect. She crossed the room with small, shuffling steps, until she was standing a few inches from me. The fact that I was a vampire fazed her about as much as it had Sienna and Levi, which was to say, not at all.

"I sent Ronnie out," she said at a whisper. "It will take Levi a few hours to find him. You need to be gone before he knows you are even thinking of leaving or you'll stand no chance. He won't let you go if he senses your intent."

"What's going on?" I asked, starting to get uneasy.

"Just go," she said. "Please. Sienna will be crushed, but she'll understand."

"But why?" I wasn't sure if I was asking why I should go or why she was so insistent on pushing the issue. Did it really matter either way?

"Because if you don't go now, you'll never find the nerve to leave."

I didn't know what to say to that. Deep down, I knew she was right. I was already struggling with it. If Levi were to tell me to stay, I had a feeling I would.

Eilene stepped back. "Please," she said. "I don't want you to get hurt."

Before I could say anything to that, she turned and shuffled up the stairs as fast as her tired legs could take her. I watched her go, half-expecting her to collapse from the strain, but she made it just fine.

I numbly turned and headed back into my room. I wanted to stay, I really did, but I knew Eilene was right. The demon mark would force me to leave one way or the other, and now was as good of a time as any, especially since Levi was out of the house.

I stood at the edge of the bed, wondering if there was some way I could put this off. To leave now would feel like I was abandoning Sienna or turning my back on what Levi has tried to do.

But I couldn't stay—not as long as I had Beligral's mark.

With a heavy heart, I opened the closet door and began to pack for the journey home.

3

I felt like a thief in the night as I slipped out the front door and around to the garage where my Honda DN-01 was waiting. It had been so long since I'd ridden the motorcycle, I'd almost forgotten what it was like to sit astride it.

I brushed dust from the seat and a sense of longing came over me. I didn't know why I hadn't ridden around town on those long nights when I didn't have anything else to do. Maybe it was because the bike was as much a part of who I used to be as my weapons. I'm not sure. I only know that standing there in front of the machine, I only wanted to go for a long, slow ride.

I tucked the bag I'd packed away and mounted the motorcycle, relishing the feel of the seat beneath me. It felt strong, powerful, and I hadn't even started it yet. Something stirred deep inside, something that longed to get out.

I was still wearing the sweater Sienna had given me. I'd considered changing into my old clothes but decided against it. I wasn't going home for good. To change clothes felt too much like shedding everything Delai had given me. I couldn't do that; not if I expected to return.

The night was dark and overcast, making the garage

nearly pitch-black. I could see well enough. My vampire-enhanced vision made sure of that.

I gently stroked the bike, brushing away dust as I did. I should have taken better care of the motorcycle. Even if I didn't plan on riding it, I should have made sure it was kept in tip-top shape. I'd always taken pride in it before. Why should that have changed?

I sighed and walked the Honda out of the garage. There was only a light dusting of snow on the ground, and the driveway and road were perfectly clear. Lights from the main part of the town shone through the trees across the road. They sparkled off the ice on the branches, causing the trees to appear to glow.

My breath plumed in front of my face as I took a deep breath and let it out in a huff. It was a lot harder leaving than I'd expected it would be. I'd known it wouldn't be easy, but even the simple act of starting the motorcycle was just this side of impossible.

Sienna.

She was the reason I was struggling so hard with leaving. I hadn't said good-bye. Would she understand? Would she be angry with me?

I didn't like the idea of upsetting the girl. How hard would it have been to go tell her I had to go, to promise her I would be back? Leaving like this made me feel like I was abandoning her. I'd already abandoned far too many people and I had no intentions of doing it again.

Levi was another issue entirely. While I appreciated what he'd done for me, he wasn't what was keeping me here. I'd miss his kind words and patient demeanor while I was gone, but it wasn't like I was leaving forever. I just had to remember that.

I knew I should have left right then and there. I'd made up my mind already that I was going to go, so there was no reason to sit there any longer than I had to. I was only making things harder by not leaving right away.

But it felt like I was waiting for something. As I sat in the driveway, I knew something was going to happen.

It wasn't until the outdoor light clicked on and the front door flew open that I knew what it was.

"Wait!" Sienna came running out of the house wearing only a thin, long-sleeved shirt, pajama pants, and a pair of socks. She ran across the yard, oblivious to the snow on the ground.

I almost started the motorcycle and drove off before she could reach me. I might have wanted to see her again, wanted the chance to say good-bye, but now that the chance was here, I was scared. Could I really leave her behind like I'd left so many others before?

"Take me," she said, coming to a stop next to me. "I want to go with you."

"I can't." A fist clenched in my gut, squeezing my insides until I felt like I might puke. My gaze flickered to the open front door. Eilene stood there, arms crossed over her chest. She was shaking so badly from the cold, I was afraid she might shake completely apart.

"Please," Sienna begged. "I can't stay here without you. I can't live with him anymore."

"Sienna." The warning was clear in Eilene's voice, though she made no move to come after the girl.

"I wish I could." I reached out and brushed a strand of hair out of her face. Tears were forming in the corners of her eyes. It nearly broke my heart to see her so upset because of me. "I have something important I have to do. I'll be back as soon as it's taken care of. I promise."

Sienna started shivering. Her socks were soaked completely through; her teeth were chattering. I longed to pull her in close for a hug, but knew if I did, I'd lose my nerve and wouldn't be able to bring myself to leave.

"Go inside," I said. I had to stay strong. I couldn't give in. "Keep your mom safe."

Sienna glanced over her shoulder once before turning back to me. "I'll miss you." She spun and hurried back toward the house, shoulders heaving as she broke down into sobs.

I can't live with him anymore.

Eilene watched her daughter for a moment before she made her slow way toward me. Her feet shuffled in the snow as if it was too much effort to lift them.

"Don't come back," she said as soon as she reached me. "Do us all a favor and never even think of us again."

She stared into my eyes, dared me to argue; then she turned and walked back to the house, leaving me sitting in stunned silence.

I wanted to call out to her, apologize for whatever I'd done to upset her so much. I'd always thought Eilene liked me, even if she never really showed it. Hearing her tell me to leave and to never come back stung so bad it felt as though she'd slapped me.

Maybe I'd always been wrong about her. Maybe she was thankful to have me out of her house, out of her life. Could I have been the cause of the trouble with her marriage? Maybe Levi did spend too much time with me.

I started the Honda feeling all sorts of miserable. I felt bad for leaving Sienna behind. I felt bad for the trouble I'd caused Eilene.

As much as I wanted to stay to fix things, I knew I had to go and take care of my demon problem. I couldn't let the pain come again, couldn't let things get worse, simply because I wanted to fix things between me and a family that had never really been my own.

But it was still hard. As I pulled out of the driveway, the knotted fist in my gut hardened. It felt like I was leaving forever despite the fact I desperately wanted to return. No matter what I did, it felt like I was betraying someone.

Delai was a blur as I sped down the road. The town

never slept as far as I could tell, and I saw more than one face peer out at me from a window. I feared someone would alert Levi about my leaving and I'd have to explain myself to him before I could get away. I wasn't so sure I could talk my way past the big man. I wasn't sure I wanted to.

I turned into the main part of town. While the snow was light, it seemed to shine with its own warm glow, making the town appear that much brighter. DeeDee's was packed, and I hunched my shoulders as I drove past, hoping no one would notice me.

The farther from Levi's house I drove, the more I realized this was the right thing to do. I should have gone back home to at least check on Ethan before now anyway. Leaving him alone like I had was beyond irresponsible. He relied on me as much as I'd relied on him. I should have been smarter than that.

Headlights suddenly flared behind me and I didn't have to guess to know who was now following me.

I didn't even hesitate. I sped up, wanting nothing more than to put as much distance between me and the rumbling truck at my back.

The truck coughed as Levi sped up to match my speed. The horn blared repeatedly and I could hear him shouting, though I couldn't make out what he was saying. I knew if I were to stop to listen, he would find a way to calm me down, to talk me back to his house, where I'd never leave.

I bore down harder, leaning forward to reduce resistance. The headlights fell farther behind and Levi laid on the horn in one long, hard blast.

Some of my old anger flared up. Why in the hell was he chasing me like this? Why couldn't he just let me go and take care of my problem? He knew something was wrong. Why not let me fix it without having to explain myself first?

I would have sped up, but I was already going too fast. Levi was losing ground quickly, but he wasn't about to give up. I could hear him still shouting and wondered if I'd finally broken that calm demeanor he always had. It would almost be worth getting talked out of leaving just to see.

I approached the intersection that would take me out of Delai. There was a stop sign ahead, but I refused to stop for it, knowing if I did, I'd have a hard time moving forward again. I barely slowed down as I took the turn.

Tires screeched as I just missed getting hit by a car. I skidded sideways, nearly went off the road, but managed to get a foot down in time to catch my balance. If I'd been a normal human, I could easily have been killed by that stupid move. As it was, pain shot up my leg and my knee buckled, but I managed not to tip over.

My wheels caught and I shot down the road, ignoring the angry blare of the horn from the car I'd nearly collided with, as well as Levi's final shouts.

I glanced back once I was sure I had control of my bike and saw Levi's truck idling well back from the road sign. He was standing next to his truck, staring at me. Even from as far away as I was, I could see the frown on his face and the anger radiating off him in waves.

I looked away, feeling somewhat satisfied at his frustration. He shouldn't have chased me if he didn't want to lose.

The snow was coming down a lot harder outside the little town. There was at least a foot on the ground, and it was turning to slush on the road. It was a miracle I hadn't crashed coming out of that turn so hard. Even vampire reflexes were no match for ice and snow, especially with so much momentum involved.

I slowed down now that I knew Levi wasn't following me. It would be just my luck to keep from crashing out of that reckless turn only to hit a patch of ice on a straight stretch and lose control.

The miles crept by and the tension eased from my shoulders. I still felt bad about leaving Sienna behind, but I no longer was upset about leaving Delai itself. In fact, I felt good about it. I had no idea why I'd had such a hard time leaving before. It was only a place. While the vamps and wolves weren't there now, they'd eventually find the sleepless town and take over like they did everywhere else.

As the tension about Delai eased, another worry started to creep up on me.

Ethan.

I never should have left him. Would he still be living at the house after all this time? Would he even want me back if he was?

I was terrified of what I'd find when I returned home, to my real home. What if Jonathan had attacked him? The silver paralysis might not have lasted long enough for Ethan to find a place to take him. In his injured state, the werewolf might have been overcome by hunger and killed Ethan in a blind rage.

I found it unlikely, but the idea just wouldn't leave. If it hadn't been Jonathan, it could easily have been someone or something else. I should have taken charge, should have taken care of Jonathan and made sure Ethan was provided for before leaving. I never should have walked out without telling anyone.

Of course, I knew why I'd done it. I'd killed my brother. I had to run or else that simple fact might have weighed on me until I'd broken down completely. Delai was the one place I'd known I could go to escape the mess of my life.

I sped up as much as I dared, wanting to just get home and make sure Ethan was okay. I felt the tires slip more than once, but it was never more than I could control.

The miles whipped by and the snow got thicker. Some of the side roads looked to be completely untouched, and I was worried what I'd find when I got near the road leading to my house. If no one had salted it, I might end up having to walk a large chunk of the way home. There was a reason I rarely went out during the winter. The Honda just wasn't built for it.

I tried not to think about it as I neared my street. I focused on the road, solely intent on getting as far as I could. If I had to walk, then I'd walk. I'd dealt with worse weather before. I could deal with it now.

I nearly sobbed in relief when I saw the cinders on the street leading to my house. There was still some snow on the road, but it was mostly slush.

There were tire tracks in the snow, which made me nervous. There weren't too many houses down my street, and most of the ones that were there were abandoned. And there were far better ways to get where you were going than to try to navigate the old road. I feared whoever was driving the road was coming from my house.

I knew I was probably being paranoid. Ethan could have bought a car since I was gone. Someone could have moved in down the street a ways. Hell, it could have simply been the salt and cinder trucks making a few passes that had left the tracks.

Still, I didn't like it. No one was supposed to know anyone lived in my house on the hill. The few that did thought Ethan and I were just a harmless couple who kept to themselves. Now that I was gone, had someone come to verify our cover story?

I wished I had my weapons on me. Anything could be waiting for me back at the house. I didn't like going in so unprepared. I hadn't been gone for just a few days. I'd been gone for months. Anything could have happened in that time.

I reached my driveway and my trepidation increased tenfold. While the cinders and salt continued on down the road, the tire tracks turned into the drive. They looked recent.

I struggled up the hill toward the house. Ice had formed in the tracks and it caused the tires of my Honda to slip. Finally, I gave up and shut off the engine. Besides, the motorcycle made too much noise despite the fact Ethan had modified it so it wasn't nearly as loud as a normal bike. If it wasn't Ethan in the house, I didn't want whoever might be there to know I was coming.

I walked the motorcycle to the side of the road and left it behind a tree. If everything was okay at the house, I'd come back to get it. If not . . . it might not matter where I left it.

I flexed my fingers to loosen them. I'd been gripping the handles of the bike so hard, they'd started to lock up. And the cold didn't help. It might not bother me as much as it would a Pureblood, but the cold still got to me. Just because I was a vampire didn't mean I was impervious to the elements.

I kept low as I worked my way up the driveway. I made sure to step in the tire tracks so I wouldn't leave footprints behind. If someone were to come up the driveway, they might not see the Honda parked behind the tree, and I didn't want them to know I was there until I was ready for them.

There were lights on in the house and my pulse began to hammer. The light upstairs was faint in Ethan's bedroom window, as if his door was open and the hall light was on. There were no lights on in the living room, but the TV was on. Its flickering light caused shadows to shift and move as I approached. No one moved within the lights.

I didn't have my garage door opener on me, but I headed for the garage anyway. I peeked through one of the windows and saw a car parked in my usual spot. The station wagon was beat-up and the paint was peeling. I'd never seen it before in my life.

Everything else in the garage was the same. I gave the car one last hard look before turning toward the house.

I could just make out faint footprints leading from the house to the driveway. I couldn't tell if they were a day old or only a few hours. I was pretty sure they meant someone else had been here in another car at some point.

I slid up along the side of the house and peered in through the window to the living room. The heavy drapes Ethan had installed were closed, making seeing anything inside impossible. I could just make out the glow of the television through them.

I moved to the front door and gingerly touched the doorbell box. The front door appeared to be the same as when I left it, but someone could have changed the locks; I wouldn't know until I tried to get in. I ran my finger under the box and found the tiny switch beneath. I pressed it so I could lift the doorbell, exposing the fingerprint reader Ethan had installed months ago. I ran my finger down it and was rewarded with the sound of the door unlocking.

I waited a moment to see if anyone inside had heard, but if they had, they didn't come charging at the door. I licked my lips, wishing I had as good of a nose as a werewolf. It would make my life a whole hell of a lot easier if I could sniff out who might be inside.

I held my breath as I turned the doorknob. It barely made a sound as I turned it all the way. I waited a heartbeat before throwing the door open.

Warm air blew over me as I burst through the doorway. I spun to look over the half wall that separated the living room from the entryway, toward the TV where I fully expected to find a stranger waiting.

There was a blur of movement as someone leaped to their feet from where they'd been lying on the couch. He spun to face me, eyes instantly turning a feral yellow. He started to bare his teeth before his face froze in surprise.

No, it definitely wasn't Ethan.

It was a werewolf.

4

"Where is he?" I snarled, stepping around the half wall. While I didn't have my weapons, I did have my teeth and hands, which could be deadly enough. If it wasn't a wolf I was facing, it would have been more than enough.

The feral yellow eyes studied me for a second before bleeding back to pale blue.

I knew the werewolf, though that didn't mean I had to like him. Jeremy Lincoln had jumped me one night after I left The Bloody Stake. He'd thought I would be a challenging snack. He was quick to learn I was much more challenging than he expected.

After I scared him to near starvation, the Luna Cult took him in. I was reprimanded for what I did to him, but hey, if I hadn't stepped in, who knew where the wolf would be today. He probably would have ended up dead or under the control of a vampire house somewhere. I'd helped him in my own little way.

Of course, knowing me is a hazard all in itself. He'd helped capture my brother and nearly died in the process. Thomas had come in with a pack of his Tainted and nearly tore the arm off the kid's shoulder before the rest of us were able to take control of the scene.

My eyes flickered to the empty sleeve where Jeremy's arm should have been. He'd been taken to Doctor Lei in the hopes his arm could be saved. It appeared her attempts had been unsuccessful.

"Where's Ethan?" I asked, pushing back the pity that tried to slip past my anger. I couldn't feel sorry for the wolf who might have killed my friend.

Blood dripped from my lip where my fangs had pushed through the gums. I took a slow step forward, ready to tear him apart with my bare hands. If I'd had my weapons on me, he'd have been dead already.

"He's fine," Jeremy said. His eyes traveled to the stairs behind me, but I kept my gaze locked on him. There was no way I was going to glance back, giving him a chance to make a move. One armed or not, he was still a werewolf.

I stalked into the living room and looked around. The TV was tuned to some reality show with a bunch of half-naked guys and girls lying around a beach. The sound was turned so low only a wolf could hear it. I didn't need to hear it to know he wasn't watching for the dialogue.

A rumpled blanket and a pillow lay on the couch. A large bowl with a few popcorn kernels in it sat within easy reach. A glass sat on either end table, one empty, the other almost full. Neither was on a coaster, and for some reason that only pissed me off more.

"Did you kill him?" My gaze traveled back to the young werewolf. What the fuck was he doing in my house? His hair was sticking straight up on one side from where he'd been lying down. He had probably been dozing since he hadn't heard me approaching.

Jeremy backed up to the window. He glanced behind him and for a second, I was sure he would try to leap through it.

"No," he said, turning back to me.

"Did you think you could just move in and take over the

house once he was gone?" I prodded, my anger growing. This was *my* house. Just because I'd been gone for a few months didn't mean the monsters could start moving in.

"I didn't touch him," he said. He was looking more and more nervous by the second. He glanced toward the stairs and nodded toward them. "I'm sure he'll be down in a minute."

A rumble built in my throat. I took a threatening step forward and bared my fangs. It had been so long since I'd killed anyone, the urge was taking me over. In Delai, Levi had kept me calm. Here, I didn't have his influence. Right then, it felt like every last urge I'd suppressed in the small town had come roaring back, slamming into me like a train. All I wanted to do was kill, to avenge Ethan, my brother, anyone who had died because I'd been too weak to save them.

Jeremy didn't run; I had to give him that. He stood his ground, shirt skewed to one side. His sole arm was held out in front of him, fingers splayed as if he thought it would ward me off.

My muscles tensed, ready to spring. If I couldn't take a one-armed wolf, then I didn't deserve to live anyway. Why else would he be here if Ethan wasn't dead and gone?

"Kat?"

Ethan's voice stopped me before I could attack. I'd been so sure the wolf had done something to him, I didn't truly believe it was his voice I heard at first. I turned slowly, keeping myself placed so I could keep an eye on the wolf.

Ethan stood at the bottom of the stairs wearing pajama bottoms, a dirty Superman T-shirt, and socks that had started to turn brown. He had a toothbrush in his hand and he had foam in the corners of his mouth.

A sudden gush of emotion rolled over me. I forgot about the wolf, something I would have never done if

I'd been on my game. His hair was disheveled, but otherwise, he looked complete and whole, undamaged by the wolf I'd just about killed.

"Holy crap," he said, coming the rest of the way into the room. "I thought I heard your voice." He licked the foam from the corner of his mouth and swallowed it. "I thought you were dead."

I staggered toward him, surprised by how much I really had missed him. The sight of Ethan alive had me just about in tears. He was like family to me—*was* family for all intents and purposes. I never should have left him alone for so long.

Ethan rushed across the short distance between us and threw his arms around me. I stood stiff against him, unsure what to do. I was afraid if I hugged him back, I would squeeze him in half. Tears filled my eyes and I fought hard to keep them at bay. I so didn't need to be crying in front of him, especially with the werewolf watching us.

I settled on patting him on the back with one hand, leaving the other to hang dead at my side. I had no idea why I'd been so sure Jeremy had killed him. I mean, the wolf had helped me with my brother. Other than that first night we'd met, he'd done nothing but try to be helpful.

Ethan stepped back and the joy in his face faded, only to be replaced by anger. "Where have you been?" he demanded, shaking his toothbrush at me. "I was certain you'd been killed. Do you know how hard it's been here without you?"

"I'm sorry," I said, and I meant it.

He grunted and turned away. He took a shuddering breath, and I knew without seeing his face that he was crying. Ethan wasn't just important to me. *I* was important to him too. I was his only family. Count Valentino had killed both our families. It was the reason we'd ended up living together. Two broken people who had drifted together, hoping the other could fill the void left behind by those who were murdered.

And I'd abandoned him. I was all he had in this world, aside from the demon, and I'd left him to fend for himself. I felt awful.

The sound of something moving behind me reminded me Jeremy was still here. I spun around to face him, my guilt being replaced by anger. "Why is he here?" I asked. A growl entered my voice, something I hadn't quite intended.

Jeremy immediately stopped moving and raised his hand. He looked from me to Ethan and back again. He wisely kept his mouth shut. If he had tried to explain himself, I might have leaped at him.

"He's here doing what you haven't been," Ethan said. The bitterness in his tone caused me to turn back to face him. "He's protecting me."

"From what?" I didn't know if I should be pissed or happy that someone had decided to watch over Ethan in my absence. It was stupid, really. I should have thanked Jeremy, but I couldn't help but feel as if I'd been replaced.

Anger warred with relief and confusion. I wasn't sure what to think, whom to be mad at. It was as if my emotions had gone haywire, pushing me from one end of the spectrum to the other with the slightest of provocations.

"From everything." Ethan picked up the glass on the end table nearest him and downed it. His hand was shaking bad enough he spilled some down his chin. "When I came back and you were gone, I didn't know what to do. I panicked."

"But him?" I jerked a thumb at the werewolf. "Why him?"

"Because that's who Jonathan sent."

Jonathan. The name filled me with both anger and longing. Part of me wanted to see the Luna Cult Denmaster, to make sure he was okay. He'd been cut by one of my swords, cut by my brother in a mindless rage. He could have died that night. He'd only wanted to protect me.

But another part of me hated Jonathan for what he *didn't* do. He didn't save my brother. He'd fought him, nearly got killed by him, forcing me to act. He might not have pulled the trigger, but because of his actions, I had.

My brother was dead because of him. Part of me knew I was shifting the blame, but I couldn't help it. I'd blamed myself for so long, I wasn't even sure whose fault it really was anymore. Maybe if Jonathan hadn't arrived that night, things would have gone differently. Maybe if he'd shown up earlier . . .

Bitterness filled my mouth and I wanted to spit. I didn't care whose fault it was. Thomas was dead. Anyone who had a hand in it, no matter how indirectly, deserved some of the blame.

"Look," Ethan said. He sat down on the couch, though I noticed he sat on the edge as if he was afraid I might lunge at him. "It was hard enough for me figure out where to take your friend. He managed to talk enough to tell me where to go. The woman he had me take him to had only half a face." He shuddered.

Doctor Lei. I'd met her once. She'd sewn me up after my first run-in with Thomas left me with a major gash on my back and a few minor cuts here and there. I still had the scars, but at least I'd survived. It could have been a lot worse.

"Once she got him inside, she called someone to take me home." He was starting to sweat, as if the memory of leaving the house was making him nervous. His agoraphobia could get pretty bad sometimes, and I was sure it had been at its worst that night.

"Driving there was bad enough," he went on. "I don't think I would have made it home without freaking out. She gave me something to calm me down, and some big dude drove me home. When you weren't here to take me in, he got pretty mad."

The only "big dude" I could think of that Doctor Lei might have called would be Nathan LaFoe, Jonathan's second.

I'm not sure if I was thankful to Nathan or not. If he drove Ethan home, that meant he knew where I lived. I wondered how many in the Cult were privy to that information these days.

"He was back the next day, though he wasn't happy about it." Ethan was playing with his fingers, agitated. "He never told me his name, never even talked to me, but at least he made me feel safe." He allowed himself a small smile. "Well, sort of safe. Guy was scary."

And a werewolf. I didn't know if he made that fact known to Ethan or not. I tried to remember who all Ethan had met. I was pretty sure only Jonathan had been to the house before, but I couldn't be positive. So much had happened in such a short amount of time, my memory was fuzzy.

I eased down onto the couch beside Ethan. My hands were shaking and I had to clench my fists to make them stop. Jeremy relaxed a bit by the window but didn't move, didn't speak. He only watched, his face impassive.

"So, anyway," Ethan said, "one day the big guy didn't show up. Jonathan came instead and brought Jeremy with him. He told me Jeremy would stay here with me until you returned. I think by then we all thought you were dead."

The bitterness returned, but I kept my mouth shut. If I only would have stayed home, none of this would have happened. Too many people knew where I lived now. I didn't care that they'd helped me on more than one occasion. They were werewolves, and that meant they were dangerous.

"He's stopped by a few times to check for you, Kat."

Ethan slid a little closer and rested a hand on my wrist. I flinched but didn't pull away. "He never came out and said it, but it's clear he really does care about you."

"Fuck him," I said, shooting off the couch. I didn't want to think about Jonathan, not for a long time.

Everyone went silent. I kept my back to the room, afraid of what I'd see when I turned around. I couldn't bear to see their pity or their anger at how I was acting. I'd been a fool. I knew that more than anyone.

"I could leave," Jeremy said at a near whisper.

"Yes."

"No."

Ethan and I spoke at the same time.

"Kat, he's here because you weren't. I sort of gave him the spare room."

I turned, anger flaring. "You what?" I took a step forward that was a little too threatening for Ethan's liking. He quickly stood and stepped around the side of the couch.

"He needed a place to stay. I wasn't going to force him to sleep on the couch or give him your room or anything. It was the right thing to do."

"Ethan," I growled, growing angrier by the second. "You are letting a fucking werewolf live with you? In *my* house?"

"It's no different than when I was living with a vampire," he said, moving behind the couch. "He hasn't threatened me or looked at me like he wanted to eat me or anything."

I froze, realization creeping in. I was stalking him, threatening him. I looked down at myself, at my closed fists, at my stance, and hated myself for what I'd become. I was letting my emotions get the better of me.

I knew I'd never hurt him. I'm sure he knew that too. But that didn't make my actions right. I was pissed at him because of what *I'd* done, of decisions *I'd* made. I couldn't fault him for wanting someone else around while I was gone. I was the one in the wrong here.

"Shit," I said under my breath. "I'm sorry." I forced my fingers open. I had a feeling I was going to be saying that a lot over the next few days.

"Maybe you should take some time to settle in," Ethan said. "It's going to be morning before long. I was just about to head to bed myself." He brandished his toothbrush as if for proof.

I nodded, too upset to speak.

"I will need to talk to you about something tomorrow night," he said. "Something important." Ethan's face grew serious.

I groaned. "What's happened?"

"Not tonight," he said. "It can wait. There's nothing you can do about it until tomorrow anyway."

"Ethan," I warned, some of my anger flaring back.

He shook his head. "Sorry," he said. "Having you back is a lot to absorb right now and I don't want to get into anything else." He gave a weak laugh. "Some night, eh?"

I started to protest again but knew it was pointless. Ethan was right. It was too late for me to do anything. I could use a day to rest, to get reacquainted with being home before he dumped something else on me. I wasn't even sure I really wanted to know, especially if it meant I would have to stick around longer than I'd originally planned.

"Okay," I said. "You're right."

"Get some rest," he said. "I'll explain everything tomorrow night."

"I've got to get my bike," I said, resigned. I didn't look at either of the two men as I turned and walked out of the house.

The cold air hit me hard and I shivered. I sulked all the way down to my Honda and began pushing it up the drive, thankful no one had bothered it. If Jeremy was there, who knew who else might be lurking somewhere in the dark.

I pressed the button to open the garage and walked the bike inside. The beat-up car sat in my space, and I had half a mind to make Jeremy move it since I was pretty sure it was his.

I parked my motorcycle beside the station wagon and grabbed my bag before trudging my way back into the house.

I almost didn't make it inside. I just about turned around, got back on my bike, and drove off. I wasn't wanted anymore. Ethan had replaced me. Why should I stick around if someone else had already taken my place?

I wasn't sure where the thoughts were coming from, and they only served to piss me off. Blaming Ethan for this was about as effective as running away again. I couldn't do that to him. He deserved to know where I was going this time.

Besides, I still needed to talk to his demon.

I went the rest of the way inside, bag thrown over my shoulder. I glanced in on Ethan and Jeremy as I made my way to the stairs. They were both sitting on the edge of the couch, turned so they could watch me walk by. They turned the TV off and turned a lamp on in its place.

I didn't say anything as I headed up the stairs. I didn't need to. In the short time I'd been back, I'd already said too much.

I glumly made my way to my old bedroom, stepped inside, and closed the door firmly behind me.

5

It was strange to be back in my old bedroom. Everything appeared to be where I'd last left it. I don't think Ethan had come in even once. The clothes I'd tossed in the dirty hampers were still there. A towel I'd left hanging from the bathroom doorknob remained. It was like I had never left.

I dropped my bag on the floor and sat heavily on the bed. Dust plumed into the air and settled around me. More dust covered the nightstand and dresser, further confirming the idea that no one had been in the room since I'd been gone.

The room smelled different than the one I'd been living in the last three months. I could smell old blood and death here. It had permeated the walls of my bedroom. There were a few speckled dark spots on the carpet where I'd bled from countless wounds. No amount of cleaner could fully remove the stains.

Maybe it was time to have the carpet replaced, the walls redone. It would probably never get rid of the smell completely, but it might help make the air more breathable. I couldn't believe I'd never noticed it before.

I sighed. What good would fixing up the room do? I didn't plan on staying much longer than it would take to talk to Ethan's demon. Once I'd paid off my mark, I fully planned on going back to Delai. I didn't care that Eilene didn't want me to return. I couldn't stay away, especially knowing Sienna would be waiting for me.

I knew I should have talked to Ethan about the demon already. He could have summoned him that very night. It didn't matter if he was tired or that Jeremy was around. I could have taken care of the mark and been back on the road the moment the sun went down again. Then I wouldn't have to worry about the troubles of my old life ever again.

Footfalls sounded in the hall and I tensed. They stopped just outside my door, and there was a long pause before whoever was there turned and walked away. A moment later, Ethan's bedroom door closed.

A sudden flood of guilt washed over me. I staggered up from the bed and ran to the bathroom, sick with it. I made it just in time, falling hard onto my knees to throw up in the toilet. I heaved until there was nothing left, gagging and spitting until my throat was raw. I slumped against the porcelain, too weak to rise.

Something was wrong. I could feel it deep in my gut, what was left of it anyway. I didn't know if it was the demon's doing or if it was something else, but there was something definitely wrong with me. It went way beyond guilt. It wasn't the anger at having a wolf in my house. It was something deeper, something I couldn't explain.

I lay there, shuddering like a junkie again, wishing I would just die. It was like I was suffering from withdrawal, but I had no idea what it was I was pining for.

I'm not sure when it happened, but night eventually turned to day. The sun's rays couldn't penetrate the heavy drapes hanging on my bedroom windows, but they still made me that much weaker. I stretched out on the bathroom floor, half afraid that if I tried to get up, I'd throw up again. I put an arm over my eyes and just lay there, hoping it would all just end.

I struggled to make it through the day. Every time I thought about getting up and going to the bed, I'd start to get sick and would end up with my head in the toilet. Nothing else came up, but that didn't make the experience any nicer.

As the sun finally went down, I started to feel better. I was able to sit up without my stomach churning. Lying there had cleared my head a little. I wasn't nearly as confused as I'd been the night before. I could think straight and thankfully didn't feel like throwing up again.

Still, I felt dead and empty inside. Nothing seemed important. I worked my way to my feet and stripped out of my clothes. I tossed them toward the hamper and missed. I couldn't find it in me to care.

I turned on the shower, jacked up the heat so that steam filled the room almost instantly. I stepped inside to let the scalding hot water batter some sense into me.

I'd been a fool the night before. I'd let things get to me more than they should have. Maybe I was still affected by the Madness of the full moon. It didn't always just go away like magic. Sometimes it lingered.

The water ran cold and I turned off the shower, feeling a little more rejuvenated. Something still seemed off, but it wasn't nearly as bad as before. Maybe once I figured out what was wrong, I could fix it.

I left the bathroom and went to get some clothes. I started for my closet but stopped before opening the door. I didn't want to wear those things. My old clothing reminded me too much of a life I thought I'd left behind months ago. Could I really slip back into them and become the killer I'd been before?

No. I couldn't do it. I turned away from the closet and went to the bag on the floor. I ripped it open, tearing the zipper from its seams, and dug in it until I found a set of clothes I could handle. Sienna had bought them for me and as I slipped them on, I felt much better.

As I left the bedroom, the shower down the hall started up. Ethan's bedroom door was open, as was the spare bedroom door farther down the hall. I glanced in each, finding no one in either. Ethan's was still a mess, as if he'd never learned how to clean up after himself. The other room was much more orderly, almost to the point of being empty.

I glanced toward the stairs but didn't see anyone. I felt like a stranger in my own home, which didn't help my emotional state. I needed to see what I'd been replaced by.

Jeremy's room didn't look any different than it had when it was only a spare bedroom. The bed sheet was the same ugly green I'd put on years ago. Nothing sat on the nightstand or dresser. I peeked inside the dresser and found a few pairs of jeans, three pairs of boxers, and some balled-up socks. There were no journals or anything I could read to get a sense of Jeremy's motives.

I frowned. What did I really think he wanted? It wasn't like he was going to try to recruit Ethan into the Cult. I was sure they didn't work that way. Could he really only be here to watch over Ethan like he said? Or was there more to it?

I moved to the closet next, unable to keep myself from prying further. I had to know. Two pairs of boots sat on the floor just outside the door. Two plain T-shirts hung from wire hangers in the closet. There was nothing else inside.

"You won't find anything."

I jumped and spun around. Jeremy stood in the doorway, towel wrapped around his waist. His hair was still dripping wet. Water ran into his eyes, but he couldn't wipe it away without releasing the towel.

"I was just curious," I said, hiding my embarrassment. I never should have snooped. "Doesn't look like you plan on staying long."

He shrugged. "Guess not."

My gaze traveled from his face to the lump of scar tissue where his arm had once been. The wound hadn't been a clean tear. The flesh still looked angry and jagged, despite how fast he healed as a werewolf.

Jeremy saw me looking and turned so I could get a better look at the damage.

"Lei did all she could," he said. "But it wasn't enough." He sighed and stepped aside. "I'd like to get dressed now."

Suddenly, I realized how awkward the situation was. He was practically naked, which was bad enough. Having exposed the wound that I might as well have caused myself was even worse.

I lowered my eyes, but not before I saw his well-muscled chest and abs. I never remembered him being that toned. Then again, I'd never seen him without his shirt before. Or maybe he'd started working out as a way to compensate for his missing appendage. Did it really matter either way?

"Sorry," I said, feeling all sorts of miserable. I walked past him, painfully aware that the thin towel was the only thing keeping the entire event from being mind-numbingly embarrassing for the both of us.

Jeremy closed the door behind him, leaving me standing alone in the hall. I stood outside the door and listened as he started to get ready. I wondered how hard it was for him to put on his shirt and pants with only one arm. It couldn't be easy.

I really did feel bad for him. While I might have threatened him the first time we met, I never really wanted harm to come to the kid. His life would never be the same now. Just because he was a werewolf, didn't mean he could easily overcome being a cripple.

I sulked my way down the stairs to the smell of fresh coffee. Ethan was sitting at the dining room table, sipping slowly from his favorite mug. An untouched bagel sat in front of him.

"Feeling better?" he asked. He was still wearing the

clothes from the night before, and his eyes were dark and sunken in. It was obvious he hadn't slept.

"Some." I sat at the table and stared at him. He looked terrible and I knew I was the cause. "I'm sorry," I said. "For how I acted last night. I was a mess."

"You and me both." He gave me a wan smile.

"I was an idiot. I never should have left without telling you."

He shrugged the comment off but didn't say anything.

We sat in silence until Jeremy came downstairs. He went into the kitchen and poured himself some coffee. He returned to the dining room and leaned against the wall instead of sitting with us.

"Not to sound ungrateful, but why'd you come back?" Ethan asked, setting his mug down. A flurry of emotions ran through his eyes, but most of all, I saw betrayal.

My hand went to the spot behind my ear. He saw the motion and I didn't have to say a thing.

"Oh," he said, his face falling. "I should have known."

I felt sick. It was obvious Ethan had hoped I had come back for him, not because of some promise I'd made to his demon.

"Yeah," I said, feeling guiltier than ever.

"He can be persuasive." Was that bitterness in Ethan's tone?

"I noticed."

He sighed and closed his eyes. I felt like shit having not told him how much he meant to me first. This might have been so much easier if I had.

I considered telling him how I really felt, but instead I looked away. I couldn't bring myself to look at him. I knew I should have said something, but with Jeremy standing there, everything I could think of saying made me sound weak. I refused to do that in front of a werewolf.

"You probably should have stayed gone," Ethan said. "Things here have been getting pretty dangerous."

My gaze flickered to Jeremy.

"No, not him," Ethan said, rolling his eyes.

I felt like a fool. I hadn't meant to imply I thought Jeremy was the problem, but it was hard not to. I'd spent my life killing wolves, and here I was letting one hang around while I ate breakfast.

"Someone is looking for you," Ethan said. "It's why Jeremy has stayed as long as he has. It isn't safe."

"Who?" I was confused at first, but anger was quick to follow. I hated the idea that someone was looking for me when I wasn't even there.

"I don't know," Ethan said. He glanced toward Jeremy, who was still leaning against the wall, though his posture was much stiffer now.

"A vampire Count is all we know," he said, his voice tight.

"No idea which one?"

They both shook their heads.

"Whoever it is, they're pretty upset about something," Ethan said. He tried to play it off with a laugh, but it came out sounding strained.

"We've lost a few in the Cult because of it," Jeremy added. I could hear the accusation in his voice. "They killed Paul while questioning him." His jaw tightened at the last.

It took me a moment to figure out who Paul was. It wasn't until I thought back to when I'd seen Jeremy at the Den the first time that I remembered. He was a werewolf around the same age as Jeremy. I'd only seen him at the Den once or twice, though I never actually talked to him. It appeared I'd never get the chance.

"We were hoping the search would die down once word got out you were dead."

I stared at Ethan. "Dead?"

"As good as," he said, looking away.

"I'm not dead."

"Well, we know that now." He gave a nervous laugh. "And even if we'd known where you were hiding, we would have said the same thing. From what we've been able to figure out, you don't want to get involved in this. We're talking a Major House here, maybe even a Royal."

"I wasn't hiding." I closed my eyes and tried to focus. How could this be happening? "Why would someone suddenly be looking for me? I haven't killed anyone for months."

Ethan gave me a worried look. "Maybe because everyone still thinks you killed all those vampires and werewolves a few months back."

I groaned. I'd almost forgotten that we hadn't done anything to clear my name after we discovered Thomas had been committing the murders. Only a handful of people knew, and they weren't about to spread it around.

"Okay, fine," I said. "But the killings have stopped, haven't they? There's no reason to keep looking for me."

"I don't know why," Ethan said. "But whoever it is, they're not giving up."

I knew what I needed to do right away. "I need to talk to somebody." I stood, angry I was being forced back into my old life. I couldn't let this go and turn my back on everyone again.

Ethan rose right along with me. "Do you think that's wise?" he said. "You should probably stay here until Jonathan gets here. He might know more."

I glared at him. "No," I said. "If someone is looking for me, then I'm going to be the one to take care of it. No one else needs to get involved."

"At least let me summon Beligral for you."

My gaze flickered to Jeremy, but he didn't seem to be bothered by the mention of the demon's name. Maybe Ethan had already told him about what he did in his lab at nights.

"I don't have time," I said. "Tell him I'll get around to

him soon enough." I rubbed at the spot behind my ear, hoping the demon would wait.

"He won't like it."

"Tough shit."

I started for the door but stopped. I couldn't go out dressed as I was. While I might fit in with the normal populace, I would feel sorely underdressed without my leather. And there was no way I was going to do this without my weapons.

I turned toward the stairs and took them by twos. I headed straight for my bedroom, not bothering to close the door behind me as I shed Sienna's clothes. I opened my closet and removed my hunting clothes. I held the leather for a long time, nervous about putting the blood-stained clothes on again, but decided it was the only thing I *could* do.

I couldn't go out as Kat Redding. It had to be Lady Death.

I got dressed as quickly as I could. As soon as I was dressed, I paused, feeling as though something was missing. It took me a moment to realize I no longer had a long black coat to throw on over everything. I cursed under my breath but didn't let it stop me.

Ethan was waiting for me in the basement. Jeremy was nowhere to be seen. A sword, as well as my belt with two knives hidden in sheaths built into the leather, waited for me on the table. Beside both was one of my modified Glock 17s, already in a shoulder holster.

"You'll definitely be needing these," Ethan said, smiling despite the trepidation I heard in his voice.

I couldn't help but return the smile as I began strapping on my weapons. The sword would be obvious without my coat, so I left it on the table. As much as I hated going without it, it would draw too much attention. I could wear the heavy coat Sienna had bought me to conceal the shoulder holster.

Within minutes, I was ready. I'd thought putting on my old things would feel strange, but I felt oddly at home. I never realized how much I missed having the comforts of my weapons close against my body. If that didn't say what kind of person I was, then nothing would.

"I'll be back soon," I said.

Ethan nodded and remained downstairs as I headed up the stairs to grab my bulky winter coat. It didn't quite match the rest of my outfit, but it would serve well enough.

I double-checked to make sure I had everything, took a deep breath, and then walked out the door.

6

Despite my agitated state, a wave of serenity passed through me as I pulled into The Bloody Stake parking lot. While it might not be the safest place in the world, it was surprisingly one of the few places I could go to relax and forget my troubles, though tonight I was there for another reason entirely.

The bar still looked the same as the last time I saw it. The flickering neon lights in the windows, the grime that covered most of the outside, the big moving sign with a woman repeatedly staking an overdressed vampire, they were all indications that no matter how much everything else had changed, Bart Miller never would.

I parked just inside the lot, as far away from the trash bin as I could get. It reeked of stale beer and garbage left out too long. I could smell it even from the road. The smell completed the image that The Bloody Stake was as sleazy as they came.

Of course, an image was all it was. Inside, the floor was cleaned regularly, the tables were always polished. The chairs and booths were comfortable and sturdy. The subdued light kept the atmosphere calm, or at least as calm as it could be when hungry vamps and wolves were sitting at a table next to a likely victim.

And that was part of the charm of the place. Danger lurked around every corner, and yet the danger typically behaved itself here. To do anything else was to invite a quick and painful death.

I crossed the parking lot, feeling self-conscious in my heavy coat. I doubted anyone would care what I was wearing, but still . . .

The doors opened without a sound and Bart's eye immediately fell on me from where he stood at the bar. He looked like a street brawler, thick all around, with a scar running down the right side of his face. He had a limp that I noticed was a little more pronounced than usual. I wondered if there had been a fight while I was away.

I took a quick glance around the room. I'd seen most of the patrons here before, but I didn't know their names. People didn't come to The Bloody Stake to socialize. You could sit down and talk, sure, but to give someone your name was just asking them to track you down and eat you later.

Mikael Engelbrecht sat at his usual table. He was talking to someone, which wasn't too surprising. He was a snitch who did his business from the same booth every night. I'm not even sure he ever moved. I don't even think I've ever seen him get up to go to the bathroom.

Usually when I came in, he was fingers deep in some young thing, and I mean that literally more often than not. It was pretty disgusting, yet no one else seemed to care. Mikael had his own sort of charm, albeit a greasy, slimeball sort.

Tonight he wasn't with one of his girls, which meant he was working. I was sure the girls were somewhere nearby, waiting for him to be done so they could cozy up next to him again.

I went to the bar to wait for Mikael to finish his business. If I wanted to learn anything about who was hunting me, Mikael would know. Aside from the wolves at the Luna Cult and Ethan, no one but Mikael knew who I really was.

Well, that wasn't entirely true. Adrian Davis, the Luna Cult defector and all-around pain in the ass, did. He was the only one I didn't trust not to talk. But he *had* kept my identity a secret before when it would have benefited him to give me up, so there was still a possibility he had yet to blab.

Bart had a beer ready for me before I even sat down at the bar. He held it back while he looked me up and down. I let him, not wanting to cause any problems. Bart was one of those guys you didn't reprimand or refuse if you wanted to come back to his establishment. He did things his own way, and I didn't begrudge him for it.

"I didn't expect to see you again," he said, low enough so that I was the only one who could hear. He set the beer down and pushed it toward me.

I gave him a smile and took a sip from the bottle. It felt good going down. I'd forgotten how much I enjoyed just coming to the bar and sitting.

"I missed this place."

Bart didn't return the smile. In fact, his usual glower deepened. "Can't say I missed you." He glanced over my shoulder as if someone was there, but when I turned to look, no one appeared to be paying us any mind.

When I turned back around, Bart was standing at the far end of the bar, pointedly not looking my way.

I grumbled to myself and continued nursing my beer. At least he hadn't thrown me out. I'd caused enough trouble in his bar in my time. It had never been quite enough that it would earn me a shotgun blast to the head, which was Bart's usual way of dealing with trouble, but I'd been asked to leave more than once. It was only a matter of time before he told me not to come back.

Still, it bothered me that he'd dismissed me like I no longer mattered. Bart and I were never really friends, but we had that sort of relationship that spoke of mutual respect. He might not know who I was, but he knew *what* I was, and he never once held it against me.

I checked on Mikael a few times as I drank. He was still talking to the man, a slimy smile spread across his face. He hadn't noticed me yet or he would have motioned for me to wait. I was sure he would want to talk to me after I'd been gone for such a long time.

My eyes passed over the guy he was talking to, not really taking him in. I couldn't even hear a murmur from his booth. They had to be talking in near whispers for me not to hear even the slightest grumble.

I shook my head and returned to my beer. It was none of my business anyway. If Mikael caught me looking and thought I was trying to eavesdrop, there was no telling what he would do. He took pride in keeping things between just him and his clients. He would never sell anyone out as long as they were lining his palms with green.

I wondered if he'd kept my secrets safe over the last few months. He could easily have decided I was dead and started sharing what he knew to those willing to pay. I just had to hope he had more faith in me than that.

I finished my beer and tapped the bottle against the bar to get Bart's attention. He frowned my way, seemingly irritated at having to serve me, but he retrieved a fresh bottle. He set it down in front of me and scooped up the empty in one quick motion. Before I could say anything, he was back across the bar, pretending he didn't know me.

I just about threw the bottle at him. He could be unhappy about me coming around, fine, but I wished he wouldn't make it so clear to anyone who bothered to notice.

I was so busy sulking, I never noticed the man Mikael had been talking to had gotten up and left. I was glowering down at my beer when a hand gripped me by the arm and someone whispered harshly in my ear.

"What are you doing here?"

I immediately grabbed for the hand holding me, but caught empty air. I flew off the stool and spun around, hand going to my waist. Drawing my weapons in The Bloody Stake would get me killed almost as fast as I could unsheathe the knife, but instincts had taken over.

Mikael stood a good three feet away, staring at me. The entire bar fell silent, anticipating a fight. I think most of the patrons came to the bar in the hopes of seeing someone lose their head.

"What the hell?" I said, easing my hands away from my knives. I glanced back at the bar to see my beer spilling out on the countertop. I must have knocked the bottle over when I'd jumped up. "Don't sneak up on me like that."

Mikael frowned and looked around. Everyone shied away from his gaze and went back to what they were doing as if they were afraid to have him acknowledge them. Maybe they were. Mikael might have dirt on every single person in the room, and most people wouldn't want their indiscretions to get passed around.

"Let us sit," he said, turning his back to me. He returned to his booth and sat down, looking far more concerned than I'd ever seen him.

I brushed down my coat where he had touched me. I was surprised he'd reacted so fast. A normal Pureblood would never have been able to pull away in time, yet Mikael had managed to avoid my grasp and flutter back a few steps before I could fully turn around. The weaselly man was a lot more agile than I'd ever given him credit for.

I made my way over to the booth and slid in across from the Swede. He was fidgeting, which wasn't like him. Usually Mikael was completely composed, ready to deal. He always seemed to be in complete control of the situation, and yet, somehow, I'd thrown him off his game.

I didn't like that at all.

"What's going on?" I asked. "Everyone is treating me like I have the plague, and I want it to stop."

"Close enough," he said. "I really wish you wouldn't have come here, my sweet." He looked around the room, scanning as if he was worried someone would see us together.

"I really wish people would stop saying stuff like that." I took a deep breath. "What's going on?"

His eyebrows rose and he stared at me like I must have gone completely batshit. "Don't you know? How could you not know?"

"Know what?"

He ran a hand through his hair. It came away greasy and he absentmindedly wiped it on his shirt. He grumbled something Swedish before switching back to English.

"You are a wanted woman," he said, leaning forward. "If anyone knew I was talking to you, it would be my head."

I didn't like the sound of that. "Hasn't it always been that way?"

His frown deepened. "Of course, but it is much worse now."

"Is this about whoever is looking for me?"

He cocked his head to the side. "So then you know?"

"Not enough."

"Obviously, or you wouldn't be here." He sighed. "You should have stayed dead."

I ground my teeth. "I wasn't dead."

"Then in hiding."

"I wasn't hiding either."

Mikael huffed and shook his head. "Whatever you want to call it, it was better that you were gone. You can't fight this. Maybe you should go away again, my sweet. It would be better for everyone."

"Just tell me what's going on so I can fix it." I really didn't like where this conversation was going.

He looked like he was going to say something rude but changed his mind at the last second. He took a deep breath and puffed it out, making his lips flap. He gave me a quick smile, letting some of the old Mikael show through.

"All debts are paid, okay?" he said, assuming a businesslike manner. "You owe me nothing anymore."

"Okay," I said, my heart plummeting. Did this mean he was cutting ties with me? Without Mikael's information, I would have been dead years ago. And if he thought he was going to sell what he knew about me the moment I walked out the door . . .

"No," he said. "I am not planning on telling anyone about you. It would not be good for me if some of the powers-that-be knew I had been feeding you information. Enough suspect already."

I grunted.

"But I don't want you coming back here. At least not until this blows over, if it ever does. I have a feeling you will be dead before you are clear of this."

"How about we stop all of this talk about me dying, okay?" I said, growing more and more agitated. "Just tell me who's after me and what I can do about it. I'm tired of everyone telling me I need to go hide away somewhere."

He closed his eyes and remained quiet for so long, I was starting to think he might have gone to sleep. Finally, Mikael opened his eyes and stared directly at me. It felt like he was dissecting me, bit by bit, churning through my every memory, my every thought.

I couldn't help it; I looked away.

"Her name is Countess Baset," he said. "She was once the head of a Royal House, but something happened and she fell down the ranks. I don't know what caused her fall and I don't care. Baset is still a Major House, an extremely dangerous one. No one messes with her and survives."

The name was familiar, but I couldn't place it. I'd known all the names of the Major and Royal Houses before, but things often change, new powers come into play, and they all had started to meld together in my head.

But to have once been a Royal House and to have fallen without being destroyed was a major accomplishment. Normally, a House that high up would need to be destroyed before they'd ever settle at becoming something less than they once were.

"You *must* be aware of the danger," Mikael said. "She is not to be trifled with, yes?" He looked at me pleadingly. "You must leave, must not come back. Countess Baset *will* kill you, and everyone you have ever had contact with will suffer."

"Why is she after me?" I asked, firmly. I was *not* going to run away. I'd run enough already.

Mikael stared at me long and hard. The music blaring over the speakers drowned out the other conversations around us. No one was paying us any mind and I was really starting to wonder if it was natural. You'd figure someone would be curious once in a while. Even I hadn't paid much attention to the guy Mikael had been talking to earlier. Hell, I couldn't even remember what he looked like.

"Listen to me, Lady Death." Mikael spoke slowly, as if he was desperate for me to understand exactly what he was saying. "You cannot win this."

"We'll see."

"No!" he said, slamming his fist onto the table. "Listen to what I say. You will not survive if you stay here. Baset is no longer what she once was." He said it like I should know who or what she had been, other than a Royal. "The meaning of her name no longer applies. You must not stay."

"Tell me why she's after me and I'll decide whether or

not I should run away like everyone keeps telling me to." There was a bitterness in my voice that surprised even me. This whole thing was really starting to get to me.

Mikael sighed. He leaned back and looked around the room as if checking to make sure no one was listening. I followed his gaze to see that not a single eye had turned our way despite the raised voices.

"It's simple," he said. He licked his lips and swallowed, hands shaking on the table in front of him. "You killed her lover."

7

I absorbed that for a few seconds, not quite sure what to make of it. I've killed lots of vampires. It's hard to say who had been Countess Baset's lover, though I didn't recall killing anyone so high up in the vampire ranks. I was pretty sure an ex-Royal wouldn't be sleeping with anyone too far beneath her in the ranks. It just wouldn't be proper.

"Who?" I finally asked, stumped. The closest name I could come up with was Count Tremaine, and it was highly unlikely he'd been her lover. I'd seen nothing that would indicate he had any affiliations with anyone outside his own House, especially since his own had been so recently crippled.

Mikael smiled. It wasn't pleasant. "I'd think you would know," he said. "Countess Telia created such a problem for you before, it would seem you should remember her."

"I didn't kill her."

"No one knows that but a handful of people, yes?"

He had me there. "But I thought you said it was Countess Baset's lover I'd killed. Or am I missing something here?"

Mikael laughed. "No, you are not missing a thing." He sobered quickly. "But your sense if you think you can do anything about this problem." He folded his hands on the table in front of him. "Telia was Baset's lover, had been for years until the rumors of her death by your hand started."

I frowned. I had no problem with Baset's choice in bed partners, but something else was bothering me. "I thought Telia broke off from another House?"

"She did."

"Baset's?"

Mikael nodded.

"If she broke off from Baset, then why would the other vamp care whether or not she was dead?" I couldn't seem to wrap my head around it. "Were they still together despite the defection?"

"In a way," Mikael said. "Telia broke off because she wanted power of her own. Baset loved her, so she let her go in the hopes she would rise through the ranks and they could form an alliance. Both would have been able to obtain Royal status, or at least that was Telia's hope. I don't know the details of the split or how they planned to accomplish their goals, but they did have a plan."

I guess it made sense in a way. I'd wondered before why Telia's old House hadn't come after her when she split. I guess if the defector was someone you loved, it would be hard to let go.

But I still didn't like it. While I might have been planning on it, I never killed Countess Telia; my brother did. Only Mikael, Adrian, Ethan, and the Luna Cult knew that for sure. I really should have done more to clear my name.

Then again, why would I? I was Lady Death. I killed vampires and werewolves all the time. I'd never apologized for it before. In fact, Telia's death had only added to my infamy.

And then there was the fact that a Major House was actively looking for me, scaring the hell out of everyone

I knew. There was no way that could be good. Sure, the major players had kept an eye out for me before, but Jonathan had said they liked having me around. I kept the lesser Houses in line so the big ones didn't have to.

"Thanks for the info," I said, rising. "I'll pay you when I have some cash on me."

Mikael shook his head. "No, this information is free. It might be the last you are alive to receive."

And on that happy note, I left.

Bart never looked my way as I made my way to the door, but I could tell by how his shoulders relaxed that he was happy I was leaving. A few patrons glanced my way, but as far as I could tell, no one would come chasing after me the moment I was down the road. I'd left The Bloody Stake often enough with someone following me out the door. I didn't care to repeat the experience.

I was a mess of emotions on the ride back home. I had to take it slow. Snow was starting to drift into the road and the wind was picking up. I really needed to get some sort of cold-weather vehicle for days like this.

I had half a mind just to say, "Fuck it," and drive straight to Delai. If I didn't need to talk to Ethan's demon so bad, I might have. I was tired of all the bullshit that went with being me. It seemed like someone was trying to kill me every night, even if I wasn't trying to kill them. That was something I hadn't had to worry about at Levi's house.

I ground my teeth and sped up. Maybe Delai wasn't such a good thing for me. It was making me soft. I wasn't someone who sat around, watching the television or reading quietly in my room while people were dying a few miles away. That just wasn't me.

I killed people. I kept the vampires and werewolves from taking complete control of my little slice of the world. They held a large portion of it, sure, but at least I kept the worst of them at bay. The day still belonged to the Purebloods. I planned on keeping it that way.

I made it all the way home but had to stop and walk the motorcycle up the driveway. I was so intent on watching my step so I didn't trip over a rock or fallen branch obscured by the snow, I almost bumped into the black car parked at the top of the drive.

"Son of a bitch," I growled. I pressed the button to raise the garage door, walked my Honda inside, and waited until the door was closed again before heading for the house.

Of all the things I wanted to deal with, Jonathan Alucard wasn't one of them.

I threw open the side door and stormed inside, knowing he would be waiting for me. I wasn't disappointed.

"Kat." He was standing just inside the dining room, facing the kitchen as I came in. His glamour was up, hiding the missing portion of his skull, a chunk I had hacked off back when he was a member of House Valentino. I'd thought I'd killed him, but here he was, years later, standing in my house like we were friends.

Ethan and Jeremy were standing behind him, each looking nervous. I didn't blame them.

"Not now," I said. I tried to walk past him, but he moved to stand in my way.

"Please," he said. "We need to talk."

I kept from shooting him by taking off my coat. His gaze lingered on the gun in its shoulder holster as I tossed the coat on the table. I put my hands on my hips and gave him such a dark look, he winced.

"Okay, talk," I said. "But this better be damn good or I'm going to have to start putting holes in people who show up at my house unwelcome and unannounced."

"Then this is still your house?" Jonathan asked, all innocence.

I glowered at him. "Of course."

"I was beginning to wonder," he said. "You haven't been here for so long, I thought perhaps you'd wised up and took to ground."

"Don't you start in on me too."

He held his hands up. He was holding something in his left hand.

I felt myself soften without meaning to. The coat looked just like the one I'd worn for years. I'd managed to lose both of my old coats while dealing with the mess my brother had caused.

Jonathan saw me looking and a small smile quirked the corners of his mouth. "I thought you might like a new one." He glanced at the coat on the table. "It appears you have not replaced your other, so it seems the gift is warranted." His gaze traveled back to me. "I've waited a long time to give this to you."

For some reason, that made me angry. Just seeing Jonathan made memories of my brother flood into my head. I couldn't stop blaming him for Thomas's death. He'd been there and hadn't been able to do anything to stop it.

"Keep it," I said. "I don't need it."

Jonathan looked hurt. He lowered his hands and gave me such a pained look, I almost felt guilty for turning away his gift.

"Look," I said, trying to keep most of the anger out of my voice. "Tell me why you're here and then get the fuck out of my house. And take your maimed wolf with you."

Jeremy flinched, and I could tell I'd hurt him almost as bad as I'd hurt Jonathan, maybe more. Why was I being such a bitch when all they were trying to do was help?

Jonathan's jaw stiffened as if he was fighting off the urge to say something less than respectful. He managed to compose himself before speaking.

"I wanted to make sure you were okay," he said. "When Jeremy called and said you were back, I didn't know what to think. I was really starting to believe you might be dead."

I glanced at the young wolf. He quickly looked away, face flaming. Ethan stepped protectively near him and glared at me.

What the fuck? Ethan used to be scared of the Luna Cult wolves, had even warned me against them more than once. And now he was defending one of them? Things had really changed since I'd been gone.

I hate change.

"You've seen I'm okay," I said, shifting my attention back to Jonathan. "Now go." I tried to walk past him, but he refused to move out of my way.

"No," Jonathan said. "You're not okay."

"Who gave you the right to decide how I'm doing?"

"No one," he said. "But I can see it in your eyes, hear it in your words. Something is very wrong with you and I only want to help."

My hands balled into fists and I stepped closer to the Luna Cult Denmaster, seriously invading his space. "Nothing is wrong *with* me. It's everyone around me that's pissing me off. I'm tired of everyone telling me to hide, to run away. I never should have come back if that's the way you're all going to act."

"Then why did you?"

I closed down. I didn't know how much Ethan had said to the others about his demon. I knew Ethan wasn't a fan of the Denmaster, or at least never used to be, so I doubted he'd explained things to him. That didn't mean Jeremy hadn't, however. The young wolf could have been supplying Jonathan with all the information he wanted about my house and how I lived.

Anger flared and I had to fight really hard to keep from lashing out. I should have listened to Ethan before when he'd warned me against the Cult. Now here I was with them in my house and they'd seemingly swayed him to their side. I was losing control of my own life.

Jonathan glanced over his shoulder, apparently unconcerned by my nearness. "I'd like to talk to her alone," he said.

Both Jeremy and Ethan turned and headed for the stairs without hesitation. Ethan glanced back once, giving me a pleading look as if asking me to cooperate, before vanishing down the stairs.

"I—"

"Shut up and listen to me for a minute," Jonathan said, turning back to face me. His eyes flared yellow and I took a step back, snapping my mouth closed. I'd never seen him this angry before without some severe provocation.

"You have no right to talk to any of us like this," he said. "I'd almost forgotten how stubborn you could be."

"I . . ." This time I trailed off on my own.

"Ethan is supposed to be your friend and you left him to fend for himself. Jeremy lost his arm in an effort to help your brother. He thinks he is useless now, thinks the world has no place for a 'maimed wolf,' as you so eloquently put it. I gave him a reason to live, and I will not let you throw that away because you are too stubborn to see we are all here trying to help."

Guilt crept in past all my anger and confusion. I felt like a fool for lashing out so quickly. Just because I didn't like what they were saying didn't mean I should ignore them. They were only concerned for my well-being.

Then why did it feel like they were trying to control me?

"I came here in the hopes we could discuss this problem of yours, but I see now that it will not be possible, at least not tonight. Bad people are looking for you, and I do wish to help. No matter what you think, I want to keep you alive. I care about you. We all do."

I closed my eyes, which was something I normally wouldn't do with a pissed-off werewolf standing a few feet away, but I didn't know what else to do. I didn't know if I wanted to cry or if I wanted to scream. Jonathan's words were hitting all the right spots.

"Don't throw your life away just because you are too bullheaded to ask for help. Just because things didn't work out before doesn't mean we can't fix them now."

My eyes snapped open and anger took over. "You can't fix my brother," I said. "No matter how hard you try, you can't fix him. He's dead because we fucked up."

Jonathan's eyes bled back to their normal blue. "Be that as it may," he said, "it doesn't have to destroy us." He put special emphasis on the last word.

"There *is* no *us.*" All the anger was back. "There never will be. I just want to live my life without people treating me like I'm some sort of cripple."

Jonathan sighed. He set the coat on top of the table, next to the coat Sienna had given me.

"Keep it," he said. "It's a gift and I won't take it back." He looked at me and a profound sadness filled his gaze. "You don't have to see me again," he said. "But I will ask that you let Jeremy stay here for a little while longer. This is good for him. Don't take that away just because you are angry."

I started to protest, but he raised a hand to stop me.

"Think of Ethan," he said. "The two of them have grown close. You can't be here to protect him all the time. Jeremy can be here when you are not, can keep Ethan safe against those that would hurt him to get to you."

That hit a little too close to home.

"Fine," I said in a small voice. Somehow Jonathan had made me feel like a fool. Maybe I was. I'd been mad at so many people for so long, I was probably making things harder on myself by simply not listening and taking people's advice when they give it. "He can stay."

"Thank you." Jonathan dipped his head ever so slightly and turned and walked away.

I almost called out to him, almost told him to come back. I was the reason he was forced to keep a glamour up at all times to hide his true face. I was the reason he limped ever so slightly when he walked. I'd damaged him in more ways than one. The least I could do was talk to him civilly and thank him for all that he'd done.

But I kept quiet, knowing if I called him back, I'd regret it later. I couldn't let anyone get close to me again, not if I planned on returning to Delai once all of this was over.

The front door opened and closed, leaving me standing alone in the dining room with nothing but my guilt to keep me company.

8

You'd think some time alone with my thoughts would help me sort through the mess of emotions I'd been going through. A long day alone in my room with just myself for company could be a balm to the soul.

But it wasn't. I sat there and fumed, dwelling on things I probably should have let go. Jonathan had no right to come into *my* house and tell me how to act, what to do. It seemed everyone wanted to have a say in what I did with myself. It made me so angry, I wanted to scream.

In the end, however, I was angriest at myself for letting things get so far out of hand. I never should have up and left for Delai like I had, leaving everyone to wonder what happened to me. I understood why I did it. I couldn't face my brother's death, face what I'd become. I'd been in shock, and the sleepy little town was the only place I thought I could go for sanctuary.

And it had worked for a time. I'd felt good there, managed to overcome a lot of my pain by pretty much forgetting about it. Levi helped me keep my hunger at bay and at times, I felt like a normal person.

Too bad I always knew the truth.

What didn't help was that my hunger was roaring by the time night fell, which only accentuated my anger. I was hungry and Levi wasn't around to help me deal with it. His blood bags might taste like shit, but I'd come to rely on them so I wouldn't have to hunt.

I stormed out of my bedroom, dressed in all leather. Jonathan's gift hung from my shoulders like it had been made especially for me. It felt awkward at first, but I think that had to do more with whom it was from than what it was. After a few seconds of fidgeting, I got over it and the coat felt natural on my body.

Ethan was waiting for me in the dining room. I gave him a passing glace, one that warned him I was in no mood to be trifled with. He knew better than to mess with me when I was as starved as I was.

My weapons were sitting on the metal bench in the basement. The moment my sword was strapped on, I felt a thousand times better, felt more focused, though the hunger was still there, eating at me bit by bit. I could feel myself becoming Lady Death, putting the Kat Redding I'd become in Delai behind me.

I wasn't sure if that was a good thing or a bad thing. I hated Lady Death, hated the name, hated what she had become, yet I needed to be her to keep those I cared about safe. I couldn't pretend I could do it without her mind-set. It was kill or be killed, and I planned on being the one doing all the killing.

I turned to head back up the stairs and found Ethan standing there, staring at me.

"What?" I snapped, slipping my coat off so I could get the shoulder holster on.

"I was, uh, wondering . . ." He licked his lips and shuffled his feet. "Before you go, would you want to talk to Beligral?" His face reddened and he took an involuntary step back before I could even say anything.

I checked my Glock, put it in its holster, and put my coat back on. "No," I said as I started for the stairs.

Ethan didn't try to stop me as I passed him. He backed

against the wall and watched me, worry lining his features. He knew I was hungry, knew I was going on a hunt.

And he also knew there was a powerful vampire out there hunting for me.

I tried not to think about it as I went through the side door, into the garage. I didn't bother checking my motorcycle like I normally did before starting it up and tearing out into the cold. The tires lost traction almost as soon as I hit the driveway, but I managed to keep from crashing. Barely.

I knew a lot of my anger stemmed from the hunger and my inability to control it, yet it felt like so much more. I could blame some of it on how people were treating me, how Jonathan assumed I would want his help. I could blame it on Countess Baset for hunting me even though I hadn't actually killed her precious lover.

But there was so much more to it than that. I couldn't put my finger on it, but the rage kept building and building; it boiled in my gut so that I was a total mess by the time I decided which way to go.

Blood dripped from my gums from where my fangs had punched through. The taste only served to make my hunger flare even more. If I kept going like this, I would be a ravenous beast in no time, and that wouldn't be good for anybody.

My first inclination was to head to High Street where I knew I could find a victim that wouldn't weigh on my conscience later. I could go there, find someone in some dark alley who was probably high on something or near death anyway. I could feed on them until I was sated, and no one would bother me. I could then go on my merry way, having done a service to the Purebloods who still tried to walk the night despite the scum who usually prowled the streets.

But that wouldn't prove anything. Countess Baset was hunting for me even though quite a few people thought

I was dead. Perhaps it was time I made myself known. Let the bitch see me. I could make such a scene it would terrify her.

I found myself laughing as I shot down the road toward a part of town I rarely bothered to go.

Polaris was a place where the rich Purebloods had congregated after the Uprising. They built their big houses, tried to keep themselves safe behind large walls and fancy electronics. The mall there was huge by today's standards, as were many of the other buildings. The people of Polaris thought big was always better, and even as things fell apart around them, they stuck to it.

Still, despite their attempts at isolating themselves from the horrors of the night, Polaris had become their prison.

One of the big Royal Houses occupied the region now. Count Mephisto was pretty much top dog when it came to Royals. It didn't take him long to take control of the businesses, and the homes quickly followed. He still let the Purebloods live there, protected them from outsiders even, but that didn't mean they were anything more than sheep.

Now, the Purebloods are still rich, but they give up their wives and children upon request. You didn't tell Count Mephisto no. To do so was to invite disaster into your home. He wouldn't kill you outright, but you'd wish you were dead by the time he was done with you and those you loved.

Anyone could come and go in his territory. The parkway was open to anyone, as was the mall. You just had to abide by Mephisto's rules, and feeding on his sheep wasn't something he allowed without a permit.

It was the perfect place to prove my point that I wasn't someone to be fucked with.

The dark roads I was used to were replaced by the well-lit parkway. Expensive cars rolled down the road, kids out cruising in one of the few places they could do so. Tall buildings towered to the sky, a water fountain sprayed a foamy stream into the air. Groups of teens huddled together, scurried from place to place in the hopes that something wouldn't jump out at them from behind a tree.

Just because it was illegal to eat his sheep, that didn't mean rogues didn't try it every now and again. And who knew when Mephisto or one of his minions would head out for a late-night snack, one that wasn't as willing as the ones they kept back home in their cushy little mansions.

But beneath the calm-seeming exterior, I knew the heart of the place to be black. No matter how much he tried to dress it up, Mephisto couldn't do anything about what went on in the darkest corners of his safe haven. He wasn't the only monster that walked the streets here.

My eye fell on a huge man who was pressing someone against the wall of an alleyway. As I passed, he stepped back and the tiny thing he'd been holding slid down the wall to fall in a heap. The big vamp looked both ways and then bolted, leaving his bloodless victim behind.

My stomach growled and I had to look away. I didn't know if it was just a small woman or a child he'd fed upon, but either way, she was dead. Polaris wasn't really that much different from High Street when you got right down to it. People died. It was a way of life everywhere.

I headed for the mall since it was the most public place I could think of. If I wanted to announce my return, it would be the ideal spot. I just had to find a likely victim and make sure I could easily get away. It wouldn't do to make a scene, only to be captured by Mephisto's men before I could get away.

I found a place to park deep in the mall parking lot. The mall was huge, having grown over the years to be at least twice the size it had been when Mephisto first took over. It stayed open all night these days. Vampires and wolves shopped right along with the Purebloods, though the wares they shopped for were vastly different for obvious reasons.

I knew of at least one store that sold teenagers imported from other countries. These girls and boys were highly sought after by the vamps with the most money to burn. If I knew I could pull it off, it would have been one of the first places I'd have shut down, though I knew it would be near impossible. Killing the employees wouldn't stop Mephisto from importing children and selling them. I'd have to kill the vamp himself, and that was so unlikely as to be laughable.

I kept my coat tightly wrapped as I dismounted. I didn't want my weapons to show, especially here. I knew there were cameras, as well as crews on the lookout for those breaking the law. One glimpse of my silver weapons and I'd have the entire place coming down on me.

That didn't mean I'd ever consider leaving them behind. I'd rather risk getting caught with them than go unarmed. Anyone could jump me at any time. Safe rather than sorry, right?

I glanced around the parking lot, unsure where to go from there. I was so hungry it hurt, but I wasn't going to rush into anything.

It was surprising how busy the place was, especially when you consider how quiet most of the city is at night. Aside from the vampires and wolves lurking the dark corners, walking next to the Purebloods, it might even be reminiscent of what it was like back before the Uprising. I only wished I'd been alive that far back to have seen it.

With a sigh, I started walking for the mall. There was no sense standing around and waiting for something to happen. I was there for a reason and I just wanted to get it over with.

A pair of men stood to either side of the doors as I entered. They casually glanced my way and I knew they were looking me over to make sure I wasn't a threat. I must not have registered on their scale because they looked away almost immediately to check out an older couple wearing nearly as much leather as I was.

I made it all of ten steps into the mall before realizing how mind-numbingly stupid it would be to attack someone inside. I could walk through the mall and out the other side where there were some other stores, but that would only put me farther from my motorcycle. If I was going to do this, I was going to do it smart.

I turned around and walked right back out. The two men both raised their eyebrows at me and I shrugged in what I hoped would be an innocent manner as I passed them and headed back to the parking lot.

I walked all the way back to my Honda, checking behind me to make sure neither of the men followed me. They were still by the door, leaving me alone to consider what to do next.

The parking lot had constant traffic, people walking to and from the mall. I could easily find someone here if I waited long enough. It wouldn't be too hard to feed, to expose myself for what and maybe who I was, and then get the hell out of there.

I leaned against the van parked beside my motorcycle, crossing my legs so I looked as though I was just hanging out. No one would be fooled into thinking I was anything but dangerous thanks to my leather, but here, that might be more of a turn-on than anything.

A group of kids dressed in coats similar to mine passed by. A sweet, smoky smell trailed after them and their eyes were bloodshot. It wasn't hard to tell what they'd been doing before arriving.

One of the guys looked my way, started to look away, and then did a double take. He smiled and said something to his friends before he sauntered over to me. The rest of his friends kept walking.

"Hey, baby," he said. He reached out and trailed a hand

down the front of my coat. "Cool threads. I do like." He smiled, exposing crooked teeth.

I had to fight hard not to roll my eyes. It was just as much of a struggle not to leap out at him either. I gave him a smile that spoke of things he could only dream about.

He licked his lips and I noticed his tongue was pierced more than once. The metal piercing clanked against his teeth when he talked. "My car is back that way," he said, jerking his head back the way he had come. "Want to go for a ride?"

"Why not here," I said, stepping back beside my bike. As far as I knew, the kid wasn't dangerous, wasn't anything but a dumb teenager out looking for a little action. I moved a hand down to my waist suggestively, though I had an entirely different motive for getting my hands near my belt.

The kid's grin widened. God, he had to be no more than seventeen or eighteen. I almost told him to piss off so I could find someone else. If I hadn't been so hungry, I might have.

He stepped close, putting the van between us and the mall. The two big men at the doors wouldn't be able to see us.

I pulled a knife from its sheath. As the kid reached for me, I grabbed his hand, flipped it over, and cut into his palm. The blade was hidden back in my belt before the guy even knew he was cut.

He tried to jerk out of my grip, but I held firm.

"What the fuck?" he said. Blood bubbled from the wound. It might leave a scar, but he was in no danger of dying from it.

I gave him my best sultry look. It appeared my leather-loving friend was Pureblooded. I leaned forward and licked his palm. I came up with blood on my chin. "I'm so hungry," I said, lapping at the blood like a kitten.

He hesitated, then smiled, easing into my grip. "Go ahead," he said. His voice went husky.

I immediately latched on. He groaned as my fangs sank into his palm and I started sucking. I didn't want to kill the kid, which was what I would have done if I'd gone straight for his neck. I'd been lucky the kid had a vampire fetish, but it wasn't so surprising really, considering where we were.

My hunger screamed for more. I sucked as hard as I could, but the blood was already beginning to slow. The palm wasn't exactly the best place to feed.

I moved up his palm and found the delicate flesh of his wrist. I breathed in his scent, and mingled with the blood it had an almost euphoric effect on me. I bit down much harder than I intended.

The groans of pleasure turned into a hoarse scream. He tried to push against me, but I was holding him too tight. He'd have to cut his arm off before he would ever get it away from me.

Blood filled my mouth, sent me into near ecstasy. I swallowed mouthful after mouthful, relishing the warm, sticky taste as it slid down my throat.

It had been too long. Levi's blood bags could never take the place of a real feeding. This was as close to Heaven as I was ever likely to get.

The kid's fighting weakened and I knew I had to stop. If I kept going, I could easily kill him. The wound in his wrist wouldn't stop bleeding unless I let him take care of it.

I forced myself to pull away. I pushed him back the moment my face was free, and he slammed hard against the van. His hand immediately went to his wrist. His face was ashen as he stared at me with wide, bloodshot eyes.

"Go," I said. I could still smell his blood, and despite the fact my hunger was sated, I knew if he didn't leave now, I wouldn't be able to stop myself from finishing him off.

I didn't have to tell him twice. The kid spun and started running down the lot toward where he'd last seen his friends. He tripped over his own feet after only a few paces and sprawled face-first onto the pavement. He didn't let it slow him down. He was up and running again without missing a beat.

I wiped my mouth and looked around. A woman a few cars down was watching me. As soon as my gaze fell on her, she ducked back into her vehicle and backed out as if she feared I would chase her down. Her tires squealed as she tore out of the parking lot.

I took a few deep breaths and let the euphoria of the feeding wash over me. My head had cleared and I was starting to realize how bad of an idea this really was. I'd let too many things get to me, and I was putting myself in a dangerous situation for no reason at all.

I never should have come. Coming to Polaris to attract attention was about as smart as walking into a Major vamp's house unarmed. You just didn't do it if you wanted to live.

I started to turn to my Honda, intent on getting out of there, when I saw the two men walking toward me. At first, I thought it was the two men by the door, drawn by the freaked-out kid, but after a second look, it was clear it wasn't. These two were wearing long brown dusters and identical cowboy hats pulled down low to conceal their eyes. I didn't have to see their faces to know I was their target.

I considered jumping on my motorcycle and taking off before they got too close. I really didn't want to have Count Mephisto's men questioning me. I didn't have a permit to hunt in his territory, and I was sure it wouldn't take him long to figure out who I really was.

But I was tired of running. I had to face my problems head-on if I ever wanted them to go away.

I stepped forward to face the two men. They stopped a good five feet back, legs spread like they were in some western and we were preparing to duel. I couldn't see any weapons on them, but that meant little. They could be hiding anything under those coats.

"Lady Death?" the one on the right said. His voice was gravelly and deep. He sounded like he'd smoked for years and it had slowly started to eat away at his esophagus.

I didn't nod, didn't say anything. I just stared at them, waiting for one of them to either make a move or tell me what they wanted. I hated the idea that they knew who I was just by looking at me.

I guess my silence was enough, because the two men looked at each other and then nodded as if something had passed between them. As one, they removed their cowboy hats.

I cursed softly under my breath and took a step back as they both turned to face me. They were identical twins. Everything about them was the same, their clothes, their eyes, the dimples in their cheeks.

The knot of scar tissue on their foreheads.

"We are here on behalf of Packleader Adrian," the one on the left said. He sounded just like his brother. "You are to come with us."

And with that, they started walking my way.

9

I didn't like the idea of drawing my weapons in the Polaris mall parking lot, especially with a couple of Mephisto's goons standing at the door, but I had no choice. The two vamps by the door were far enough away, it was unlikely they would see what was going on until after the first blow landed. I hoped that would give me enough time to escape before they could call in help.

I drew my gun and kept it pointed low. Since it was small, it was the least likely of my weapons, outside my knives, to draw attention right away. No one would know I was packing silver bullets until I shot them.

Both men replaced their cowboy hats and walked slowly toward me, as if afraid I might bolt if they moved too fast.

"We're not going to hurt you," Lefty said. The way he said it, however, made it clear he wouldn't mind roughing me up a bit. Add to that the way his eyes were already a feral yellow, and I knew he was just itching for a fight.

"Stay the fuck back," I said, taking a step back so I couldn't be seen from the front of the mall. "Make another move and I'll shoot."

Righty snarled and took a step forward.

So I shot him in the leg.

The Glock I used had been modified by Ethan and his demon so that the bullets moved slower and would stick in anything they hit. The silver would then be stuck in my target, leaving a supe paralyzed until someone dug out the bullet. And while his modifications also made the gun quieter than it otherwise would be when fired, it was still loud as hell when you didn't want others to notice.

Righty screamed in agony as he dropped. He grabbed his knee, thrashing on the ground. The silver wouldn't work on Adrian's wolves, but a gunshot wound was still a gunshot wound.

I turned my gun on Lefty, who was standing with both hands in the air. A gust of wind blew the cowboy hat from his head and even though he winced at its loss, he didn't make a move to retrieve it.

"I'd turn around and leave if I were you," I said. "I'm in no mood to be fucked with. It's too cold. Go back and tell Adrian I'll deal with him when I'm damn well ready, *not* when he sends two bozos like you to collect me."

Lefty stood there, frowning. He didn't make a move toward me, which would have earned him a bullet to the leg like his brother, but he didn't turn to leave either.

"I'm serious," I said. I was growing nervous. Someone had to have heard that gunshot, and even though they wouldn't know the bullets were silver, they'd still wonder why I was shooting people up in the parking lot without Mephisto's permission.

"I can't leave without you," Lefty said. It looked as though it pained him to say it.

"You'll just have to manage."

He looked down at his twin, who had stopped thrashing on the ground. Though his eyes were still yellow, he wasn't screaming in pain anymore. He looked more frightened than hurt, and for some reason, that scared me.

"You don't understand—"

He cut off as my aim firmed on him. He took a deep

breath and bowed his head once before reaching down to help his brother to his feet.

And that's when we all heard the running footsteps.

Lefty's eyes widened as he looked behind him. "Go," he said, shooing me as if I were some annoying fly. "Get out of here."

I hesitated, undecided whether I should be pissed at how he dismissed me or if I should take his advice and run. The hesitation cost me my chance to get away clean.

Something roared on the other side of the van and I knew I had to move fast. Instead of leaping onto my Honda and tearing out of there, I stepped forward, closer to Adrian's wolves. I couldn't leave them there when I was the one who'd drawn attention to our little confrontation.

I was barely a step out from behind the van when something very large and very angry came flying over the van. It smashed into my motorcycle, and the crash of my Honda hitting the pavement as they both tipped over sent my teeth to grinding.

"Goddamn it," I said. I raised my gun and shot the werewolf in the back of the head while he was still trying to untangle himself from the wreckage.

He dropped instantly and I turned my attention to what was approaching.

There were at least a dozen of them. The wolves were already shifted and were approaching much faster than the vampires behind them. Someone in the back was carrying a shotgun.

"In the name of Count Mephisto, lay down your weapons and surrender yourselves." One of the vampires in the back spoke, his voice lofty and self-important. He didn't look to be overly concerned that I'd just killed one of the wolves.

"Get out of here," Lefty snarled to me. "You aren't any good to Adrian in the hands of Mephisto."

"And you'll be no good to him dead."

He gave me a long, hard look before he nodded once. We turned to the oncoming army.

There were five wolves in the party, as well as five vamps behind them. The other two in the back appeared to be Purebloods, but I couldn't be sure. One was carrying the shotgun. The other looked unarmed, but with the confident way he held himself, I was pretty sure he had a weapon hidden away somewhere.

The wolves stopped a good ten feet back. The vamps held their ground behind them, waiting for us to either surrender or make the first move. They knew they had us. Even if I started firing right away, there were too many of them for me to get them all before they'd be on us.

"We'll just be leaving," I said, faking a smile. "We just had a little lover's spat. It's all cleared up now."

One of the vampires in the back smirked. "I don't think so," he said. "Firing a weapon on Mephisto's property is against regulation 436." He looked me up and down. "We must confiscate the weapons and take you back with us so you can be properly interrogated."

A wolf growled, causing the rest to follow suit.

"Oh, fuck this," I said, raising my gun and firing.

I'd been aiming for the vamp who last spoke, but just as I moved my arm, all five of the wolves straightened. The one in front of the vamp I was aiming for took the bullet and he dropped, shuddering from the silver bullet lodged in his chest.

The other four wolves didn't hesitate. They charged forward, dropping to all fours to increase their speed. They were on the twins so fast, I didn't get a chance to fire another shot before the melee began.

The vamps held back, but spread out so I couldn't drop them in a couple of quick shots, and the Purebloods behind them moved to hide behind cars.

I had to think fast. The twins weren't going to hold their own against the wolves, but I knew if I left the vamps alone, they'd find a way to get to me while I was distracted by the wolves.

I growled deep in my throat, frustrated that I had to make the decision.

I drew my sword as I fired two quick shots. One took a wolf fighting Righty in the head; the other nicked Lefty's shoulder and flew off harmlessly. He howled in pain and glared over his shoulder at me. I shrugged and mouthed an "oops" before turning my attention back to the enemy.

Righty had fallen and struggled back to his feet. His cowboy hat was somehow still on his head despite the wind and the fight. He started to say something, but before he could say much more than "Th," a loud blast took his head clean off his neck.

I immediately fired. The Pureblood had made the mistake of watching the results of his shotgun blast and my bullet took out his eye.

The vamps, apparently having seen enough, charged. I managed one shot, which went wide, before two of them were on me. They each had wicked curved blades in hand. Even though they weren't silver, the blades looked more than sharp enough to get the job done.

I swung my sword to meet the first attack and then just barely managed to twirl out of the way of the second. If I'd had my knife in my other hand, I might have been able to jab one of the vamps in the ribs. As it was, I managed to twist my wrist just enough to fire a shot. It hit him in the ass and he cried out as he dropped.

I managed to avoid another attack from a curved blade and turned just in time to see one of the vamps who'd held back come charging in. I raised my hand to fire, but the vamp I dodged came at me and hit the top of the gun with the hilt of his blade, knocking it from my hand.

I didn't have time to draw another weapon. I dropped low and swung out my leg, catching in the calves the vamp who'd knocked my gun free. He tried to catch his balance but stepped on the dropped gun. The Glock shot out from under him and went flying under the van as the vamp fell hard, cracking his skull on the pavement.

The oncoming vamp howled as he leaped at me.

Rookie mistake.

I braced myself and settled my sword so the point would meet him on his downward arc. His eyes widened and he tried to twist in midair, but instead impaled himself on my sword. I jerked back in time so he wouldn't slide all the way down, trapping the blade beneath him. He fell to the ground, shuddering.

I spun to face the vamp I'd tripped to find him lying there, eyes dazed. Blood oozed from his skull, which was oddly misshapen. It wouldn't kill him, but it should keep him down for a good long while.

I couldn't take the chance that he'd recover enough sense to rejoin the fight, however. I stabbed him in the chest just to make sure he stayed down, before turning to face the others.

Lefty was just barely holding his own against the remaining wolves and vamps. He'd shifted, but it was clear he wouldn't last long if I left him, which I wasn't about to do. I'd created this mess by firing my gun. I planned on cleaning it up, even if it meant saving one of Adrian's men.

I took a step forward and one of the wolves noticed me. He broke away from the fight to leap at me. Before I could raise my sword, Lefty lashed out, catching the wolf in the back with a claw. The sound of snapping bone followed and the wolf crumpled to the ground, spine shattered.

Lefty grinned at me as I moved to fend off another vampire. He started to turn back to his own fight just as something small hit him square in his chest.

The wolf looked down at the tiny feather, turned to look at me, and then slumped to the ground, out like a light.

I looked up in time to see the last Pureblood duck behind a car . . . And the two dozen wolves running up the aisle.

"Shit," I said, retreating. There was no way I was going to be able to handle all of them on my own.

I knew Lefty was still alive, knew he'd stuck around to defend me for some reason. I felt bad leaving him behind, even if he was one of Adrian's thugs who had been sent to bring me in. The guy had at least been somewhat respectful. It was more than I could say about a lot of people.

But I couldn't stay here. If Mephisto caught me, I'd be done for. Nothing Ethan or Jonathan or anyone else could do would save me.

I turned my back on the vamps and wolves, and ran to my bike. I felt something hit my coat, but whatever it was didn't poke through. The dead wolf was still tangled in the wreck, and I yanked on him as hard as I could.

He was heavy, but not so heavy that I couldn't move him. He trailed a thick stream of blood, spilled it over my seat and into the workings of my Honda. I winced, knowing it would be a bitch to clean out and the smell would probably never go away.

A wolf dove at me just as I righted the motorcycle. I still had my sword in hand and used it to knock him away, though I didn't manage to cut him. He landed on his feet, spun my way, and charged again.

This time he wasn't so lucky. I drew one of my knives and before he could so much as open his mouth to howl, I threw it. The knife took him in the throat and he dropped, mid-leap.

I knew the others were just behind me. I leaped on my bike, drawing my other knife, knowing chances were good I'd have to throw it, leaving me dangerously short on weapons.

But no one came. I started the motorcycle and turned so I could flee, only to find all the remaining wolves and vamps on their knees. I hesitated, wondering what was going on; then I saw him.

The vamp was tall, dressed in flowing black silk. He wore sunglasses despite the fact that it was snowing and nighttime. He was staring at me, and what I could see of his eyebrows were furrowed, as if he wasn't quite sure what he was looking at.

Mephisto. It could be no one else.

My blood ran cold and I didn't know if it was because of his intense stare or if it was something else, something magical. I decided I didn't want to wait around to find out.

I gave the Honda as much gas as I dared and sped out of the parking lot. I waited for a shot to be fired, for something to leap out and tackle me, but nothing happened. I hit the road going far too fast and nearly collided with a salt truck. A horn blared, but I barely heard it over the pounding of my heart.

I was halfway down the road before I even dared to breathe. I slowed down and nearly collapsed. Why had Mephisto let me go when he had me trapped? Chances of me escaping with so many of them right behind me were slim. He could have had me.

I'd been stupid. I never should have gone there, never should have fed that openly. I didn't know how Adrian's wolves found me, and quite frankly, I didn't care.

After what I'd just seen, I was happy I was still alive.

I tore down the road, my heart pounding. With the way my life had been going lately, I wasn't sure I could say that for much longer.

10

As I rode home, I started getting pissed all over again. It wasn't so much about the fight or about Adrian's wolves coming to gather me. I'd brought that on myself by going out like I had.

No, I was fuming over something else entirely.

I'd always been someone who did what I thought was right. I did whatever I wanted, how I wanted, and when I wanted. I never bowed down to anyone, never let myself get distracted from what needed to be done. I was focused.

Yet somewhere along the way, I let others in. I'd gotten weak, let others dictate how I lived my life. They didn't come out and say it, didn't even tell me what to do, but I was doing things based on what they'd think of me, how they'd react.

No more. I refused to let myself get killed because someone didn't want me to do something I knew was necessary. I never should have let Jonathan talk me into not killing Adrian. I should have shot the backstabbing bastard the first time I saw him at The Bloody Stake. But no, I just had to see what he wanted, and by then it was too late to act.

Next time I saw Adrian, he was dead. If Jonathan didn't like it, then screw him. He didn't own me. No one did. Everyone has stuck their noses into my business for far too long now. It was time I put a stop to it.

By the time I pulled into the garage, I was fuming. I'd even managed to get the Honda all the way up the driveway despite the increasing snow. It was a wonder I hadn't broken my neck with as wild as I was driving.

I turned off the motorcycle and stormed into the house, ready to start setting things to right.

"Ethan!" I shouted, throwing my coat onto the table. I started to strip off my belt but stopped myself. With what I was about to do, I'd probably want what weapons I had left on me close at hand. "Ethan!" I called, angrier this time.

I glanced into the living room and saw a wide-eyed Jeremy staring at me. He was propped up on the couch, a bowl of popcorn in his lap. The TV was on with the volume so low only a werewolf could hear it.

Some watchdog he was. He should have been on his feet the moment I'd come storming into the house, yet there he sat, like the cripple he was.

"Where is he?" I snarled, hating him more than I thought possible. Rage continued to build. I was nearly seeing red.

Jeremy's eyes flickered toward the stairs and then back to me like he didn't trust me enough to look away. He opened his mouth but closed it again when I turned away without waiting for an answer. His eyes had been answer enough.

I headed straight for the stairs. The light in the sitting room was off, but a fire was burning. It warmed the room considerably, and its comforting flicker eased my anger somewhat, but it couldn't fully quench it.

What I'd give to be able to sit in front of the fire and just relax without wondering if someone I knew was dying because of me. Just one night to forget everything, to have peace within my home and around those I cared about.

I took a deep breath before opening the basement door.

I knew it would never happen, not while I was who I was. Someone would always be after me. Someone would always get hurt because of me.

I went down the stairs, trying really hard not to stomp.

Ethan wasn't in the first basement, so I assumed he was in his lab, most likely talking to his demon. That would make what I had to do go that much quicker.

I walked over to the door that led down into his lab and pressed the intercom button. "Ethan," I said in what I hoped was a reasonable voice. "Come up here."

There was a long pause; then his nervous-sounding voice came through the tiny speaker. "Okay."

I waited as he finished up whatever he was doing, trying my best to calm myself. I stared at the lab door, wondering why Ethan thought it prudent that I didn't have a key. It was the only door in the house I couldn't get into. The entire room was soundproof and bombproof. Nothing could get in there without Ethan letting them in.

I wondered if the reason I didn't have access was because he wanted the sanctuary for himself. Or was it because he was afraid I might break someday and wanted to be able to hide inside where I couldn't get to him?

The door opened and he stepped out, eyes wide. I almost punched him because of it. I was so tired of people looking at me that way.

And he wasn't sweating, which only served to upset me more. Whatever he'd been doing, it hadn't involved his demon.

"I want you to summon Beligrow."

"Beligral."

I glared at him.

"Sorry."

"I want you to summon the bastard so I can talk to him and get this fucking mark removed."

Ethan glanced toward the lab door. He'd closed it when

he'd come up. "Are you sure that's a good idea right now? You seem a little . . ." He winced.

"Why the fuck wouldn't it be?"

He opened and closed his mouth a few times, then visibly slumped. He knew there was no chance he was going to talk me out of this, not with the mood I was in.

"Um, okay," he said. "Let's go." He started to open the door but stopped. "You'll want to leave your weapons here."

"No."

He blinked at me like I'd spoken in Swahili. "What?"

"I said no. Your goddamn demon can deal with the weapons. If I wanted to kill him, there's more than enough lying around down there to get the job down."

Ethan paled and licked his lips. "He won't like it."

"I don't give a fuck about what he likes and doesn't like." I was breathing hard now, so angry I wanted to hurt someone. "I want this mark taken off me and I want it done now."

Ethan scrambled to get the door open and rushed down the stairs ahead of me. I stalked after him, my anger back in full force. How hard would it have been for him to simply do what I asked him to do without arguing?

A drawer slammed as I reached the hard concrete floor. Ethan turned back to me, red-faced. I didn't want to know what he'd just hidden from me, I really didn't.

"Summon . . ." I trailed off as my eyes took in the rest of the room.

A lot of the stuff was the same. The shelves with the darkened containers were still there. The workbench was in the same spot, as was the circle on the floor with the recliner planted firmly in its center.

But the cage across the room was new.

I stared at it, dumbfounded. Why in the hell was there a cell in Ethan's lab? A silver one at that.

"Ethan," I said warningly.

He gave a nervous laugh. "I knew you'd hate it," he said. "But Jonathan thought it would be a good idea in case something like . . ." He coughed and changed what he'd been about to say. "In case we have to hold someone," he finished lamely.

"Why would we need to hold anyone down here?" I was nearly growling my words by now.

"It works wonders during the full moon," he said. "Jeremy comes down here and it keeps him from going all crazy on me. Well, he's still crazy, but he can't eat me while he's inside." Another nervous laugh.

I had to close my eyes to keep from exploding. I hated cages. I didn't care whether Ethan decked it out with all the comforts of home or if he kept it as a bare stone floor as it was now. It was still a cage, meant to hold people inside against their will. I'd been trapped in more cells than I cared to remember.

But it did make sense. If we'd had the cell when we'd caught Thomas, he'd still be alive today. He might even have recovered. I should have thought of it before.

"Fine," I said, opening my eyes, though I pointedly looked elsewhere in the room. Maybe if I refused to acknowledge it, it would go away. "Summon your damn demon so we can get this over with."

Ethan nodded and rushed over to his desk. He withdrew his fleshy candles and his sidewalk chalk, and went about setting up the circle.

I watched him for a few moments before I couldn't take the silence anymore. "Is all of this really necessary," I said. I was tired of waiting. I'd waited too long already.

He glanced at me as he set one of the candles. "What do you mean?"

"All the candles and circles and chanting you do. Isn't there an easier way?"

He laughed again, but it was still nervous sounding.

"Not really," he said. "But it helps me focus. I've done it this way since I was little." He sort of mumbled the last.

I didn't know much about Ethan's life before I'd met him. I suspected his demon summoning was the reason Count Valentino had kept him locked up and hadn't fed on him like he had the others. I'm not sure if there was more to it than that, but honestly, there really didn't need to be. It kept him alive when the rest of his family had died.

Ethan set the last two candles and turned to face me. "It isn't the words or the ritual that summons the demon, really. It's the will of the summoner, the desire to bring the demon into this realm that matters."

I cocked an eyebrow.

"So, let's say Bob the neighbor finds a ritual in a book. If he doesn't believe in it or doesn't want it to work, he could repeat it over and over and nothing will happen. The summoning comes from within the summoner. You have to believe in it *and* want it to work at the same time. After that, it's cake."

"So that means you wanted to summon a demon as a kid?" That seemed wrong on so many levels.

Ethan's face reddened. "I didn't have many friends," he mumbled as he turned to start the ritual.

I felt bad for him. How bad of a life did he have that he had to resort to summoning demons to keep himself occupied? Did someone show him how to do it or did he go looking for it himself? I just couldn't picture a young Ethan looking for trouble of this sort.

I'd seen him do it before, but watching Ethan perform the summoning was hard. I couldn't believe he of all people was capable of doing something so inherently evil. The guy hardly ever cursed and here he was doing so blasphemous, it made *me* look like a saint.

Ethan drew a chalk outline around the silver circle on the floor, careful not to step inside. He'd said it was only precautionary, but I wondered how true that really was. I'd seen his demon. The thing was scary.

He started his chant, keeping his voice low so that I never could quite understand what he was saying. The foul candles flickered, giving off the smell of burning flesh. My stomach curdled at the thought that they might have been someone once. No matter how innocent I thought Ethan might be, there was a dark streak in him that was scary as hell.

The room started getting hot, and the mark behind my ear started buzzing. It felt like I had some sort of small vibrator beneath my skin and I reached up to touch the bumps. They were more pronounced now, as if they were trying to tear free of my skin in response to the summoning ritual.

A dark speck appeared in the middle of the circle. The room got almost unbearably hot. Ethan was sweating so badly his shirt looked as though he'd dipped it in a bucket of water.

Heat poured from the speck. It grew, rising vertically as if the opening between realms was being drawn by a zipper.

The mark throbbed in time with the pulses of heat. Fear bubbled in my gut, and my brain kept screaming at me to run before the demon saw me, to get out and as far away as possible. Nothing good could ever come of treating with a demon.

I held my ground even as the dark portal opened and a wave of heat poured out. It was like standing in front of the sun. Oppressive heat washed over me and I cringed back.

The demon emerged.

11

My eyes burned and watered, but I forced myself to watch as Beligral stepped through the portal. There was a hint of red skin, of horns, and of black, demonic wings, but before the image could truly form, he turned into a seemingly dapper man, dressed smartly. Only his sharp yellow teeth and red eyes gave him away as anything but normal.

I knew for a fact the human appearance was fake, a glamour cast to fool the eye, but I wasn't sure about the other demonic visage. Did he do that only to confuse me about his true appearance? Or was he really as nightmarish as he appeared to be?

Part of me never wanted to find out.

As soon as he was through the black portal, Beligral turned to me and bared his teeth in what I took to be a smile. The tear between realms sealed itself behind him, leaving behind the heat and the demon trapped within the circle.

"Well, well, well," he said, leaning forward on a cane that seemed to appear from nowhere. Knowing him, it probably had. "Look who finally decided to make an appearance. I'm so glad you could join me on this most glorious of nights." He took a deep breath and let it out in a contented sigh.

I had to swallow a lump in my throat before I could even think to speak. Every nerve in my body was hopping. I wanted to run, wanted to flee right back to Delai and never look back. My skin felt as though it was just about to melt from my bones. Ethan didn't look much better, even though he claimed to be used to the heat.

Beligral laughed and walked over to the recliner in the middle of the circle. He sat down and laid the cane across his knees. There was something on the head of the cane, but I couldn't tell what. The demon never lifted his hand enough for me to see.

"Not much for words today, I see," he said. "Sometimes my entrances can be . . . overwhelming." He bared his teeth in that smile again. "But you'll get used to it in time."

I took a deep breath and nearly choked when it burned my lungs. I knew most of the heat was imagined. Beligral probably created some of it himself just to fuck with anyone stupid enough to summon him. I had to admit, it did its job.

It took me another moment, but I was finally able to find my voice. "What do you want?" I croaked. I sounded like someone stranded in a desert with no water and no hope of rescue. I cleared my throat, which helped a little. "I got your message."

My hand went reflexively to the mark behind my ear. It felt like I was touching a hot iron and I jerked my hand away. I was surprised my hair hadn't caught on fire from the heat. I wondered if Ethan had the same sort of mark, and if it felt as hot as mine did or if the demon was only causing mine to flare for my benefit. I wouldn't put it past him.

Beligral leaned forward in his chair. That damnable smile was spread across his face. It made me want to step over the circle and punch him just so he'd stop, but that would be bad. Really bad.

"Why, I only want what is owed to me. You promised to return and I've decided it was time you repaid that debt. I can only wait so long."

"Well, I'm here now," I said. "The debt has been paid. Now leave me the hell alone." I turned to go.

"Ah, but is it?" Beligral laughed. There was no humor in it.

I managed not to shudder when I turned back to face him. "You said all I needed to do was to see you again. Here I am."

The demon stood. The cane was gone, vanished as if it had never been there to begin with. He walked to the very edge of the circle and stopped. "I know where you have been," he said, his voice conspiratorially low. "But do you?"

I clenched my teeth and refused to speak. I wasn't sure if he was talking about earlier that night or if he was talking about the last few months. I really hoped he wasn't referring to Delai, because a demon in a place like that would destroy the peace the people there had fought so hard to achieve.

"I see you don't," he said. He shook his head as if disappointed in me and started walking around the inside of the circle. "You think you know what you've been experiencing. You think you have things under control. Do you know what you've really been doing since you left here? Do you know what kind of monster you've been playing house with?" He gave me a sad smile. "I don't think you do."

I didn't say anything. I knew speaking would only make things worse for me. He'd find a way to twist my words, a way to get me to add yet another mark. I knew that was his game. I wanted my mark gone, not to add another.

Beligral sighed. "Delai is not a good place for someone like you."

Ethan glanced at me, a confused look on his face. I shook my head and continued to stare at the demon. My eyes were dried out from the heat, but I wouldn't look away again until he was gone.

"If you go back, you might never escape. That's what he does. He traps your kind in, turns them into husks that do his bidding. He will burn you out of your own body and will enjoy every moment of it. He may claim it as a cure, but we all know what he does is far from it."

I couldn't hold back any longer. "You don't know what you are talking about."

"Don't I?" He laughed. "I think I have much more experience in regard to matters of this sort than you."

"And you're a liar."

He smirked. "Tell me, what have I lied to you about? I've done everything in my power to help you. I've never led you astray."

I wasn't so sure about that. He'd claimed to do a lot of things, but I couldn't prove any of them. He'd said he tried to help my brother, but I hadn't seen or felt anything that could prove it one way or the other. I had only his word, and I sure as hell wasn't about to trust the word of a demon.

"I've invested too much in you to have you throw it all away," Beligral said. "I cannot let you succumb to his magic without giving you something to fight back with."

"You've done enough already." I growled the words, angry at myself for even getting involved in the conversation. I should have kept my mouth shut and walked out of the room when I'd had the chance.

"But clearly I haven't," he said. He resumed his seat in the chair. "If you knew what you were getting into, you would never have gone there in the first place. Since you've spent so much time in Delai, it is doubtful you'll ever believe what I have to say. The people there are no good."

I looked at Ethan. He was looking back and forth from me to the demon. He looked hurt that there was something passing between us he didn't understand. I felt like a bitch for not filling him in already. It should have been the first thing I did when I'd gotten home.

"Tell me," I said, turning my attention back to Beligral. "And then let me go. I never want to see you after this."

The demon's lips lifted in a grim smile. "Of course," he said. "I will even give you this information for free. It will be up to you if you wish to accept what I have to offer afterward."

I ground my teeth, hating how this sounded. I knew he was trying to trick me into another mark somehow. Free information is never really free when it's coming from a demon, I was sure.

"Fine," I said. "Say what you have to say."

Beligral leaned back, his cane once more resting across his knees. "Does he still call himself Levi?"

I thought I kept my face neutral, but he read my expression as easily as if I'd spoken.

He nodded. "He isn't what he appears to be. The name is as much of a lie as the rest of his world. If you let him get to you, he will turn you into one of his pets. I can already see his mark upon you."

I glared at him and tried not to let my unease show. I didn't know why, but as soon as he started talking, I pictured Ronnie, how he stared at nothing all the time, how he did whatever Levi told him to do. I didn't know if I was thinking these things on my own, or if Beligral was somehow putting the thoughts in my head.

"They say all roads lead to Delai," he went on. "It appears you've traveled that road and back again, something not many have done. It was only by my intervention that you managed to escape when you did. Much longer and he would have had complete control over you."

Beligral was staring directly into my eyes as he spoke. I knew that was a bad thing. It had to be, right?

It was a struggle, but I managed to look away. I kept wanting to look up, as if his eyes had a pull to them. I so didn't want to get trapped in his gaze.

"If you go back, he will have you. I can't keep you safe forever."

I almost laughed at that. "I don't want you messing around in my life." I looked squarely at his knees.

I could hear the smile in his voice as he continued. "I'm already in too deep. You are stuck with me whether you know it or not. You don't have to like it."

I glanced up at his face and could see the fierce glow in his eyes. They flared with an almost feverish intensity. I looked away before I got burned.

"Delai will always be there because you expect it to be. No matter how you get there, it will be waiting." He paused. "At least until you are no longer wanted. I will make sure that happens."

"Why would I want you to do that?" It was hard to sound as angry as I felt when I couldn't look him in the face. It felt too much like I was subservient to him, but I knew looking him in the eyes would only make things worse.

"Do you know what Levi is? Di'leviathan? He is older than even I."

I really wanted to turn around and walk out. How could I ever believe something coming out of a demon's mouth? I wondered if he was afraid that Levi would find a way to save me from the demon's influence. Maybe it had started happening already and that was why he'd sent the pain, to draw me back before I could be fully swayed.

But despite the desire to leave, I'd stayed. I knew from the first day I'd gone there that Delai was different. I never could put a finger on it, but it always had seemed ever so slightly off. I knew I'd never get the whole story out of Beligral, but I was sure he would at least leave me with some half-truths as long as it served his purposes.

"The slice of time he controls will always remain as long as he remains stuck between our worlds. Something has anchored him there. He cannot escape his little haven, but he isn't forced to return either. If you find out what is keeping him, most likely his summoner, then you can send him back to where he belongs."

"He's a demon?" I looked up, startled.

"No." Beligral shook his head and frowned. "Not in the way you think of demons. He comes from the same realm as I, will destroy anything he touches, much like my brethren would do if they were to escape. He is similar, but something oh so different."

"Then what exactly is he?" I challenged. It bothered me that he was being so damn vague.

Beligral smiled and waggled a finger at me. "Tsk, tsk. Do you think I would share everything I know? If you want to find out what he is, you will need to do that on your own." He looked at his nails and smiled. "I could provide you with a way."

"How?" Something inside me groaned. I really should have left a long time ago.

"I will allow you to see him for what he truly is. I will give you the Sight, something only a few have ever been blessed with. It will allow you to see past his glamours, to see into his heart. Once you see what kind of hold he has on those he's trapped, you will understand my concern."

"And what's in it for you?"

Beligral chuckled. "Nothing but your return. I will give this to you and you will see I have not led you astray. There is so much more we could do together if only you'd learn to trust me."

Yeah, like that would ever happen.

I looked at Ethan. He was shaking his head frantically from side to side, though he didn't voice his disapproval. I knew it was a bad idea to agree to anything the demon offered. He would somehow turn it to his own uses, would trap me like he'd trapped Ethan.

But I had to know. Could I really walk away without knowing for sure whether he was telling the truth?

"What do I need to do?" I asked, resigned.

Ethan visibly slumped and closed his eyes. I was disappointing him, I knew.

"Come into the circle with me. I have to touch you to impart this most wondrous of gifts."

"Not happening," I said. How stupid did he think I was? "Find another way."

"There is no other way," he said. "My powers are limited to this circle. If you wish to receive my gift, then you must cross the barrier and take it from me." He smiled, exposing his teeth again. He was almost salivating.

I considered the offer. There *was* something off with Delai, I couldn't deny that. I cared about Sienna and Eilene, and even Ronnie and Levi in a way. They'd taken me in when I felt I had nowhere else to go. They'd given me a place to live, a place to control the hunger inside me.

Yet it always felt wrong. There was something unnatural about the way Levi could calm me when I was at my most ravenous.

And then there was his family. They feared him. Could Beligral really be telling the truth? Could I take the chance that he wasn't? I couldn't leave Sienna and Eilene there if something bad was happening to them.

Beligral's smile widened as if he could hear the thoughts running through my head.

"I'll think about it," I said, wiping the smile off his face. "Until then, our debt is paid." I turned and walked out.

As soon as I was out of the lab, I slumped against the

wall. My skin felt parchment dry after having been in the oppressive heat of the lab. I waited for Ethan to dismiss the demon and gather his supplies. He joined me a few minutes later, looking grim.

"He's not happy," he said.

"I don't care."

"But you're free."

I reached up and touched the smooth skin behind my ear. The mark was gone and I hadn't even felt it go. "Yeah."

"Don't do what he wants."

I didn't say anything.

"Kat . . ."

I looked up and Ethan cringed away. "I'll do whatever the fuck I want," I said, getting pissed all over again. I was tired of people telling me what I should and shouldn't do. I was my own person, damn it.

Ethan didn't say anything. He stood by as I tore off my belt and tossed it onto the table. I gave him one last challenging stare, daring him to say something else, and then turned and stalked up the stairs to sulk alone in my room.

12

I struggled to make it through the day without going insane. I couldn't shut off my brain, even for a little bit. I tried taking a bath, which usually helped clear my head, but all it really did was make me wet. I dried off and caught a glimpse of myself in the bathroom mirror.

The old scars were still there. My back was virtually crisscrossed with them, though none was worse than the large scars on my back from where the wolf had gouged me. The scar was still red and angry looking. It ached every now and again, a constant reminder of how close I'd come to death.

I turned away from the mirror and headed into the bedroom to get dressed.

I wasn't sure what was bothering me the most. What the demon had told me was pretty upsetting, but I could always make myself believe he was lying. I was free of him and never had to go back if I didn't want to. The same went for Levi and Delai. If I decided not to risk it, nothing was forcing me to go back.

Of course, I doubted I could keep myself from returning even if I wanted to. Levi had shown me nothing but kindness since the day I'd arrived. He helped me overcome my hunger, at least a little bit. I couldn't imagine him being anything more than the affable big man he appeared to be.

Still, the doubt was there. I hated to admit it, but it was. I was free of Beligral's mark, yet I wasn't free of his influence. I knew if I ever wanted to know the truth about Levi, I'd have to go back to the demon, would have to take on another mark.

I wasn't so sure I wanted to do that.

I refused to think about the demon any longer, and thoughts of the Luna Cult immediately invaded. I wondered how they were faring, wondered what Jonathan was doing. I was still pissed at him, still never wanted to see him again, but I really didn't want anything bad to happen to him.

I growled in frustration as I finished getting dressed. I had put on my leather, a sure sign that I planned on doing something dangerous the moment the sun went down.

Thoughts of Jonathan brought much of my anger back. He left me with a goddamn watchdog. Jeremy Lincoln might have been sent here under the pretense of watching over Ethan, but I knew better. He'd been sent to *my* house so he could tell Jonathan when I returned.

Time ticked by and I only got angrier. I kept dwelling on all the bad things that had happened to me; perceived or real, it didn't matter. It seemed like ever since I returned, everyone had gone out of their way to piss me off.

And then there was Countess Baset.

I'd been hunted before. I was sure I would be hunted again; but for some reason, this one bothered me. Maybe it was because I hadn't actually killed her lover, Countess Telia, and yet she was still coming after me like I had. She might not know I hadn't killed her, but damn it, she should have stopped looking for me when it became obvious I was no longer around.

Or maybe I was just sick of vampire Houses thinking they could do whatever the fuck they wanted. Someone should have put Baset down the moment she had fallen from Royal. I should have done it myself.

Maybe I still could.

It was decided before evening. I could feel the cold seeping in from around the window, could almost smell the fresh layer of snow that covered the ground.

The shower was running, but I wasn't sure if Ethan or Jeremy was in it. Neither man was in the hall, nor were they downstairs in the kitchen as I passed. I continued down into the basement and gathered my weapons.

The smell of coffee percolating assaulted my nose as I returned to the dining room. Ethan was busy in the kitchen getting his evening breakfast started. He glanced at me out of the corner of his eye but didn't look directly at me when he spoke.

"Going out tonight?" he asked.

"Yeah."

He cleared his throat and looked everywhere but at me. I think he was still pissed about the night before. If it had been me, I probably would have been too.

"You going to the Den?"

"Fuck no."

He looked startled at that. "Um, then where?"

"Where do you think? I'm going to take care of my fucking problem."

Ethan blinked a few times, his eyes passing over me. "Okay?"

I sighed. "Countess Baset has been hunting me, as you well know. I'm going to put an end to it. Tonight."

He choked. "You're going to what?"

"I'm going to kill her." I glared at him angrily for making me explain myself. "You know full well what I do to those who think they can interfere in my life." A thought of Jonathan drifted through my head and I pushed it away.

Ethan looked away and I felt a twinge of regret. I was

treating him like shit, I knew. I just couldn't seem to help myself. Ever since I left Delai, I was angry with everyone, and half the time I didn't even know why.

"How, uh, are you going to pull this off?" he asked, finally looking at me. He looked concerned. "Alone?"

"How else?" I smiled, hoping it would ease his mind. "I'll slip in and kill her before anyone realizes I'm there. As far as a lot of people are concerned, I'm already dead." I thought back to my little escapade at Polaris. I really *hoped* everyone still thought I was dead.

"But she's the head of a Major House, isn't she?" Ethan shook his head. "I don't like this. You can't take down a Major House."

"I don't have to," I said. "I just have to kill her."

He laughed. It sounded half crazed. "You make it sound so easy." He sighed. "At least go talk to Jonathan—"

"I don't fucking need him!" I shouted, taking a threatening step forward. Ethan backpedaled into the cabinets. "Ever since I got involved with the Luna Cult, my life has only gotten more complicated. I don't need their help. I don't need anyone's help. I can do this on my fucking own."

"Okay," he said, hands held up in front of him like he thought I might hit him. "I'm sorry I mentioned it."

I took a deep breath and closed my eyes. I was taking my anger and frustrations out on someone who didn't deserve it. Again. I really needed to figure out why I was always so pissed off lately before I accidently killed someone. I'd been nothing but confused since the day I returned, and even that made me angry.

"No," I said, trying really hard not to scream. "I'm sorry. I shouldn't have yelled."

Ethan lowered his hands slowly as if he was afraid I'd snap at him if he moved too fast. Once he was sure I wasn't going to bite his head off again, he went about filling his coffee mug.

"I've just been under a lot of stress lately," I went on, feeling the need to explain myself. "We used to be fine with just the two of us. We didn't need others to help us fight our battles. We should go back to that, just you and I. It's safer that way."

"Is it really?" he said, turning back to me. "Is it really safer for us . . . or just for you? I'm not sure I want to be alone again."

I opened my mouth to respond, but nothing came out. It felt like he had slapped me.

"I understand why you feel like you have to go it alone," he said. "But I don't think it's the best thing for you." There was a long pause before he added, "I missed you."

For some reason, the last really got to me. My legs weakened and I leaned against the table. "Yeah," I said. "I missed you too."

There was a long stretch of silence; then Jeremy spoke from the stairs. "I'll call Jonathan."

And just like that, my rage was back.

"No, you fucking won't," I growled, straightening. I glared at him, dared him to disagree.

"I thought—"

"I don't care what you thought," I said, advancing on him. Even without an arm, he did good to hold his ground. The Jeremy I'd known before would have cringed and fled. "I'm not dealing with the Cult right now. Do you understand me?"

"The Cult has helped you more than you care to admit."

I stared at him, so angry I didn't know what to say. He was standing up to me, defying me in my own home. It was my choice to make. Why did these people think they could tell me what to do?

"Helped me?" I finally said. "You think they've helped me?" I laughed. "The Luna Cult has done nothing but get in my way. They've nearly gotten me killed more than once. They killed Thomas." My fangs started to pop through and blood ran into my mouth, further fueling my rage.

Jeremy flinched back and doubt crept into his gaze. "I should call him anyway." He started to turn away, but I grabbed him by his arm and spun him back around to face me.

"Why?" I said. "Why call him? I'm not going to accept his help, even if he offers it. Besides," I said, glancing at his side, "what has the Cult ever done for you? They only make everyone's life worse. Take a look at your arm . . . if you can find it."

I regretted the words even before they were out of my mouth. Jeremy jerked his wrist out of my grip and stepped back, a wounded look on his face. He stared at me for a really long time before turning and heading wordlessly upstairs.

"Shit," I said as soon as he was gone. I rubbed at my forehead, a headache coming on.

"You shouldn't have said that," Ethan said from behind me.

"No shit." I sighed. I was fucking everything up and I didn't know why. My head was so muddled I could hardly think straight. I kept making all the wrong decisions. "I should go apologize."

Even though I'd been the one to say it, I didn't move.

I didn't know what to do. I was making a mess of my home life, ruining any friendships I might have made, and for what? Just because I was pissed off at the world, I had to destroy everything? I didn't have to be alone. Why was I forcing the issue by being such a bitch to everyone?

I went to the table and sat down. I couldn't go running off after a vampire Countess with my brain all twisted inside my head. I'd end up getting myself killed.

Maybe that was the point. Did a part of me want to die? Was I pushing everyone away so that they wouldn't be hurt when I let some vampire take my head?

Ethan sat across from me, setting his coffee mug gently onto the table as if he was trying not to disturb me. "Don't get mad at me," he said.

I groaned. "What now?" I said, dreading what he would say next.

"Just promise me you'll hear me out before you yell at me."

I looked up and he looked so innocent, so concerned for my well-being, I agreed.

"Okay," he said, taking a deep breath. "I know we've gone over this before, but I really want you to listen and think about what I say."

"All right."

"You're losing yourself." He took a sip of coffee while watching my face carefully. When I didn't snap at him, he set the mug back down and continued. "All the death, all the killing, it's starting to eat you up inside. You're letting it get to you. It's making you angry all the time."

Was that it? Could it really be that simple? "And?" I said, still not sure I wanted to hear any more.

"And I want to help." He reached across the table and rested a hand on my own. I managed not to jerk away, though I wanted to. "I really think if given the chance, I can find a way so you don't have to feed. It would take one more thing off your plate, one more thing that is driving you away from everyone who cares about you."

I closed my eyes. His hand felt so warm, so comforting, it made me want to cry. I'd never end up in bed with Ethan. Just the thought was laughable, but he was my closest friend, my only friend, really.

"I don't know what you and Beligral were talking about, where you've been," he went on. "I don't care. But from what I can tell, the place sounds dangerous. Ever since you've come back, you've been worse than I've ever seen you." He swallowed hard. "And that scares me."

I clenched my jaw, determined not to interrupt him until he had his say.

"Let me search for a way to curb your cravings. Maybe I can find a blood substitute. Maybe I can find some sort of alternate source that will keep you satisfied without forcing you to kill to get the full effect." His hand tightened on mine. "Please, let me help you."

I wanted to object, wanted to tell him to piss off, but instead found myself nodding. I couldn't keep living like this. Ethan was right. I was losing myself to the vampire in me. I was becoming more and more like the Counts and Countesses I despised.

I couldn't let that happen.

"I'll start right away," he said, pulling his hand away. He sounded happy.

Ethan stood and started toward the stairs leading down into the sitting room.

"I need you to do something for me," I said, my voice so quiet I wasn't sure he'd hear me.

He stopped and turned back to face me. "What's that?"

"Go upstairs and apologize to Jeremy for me. I can't do it myself right now."

"Okay."

"And get his keys. I want to borrow his car."

Ethan hesitated a moment before heading up the stairs to find Jeremy.

I hadn't known I was going to ask for the keys until the words were out of my mouth. If I was going to go out and hunt the Countess tonight, I didn't want to risk trying to drive my motorcycle in the snow.

It took only a few minutes before Ethan was back downstairs, keys in hand. I was surprised Jeremy had agreed to let me take the car after the way I treated him. It made me regret my harsh words that much more. He was a good kid . . . even if he was a werewolf.

"Don't wait up for me," I said, taking the keys.

"Be careful," Ethan said. He was still smiling, though I could see the worry in his eyes.

"I will."

And then I did something neither of us expected.

I hugged him.

Before I could take in much more than the shocked expression on his face, I turned and headed out into the garage.

Ethan had been right on more than one count. All the death *had* been getting to me. I might have taken a three-month break from it all, but killing someone wasn't something that ever left you. It festered.

And I was treating everyone like shit because of it. I couldn't keep going on like this if I wanted to have friends afterward. It was time I stopped.

Once Countess Baset was dead and everyone I cared about was safe, I could hang up my weapons, put away the leather, and try to live like a normal person for once.

I'd thought of it before, but only in passing. I'd never taken it seriously those other times because without my work, I'd have nothing.

But this time I was sure. Once Baset was dead and all my other messes were finally taken care of, I planned to put down my weapons and walk away from it all for good.

I was going to retire.

13

Jeremy's car was a piece of shit.

It took me a good five minutes to get it started, and once I got it going, I quickly learned the heat didn't work. While the cold might not bother me as much as it would a Pureblood, I did like to be comfortable.

I shivered as I chugged down the driveway and out onto the road. I was surprised the car didn't backfire or explode when I stepped on the gas.

Of course, it didn't really speed up either.

The top speed seemed to be somewhere in the thirty-five miles per hour range. If I went above that, the entire car started vibrating. If I was forced to run from House Baset, I wouldn't get very far in Jeremy's deathtrap. Maybe the vampires and wolves would laugh themselves to death before they caught me.

But despite the horrible car and the cold, I was feeling pretty good. The moment I decided to be done with all the death and retire, it was as if a great weight had lifted from my shoulders. I felt free, freer than I'd felt in a long time. I could finish this kill and ride off into the sunset . . . figuratively speaking anyway.

I still wasn't sure what I'd do about Levi and Delai. Once Baset was dead, I'd have to take some time to figure that out. It would come down to whether or not I chose to believe Beligral. I could use the demon's gift to investigate, or I could simply just grab Ethan and go. I was sure Levi would take him in if I asked.

I pushed any and all thoughts of Delai out of my head and focused on the task at hand. I couldn't be distracted now of all times. While Baset was no longer a Royal, it was still one of the biggies. The slightest slipup and I'd be dead. Hell, even if I did everything right, there was still a good chance I wouldn't survive.

Of course, I couldn't do anything until I found out where she lived. I needed Mikael for that.

I parked in The Bloody Stake parking lot and made sure no one was looking as I got out of the car and hurried inside. I didn't want to be seen in Jeremy's beat-up clunker, especially by someone I knew.

Mikael was at his usual booth with a few girls tucked under his arms. Even though it disgusted me, I was glad to see him back to his usual self. He was so involved with them, he never even looked up as I entered. His face was nuzzled up against one of the girl's necks and she was making squealing sounds that could be heard all the way across the room.

I strode toward him, trying my best not to be bothered by Bart's glare. He watched me from behind the bar, hands gripping a glass so hard it was a wonder it didn't shatter in his hand.

I approached Mikael's booth, steps slowing as I neared. Every time I came in with him sucking on some girl's neck, it made me realize how perverted he really was. At least this time he was the only one doing the sucking. I'd interrupted him before while he was involved in much more personal business.

"Where is House Baset?" I asked, slamming some money down on the table.

Mikael jerked away from his girl and gave me a startled

look. As soon as he realized who'd interrupted him in his fondling, he frowned and shooed the girls away, never taking his eyes off me. The girls gave a collective groan as they scooted out of the booth.

"I said no more money," he said, eyeing the bills sitting on the table anyway.

"Just tell me where I can find her."

He looked around the room and, after a moment, nodded toward the empty seat across from him. "This is a Major House, remember. It would sadden me if you were to die for real this time."

"I'll manage," I said as I sat down.

He sighed. "I hoped you would have taken my advice and left. Baset is too dangerous even for you."

"We'll see. Just tell me where she is." I frowned at him. "Unless she has you in her pay?" I made it a question.

"No," he said. "Baset does not use me or anyone else for her information. Not anymore."

"Then tell me where she lives," I said, feeling a little relieved. I wasn't sure what I would do if he couldn't provide me with information on her. "I don't need anything else from you."

He studied me from across the table. The money still sat between us, untouched. "Do you wish to die?"

"What kind of question is that?"

"A simple one," he said. "Do you wish to die?"

"No." It sounded like a lie even to me.

"Because if you go in search of Countess Baset, you will die. She is said to be unkillable. Rumors are she has already died once but did not stay down. She has regained much of her power since her fall. Trifling with someone like that is not good for anyone, yes?"

"And do you believe that she somehow rose from the dead?"

He shrugged. "I do not know. She is the first Countess or Count who I cannot provide sufficient information on.

And that scares me. Usually there is always someone willing to talk, but not with her."

"I don't need information other than where she lives. I can take care of the rest myself."

"Can you?" He cocked his head to the side. "I'm not so sure; not any longer."

My frown deepened. "And what's that supposed to mean?"

"I have heard of video footage of a woman dressed in black who made quite a scene in Count Mephisto's territory. The footage is not good, does not show her face well enough to be recognizable, but I hear it has interested the Count greatly. Would you know anything about this, my sweet?"

I tried to hide the guilty look on my face. "I was hungry."

Mikael grunted a laugh. "And you risked everything for that meal? It does not seem like you."

"It was dumb, I admit it." And I hated to be reminded of it. "Can we get back to Baset? What can you tell me?"

Mikael studied me and then sighed. "All I can say is that she no longer lives where you'd think. She leads a Major House, yes, but she is ostracized, has separated herself from the others. I don't know why. She lives in isolation, as much as a vampire Countess of such power can."

"Okay. Where does she live?" I felt like a broken record, asking the same thing over and over again. I just about kissed him when he finally gave me an address.

It appeared Baset lived outside city limits, off where I knew there to be little to no one left living. I didn't like it one bit. Normally, I might like hunting a vamp where no one else was likely to spot me, but somehow, the thought of going after Baset in the middle of nowhere had my stomach doing flips.

I stood and thanked him, leaving the money on the table for him to decide what to do with. I could feel his eyes on my back as I walked out the door. I slipped into Jeremy's car, more worried than ever.

The engine coughed a few dozen times before starting and I pulled out onto the road, thankful no one had been in the lot to see me.

I felt like a fool, especially since Mikael had heard about my little escapade at Polaris. He was right, I wasn't as careful as I used to be. Something was making me stupid.

And that included this hunt. I'd gotten my information like usual, but I'd planned on going straight in and taking Baset out as quickly and as quietly as I could without scouting the place out beforehand.

It sounded like a good plan at the time, but the more I thought about it, the more I realized to go in like that was a sure way to get killed. Was my carelessness a result of something Levi had done to me? Or was Ethan right? Was I losing myself to the vampire part of my mind?

The road got rough and I was glad I'd chosen to take Jeremy's car, no matter how shitty it was. My Honda never would have survived the potholes hidden in the snowdrifts. I'd have ended up walking most of the way, if I didn't break my legs first.

While I'd decided I wasn't going to attack Baset tonight, I did want to at least scout the place properly. I always liked to know my enemy. Often, you could learn a lot about a vampire just by watching their home for a little while. It would help me discern how many wolves and vamps she had at her disposal, as well as how good her defenses were.

Baset lived out of the way like Mikael said. There had been a mini vampire war a few years back that had wiped out the area where she now lived. I didn't even know the name of the town, if it ever had one. The place had been set to the torch and from what I understood, no one survived, not even the vampires involved.

But obviously something had survived. After traveling down the road for a good twenty minutes, I saw lights in the distance. Tortured trees obscured most of the view. Their branches drooped low where they hadn't fallen off. A lot of the trees were still trying to recover from the fire. Most of them had died.

I turned off my headlights and continued down the road a little ways before turning around and parking just off the shoulder. If some of Baset's wolves were prowling around, they'd surely see the car and report back to their Countess. I was hoping the snow kept them inside, or at least closer to the house.

I got out of the car and headed for the house lights in the distance. Even from where I crouched, I could tell it was a good-sized mansion. I used tire tracks in the driveway to hide my passage until I found a small copse of dead trees I could use for cover. They still smelled of ash, even after all these years.

I kept my eyes focused ahead, never letting the lights out of my sight. I'd stand out horribly against the snow. Only the trees provided me any sort of cover. Anyone who happened to glance my way would probably see me.

I was so intent on watching for movement ahead, I nearly tripped over a headstone. I paused and looked around. At some point, I'd entered an old graveyard, though there had been no fence or sign warning me it was coming. A few trees had grown up near the headstones, sprouts struggling against the bitter cold of winter.

It was sad, really. I wondered how long the graveyard had been abandoned. No one would be able to pay their respects to the dead here, not with a vampire Countess living so close by.

The graveyard sat on the top of a slight incline that gave me a decent enough view of Baset's mansion. I decided it was close enough and moved to stand near a tree so that I would hopefully blend in better.

As far as I could tell, no one was moving around outside. There were a few cars parked out front, but no one was sitting in them. Snow covered all the vehicles, so they'd been there for quite a while. The tire tracks leading from the drive were fresh enough that I knew someone might return soon.

The mansion itself was near black. I think it had been white at one time, but the fire had blackened the entire outside. Even the roof was ashen. If the lights hadn't been on, it might have been invisible against the night sky.

The light was coming from a few upstairs windows and one downstairs. Vampires and werewolves didn't need light to see by, though their Pureblood servants did.

How the house had stood against the fire, I had no idea. Everything else around it was gone. Up close, there were no trees, nothing at all that had lived past the fire. It stood almost completely alone on the empty landscape.

The only thing left standing outside the house was a twisted swing set in the backyard. The metal legs were warped, but the chains holding the seats hadn't snapped. The plastic seats had mostly melted away, leaving behind only molten chunks that hung from the chains like rotten fruit.

It was strange to think that children might have played out there once. Because of the fire damage, it was hard to tell how old the swing set was. Had the kids played there while vampires slept nearby? Or was the toy so old the children could play, firm in their belief that the monsters were only tales told to frighten them?

I sighed and chose to focus on scouting. To think of a past I never knew wouldn't help.

I watched the grounds for a good twenty minutes and I saw no one. Not even a shadow flittered near a window. The snow drifted, the wind caused my coat to flutter out behind me, but around the mansion, nothing moved.

This isn't right.

Normally, a Major House would have wolves and lesser vamps swarming all over. There'd be someone on the roof, a few patrolling the grounds, and yet there was no one. It was as if I was looking at a setup of a house, not a place where anyone actually lived. I should have seen someone by now. It wasn't *that* cold.

I turned and started back to the car, unsettled. I would have stayed longer, but I knew those who had left would probably be returning soon. I didn't want to get caught spying on the Countess when they finally did return.

Maybe Baset's Major House standing was only in name. Maybe she knew something that kept her high on the totem pole, but left her with limited resources. No high-ranking vampire I knew would want to live all the way out here where no one could look upon their greatness. They were too conceited for that.

No one drove by as I got in the car and headed back toward the city. I pushed the car as fast as it would go, half-afraid I'd pass someone on the way. I really didn't want to get into a fight tonight, not until I was sure about what I was facing. Baset didn't need to know I was watching her.

Thankfully, I turned off the road without seeing anyone. I did wish I'd have gotten a closer look at Baset's mansion since I hadn't seen anything move, but I'd been too creeped out by how it seemed so isolated, so silent. I was scared at what I'd find when I actually stormed the place.

Hey, maybe they'd all be dead. Those tire tracks could have been left by someone who'd decided to finish her off. It wouldn't be the first time I showed up to kill a vamp, only to have arrived too late. It would be poetic in a way, considering the last corpse I'd walked in on had been Baset's lover, Countess Telia.

As I pulled into my driveway, my headlights illuminated Jeremy shivering just outside the garage. I opened the garage door and pulled inside. He followed me in and yanked open the car door the moment I came to a stop.

All it took was one look at his face to set the alarm bells in my head ringing. I immediately thought of Ethan and a knot of fear coursed through me.

"What happened?" I asked, getting out.

"They have him," Jeremy said, his face pale. "I have to go."

"Have who?"

Jeremy looked around wildly for a moment before settling his shell-shocked eyes on mine.

"Jonathan," he said. "Countess Baset has Jonathan."

14

All feeling left my body, leaving me numb and cold as I tried to absorb the information. I couldn't wrap my head around it.

Countess Baset had Jonathan.

And I'd just been there.

"I've got to go," Jeremy said. He reached for the keys in my hand, but I jerked them back.

"No."

Jeremy's eyes flared yellow. "I need to go help the Denmaster."

I took a deep breath that nearly got stuck in my throat. My mouth had gone so dry I could hardly swallow.

How could I have not known? How could they have taken Jonathan and held him while I was right there?

Of course, I had no proof that he'd been there while I'd been watching the place. There had been fresh tire tracks. They could have captured him while I was hiding in the graveyard. Who knew, if I had waited twenty minutes more, I might have seen them take him inside.

But it still felt like it was my fault, whether I was there or not. Baset went after the Luna Cult Denmaster because she was looking for me; I was sure of it. The thought that I was responsible for his abduction made me so sick I had to lean against Jeremy's car to keep from sinking to my knees.

"You need to stay here and watch over Ethan," I said. I took a deep breath. This wasn't the time to fall apart.

Jeremy stared at me with such intensity, I thought for a moment he might attack me. "I can't just sit here when my Denmaster is in danger. I have to go help."

"What do you think you'll be able to do that I can't?" I snapped.

His eyes immediately bled back to their human color and he took a step back as if he suddenly realized whom he was dealing with.

"I could search," he said, sounding much more abashed than he had a moment ago. "Nathan called and told me to tell you what happened. I—I can't stand the thought of sitting around while everyone else is out looking for him. It's not right."

I could see in his eyes that he wasn't telling me everything. "And what else did Nathan say?"

Jeremy looked at his feet. "To stay here and wait for his call."

I felt bad for the kid. All he'd ever wanted to do was help, and look where it had gotten him. He was missing an arm because of his desire to fight. He would probably lose more than that if he forced the issue tonight. He was no match for Baset. I wasn't so sure I was either.

"Then you should do as he says." I gave him a sympathetic look. "I'm assuming Nathan has assumed control of the Cult while Jonathan is missing?"

He nodded.

"I know you want to help, but you should do what the standing Denmaster wants. If something were to happen to Jonathan . . ." I left the rest unsaid, not wanting to hear it myself.

I turned and headed for the side door, keeping a tight grip on Jeremy's keys.

"Where are you going?" Jeremy sounded almost frantic as he scrambled after me.

"Getting more supplies and telling Ethan where I'm going."

Jeremy followed after me as I stalked through the kitchen and down the stairs into the basement. Ethan was setting weapons out on the table as if he knew I was going to need them. He probably already knew what was going on.

I hadn't fired my Glock, so I didn't exchange it for a new one like I normally would. I still checked the magazine to make sure it was fully loaded before slamming it back home.

"Do you know where to go?" Ethan asked.

"I think so." I grabbed a few silver packets and stuffed them in my pocket. I do my best not to use them, but with a Major House, it was unlikely I'd be able to get to Baset without spreading some of it around. The dust would burn my eyes, but as long as I was careful, I'd be okay.

As if reading my thoughts, Ethan said, "Be careful."

"Always am." I considered adding another sword to my belt but didn't want to take the time. Besides, it might impede my movement more than I'd like. Maybe when I was done with Baset I'd have Ethan add a few more knife sheaths to my boots so I could have a few more on hand in situations like this.

My movements slowed as I patted myself down to make sure I had everything. Why would I need him to check into it if I was going to retire after this? I'd been putting so many people at risk because of who I was, I wasn't sure I *could* continue, even if I wanted to.

I shook off the thought and finished double-checking myself. I'd worry about what to do with myself later. Right then, I had a Denmaster to save.

Jeremy was standing at the foot of the stairs, watching me. I could tell he really wanted to go, but I wasn't going to risk him getting hurt again because of me. It was going to be dangerous enough having him stay here. Who knew what kind of information Baset was getting out of Jonathan while we dillydallied.

"Don't let anyone in," I told him. "I don't care if Jonathan comes walking up the driveway himself, don't let him in. I don't know much about Baset. She might have ways of controlling him, and I don't want you to risk making a mistake. Do you understand?"

Jeremy nodded.

I turned to Ethan. "Keep him in the house." I jabbed a finger at Jeremy. "He's to leave under no circumstances. If he starts for a door, shoot him."

Ethan's eyes widened, but he nodded. Jeremy didn't show any reaction at all. He was looking as numb as I had felt a few minutes ago.

I spun and headed for the stairs. Jeremy stepped aside and let me pass without trying to argue his case. Both he and Ethan followed me up the stairs, watching me as if it were the last time they'd ever see me.

Who knew? It very well might be.

I wasn't sure how I was going to go about doing this. I could have asked Jeremy to call Nathan or someone else at the Den to tell them where to go. I could meet up with them and we could storm Baset's mansion together.

But I didn't. It was my fault Jonathan was taken. Nathan and I had never been friends. If we arrived too late to save the Denmaster, Nathan would be just as likely to kill me as he would Baset.

I got into Jeremy's car and prayed it would start up right away. After a few tries, it coughed to life and I backed out of the garage. I managed to turn the car around without getting it stuck and then shot down the driveway as fast as I dared. Jeremy and Ethan both stood just inside the garage, watching as I left.

As soon as I was out of sight, I gave in to the emotions

that had been tearing at me the moment I'd learned Jonathan had been taken.

Tears spilled down my cheeks and I didn't know why. I shouldn't have cared one way or the other what happened to the werewolf. I'd all but told him to get out of my life the other night, so why was it hitting me so hard now?

Blame. I knew that was part of it. I blamed myself for this mess. I might have been angry at Jonathan, but that didn't mean I hated him or wanted something bad to happen to him. Hell, if I hadn't blamed him for Thomas's death, then maybe he wouldn't have been taken. We might have worked together, might have already dealt with Baset so I could move on with my life.

Rage replaced misery and I slammed my fist against the steering wheel. This was so stupid. Why would Baset go after the Luna Cult to get at me? It didn't make sense.

Then again, maybe she hadn't searched for Jonathan. I didn't know the whole story. Could Jonathan have gone after Baset in some insane attempt to get her to stop hunting me? I wouldn't put it past him.

The rage ebbed and another emotion took its place. The tears threatened to come again, but I forced them back. I couldn't give in to my emotions now.

But I kept thinking about Jonathan's hand on my face, the way he looked without his shirt, the smell of his breath. I didn't want to live without that. The thought that I might never see his wounded face again left an empty void in my chest. It almost hurt to breathe.

I cursed and tried to force the thoughts away. Jonathan was just someone I knew, nothing more. Just because something almost happened once, didn't mean it would ever happen again. Hell, it didn't even mean I *wanted* it to happen again. I was just scared.

And that pissed me off.

I stepped down on the gas harder. The back tires lost their grip with the road and for a few heart-stopping moments, I was swaying back and forth before they caught again.

I should have taken my bike. At least then I could have used my weight and feet to keep from tipping. Inside the metal box, I was trapped, helpless to the perils of the road.

I slowed down as I turned onto the road that led to Baset's blackened mansion. I wanted to race all the way to her front door, but I couldn't risk it; not when I was this close.

I parked just off the road in the same place I'd parked earlier in the night. As soon as the car was stopped, I threw open the door, leaving the engine running.

There were more tire tracks in the driveway. I knew others had come through since I'd last been there, but I had no idea how many. Tracking like that was a skill I hadn't bothered to learn, though Thomas had always told me it would come in handy someday. I guess I should have paid better attention to his lessons.

I ran at a crouch toward the graveyard. I was still worried someone would see me. My black would stand out against the white snow. I just had to hope they were too busy dealing with Jonathan to notice me coming. I at least wanted the dead trees and gravestones as a backdrop in the hopes anyone who might glance my way might mistake me for one of them.

More lights were on in the mansion this time. There were also two more cars parked out front. I couldn't tell if the mansion supported a garage from my angle, but I was pretty sure it did. It made it hard to gauge how many people might actually be inside.

I drew both my gun and sword, and found a tree to watch the house from. There were a few shadows moving around on the inside, but nothing definitive. They could have been made by one or two people, or ten times that many. I just couldn't tell.

I scanned the grounds, searching for a guard. Like

before, I couldn't see anyone. Either Countess Baset's minions were good at concealing themselves, or she was just so cocky that she didn't think she needed them.

Then again, maybe she didn't have enough wolves and vamps at her disposal to keep a guard. I could always hope.

There was little I could do but move forward. I started toward the mansion at a brisk pace, moving as quietly as I could. My feet made light crunching sounds in the snow. If a wolf was nearby, they'd surely hear.

A muffled scream came from within the mansion and I picked up the pace. I couldn't tell if it had been Jonathan screaming or if he'd managed to get hold of someone. I wasn't sure it mattered.

Snow was falling again. It lazily fell from the sky, drifting on the wind. It wasn't thick enough to offer concealment, but there was enough that it might cover my tracks if someone was indeed prowling the grounds.

I reached the side of the house without anyone raising the alarm. From there, I just needed to get inside and find Jonathan. I ran through my options, liking none of them.

The front door was an obvious choice, but it was probably watched. Any back and side door would likewise be guarded. I could always try a window and work my way through the mansion that way. I'd done so successfully before.

But somehow, that didn't seem wise here. This wasn't a Minor House. The windows were probably trapped, either mechanically or magically. If I tried to get in through one, there was always a chance they would explode. It was an unlikely scenario, but I knew so little about Baset, I couldn't bring myself to take that chance.

My hand tightened on my gun. I would do this the hard way.

I smiled. I liked the hard way.

Keeping my back to the wall, I slid down to the corner

of the mansion. I peeked to make sure no one was there and then started working my way around to the front door. I was going to have to do this right or I would stand no chance.

It wasn't like I really thought I was going to get out of this alive. Somehow, deep down, I knew this was going to be my last run one way or the other. Either Baset or her goons would kill me, or I'd find a way to rescue Jonathan and then retire. There was no other way this could end.

The curtains were so thick I couldn't see in as I passed by the windows. I ducked under each one, not wanting to alert anyone I was coming. Just because I couldn't see inside didn't mean someone who glanced toward a window wouldn't see my silhouette as I passed.

No one stood outside the front door, but the light was on, as if Baset was expecting company that couldn't see in the dark. I checked the driveway once more to make sure no one was sitting in any of the two new cars; once I was sure it was clear, I glanced behind me to make sure I wasn't being followed.

All seemed in order and I readied myself. I would have to do this fast if I was going to do it at all.

I reached the front stoop and stopped to listen. There were a few muffled sounds coming from inside, but nothing I could discern as talking or screaming or anything. I held my breath, sheathed my sword, and then reached for the doorknob.

Kicking in the door would have been much more dramatic, but opening it would be just as effective, and it wouldn't warn anyone with ears I was coming.

I grabbed the doorknob, counted quietly to three, and then turned it, hoping it wouldn't be locked.

It moved easily in my hand.

I turned the knob the rest of the way and held it, waiting to see if someone would notice. No one called out or yanked the door open on me, so I assumed I had gotten this far unnoticed. The door opened outward, so I jerked it open and raised my gun in one fluid motion.

Two heads snapped sharply my way. I didn't have time to make out faces before I fired two quick shots. The bullets took each of the men in the head. They fell to the ground without uttering a sound.

Of course, my gun hadn't been nearly as quiet. I stepped inside and kicked the door closed behind me as I drew my sword.

A clamor arose deeper in the mansion and I headed toward the sound. If Baset really did have Jonathan somewhere, I figured that would be where most of her minions would be.

A wolf still in the process of shifting came around a corner toward me. I shot him in the head without breaking stride. His body slid a few feet on the hard floor and I stepped over him as his blood began to seep into the wood.

Shouts rose and I smiled grimly. It had been a long time since I'd fought like this. I'd forgotten how good it felt to take out some of the bad guys, though I really didn't enjoy the killing as much as I used to.

I was passing by a stairwell when someone came out of a hidden door at my side. I didn't have time to turn before he was on me. I tried to swing my sword in a vain attempt to cut my attacker, but he was too close. He spun around me, huge arms wrapping around my body, trapping my gun arm close to my side.

But my sword arm was still free.

I swung as another attacker came out of the hidden room. The vampire's grin never left his face, even as his head hit the floor. His body following a few seconds later.

I tried to wrench free of my captor, but he was far too strong. No matter how hard I fought, he always managed to keep his softer parts out of my reach. I just couldn't get an angle on him to strike him with my blade.

Another vampire came out of the room. He walked slowly and stayed well out of the reach of my sword. He glanced at his fallen comrades with disdain before turning his eyes to me.

The guy holding me loosened his grip for a heartbeat and I tried to take advantage. I snapped my head back and felt the satisfying crunch of his nose breaking against the back of my head. I tried to push free, but he managed to catch me in his bear hug again, this time trapping both my arms.

"Lady Death, I presume," the vampire said. He was wearing a black robe. In fact, everyone I'd seen had been wearing them. "Countess Baset has so wanted to make your acquaintance. She will be thrilled you have come so quickly." He stepped closer to me. Hot, rancid breath spilled over my face when he spoke again. "This way."

He turned and walked back through the hidden door. The big guy holding me kept a firm grip as he led me through the doorway. Another stairwell led up into the mansion. I just barely caught a glimpse of the robed man as he vanished upstairs.

As soon as he was gone, I dug my feet into the hardwood and refused to move. The guy holding me might be strong, but I was a vampire. I was strong too.

He grunted when we suddenly stopped. I prepared to make my move, when my captor suddenly let go of me. I started to spin, but just as I turned, he grabbed me by the wrists and twisted.

Agonizing pain flared up my arms, down into my hands. My grip loosened on both weapons and they clattered to the floor.

I didn't even have a chance to bend to retrieve them. The big man scooped both weapons up the instant he let me go.

Before I could even think to reach for one of my knives, he had my gun aimed at my head.

"Go," he said, blood running down his face from where I'd broken his nose. He held my sword gingerly in his other hand, as if afraid to touch it too much. His grip on the gun was far more secure.

I shrugged, feigning indifference. What else could I do? He had the better of me. It's what I'd expected to happen going into a Major House like I had.

I turned and headed for the stairs, knowing chances were good I'd never come back down them again.

15

I was led down a long, dark hall, into a room at the far end. The lights inside were dim, almost distracting. There was just enough light to illuminate the black-robed figures standing along the walls, heads bowed as if in prayer. Their hands were hidden within their robes so that not a hint of skin showed.

The guy with the bad breath was standing in the middle of the room. He'd lifted the hood of his robe and his head was bowed like everyone else's. From where he stood, I could only assume he was more important than the others in the room.

Jonathan was sitting in a chair beside the robed vamp. His head came up the moment we entered, and I gasped when I saw his face. The glamour he usually kept up to hide the damage to his skull was gone. His eyes were swollen nearly shut; his face bruised an almost uniform purple. Three fingers on his left hand were bent at an odd angle. There were no ropes or chains binding him, yet he remained seated as if too weak to fight.

I took a step toward him but stopped when the vamp beside him raised his hand. I wasn't sure if it was a warning or a request, but I stopped anyway. Jonathan's head dropped as if he couldn't hold it up any longer.

"What have you done to him?" I asked. My fingers twitched. I wanted to grab my knives from their hidden sheaths and bury them in the vamp's throat. I knew he was at least partly responsible for Jonathan's torture.

But I didn't move. I knew if I did something stupid, like attacking one of the people in the room, Jonathan would die. I'd probably be quick to follow.

The vamp shook his head and didn't speak. No one moved or spoke. I wasn't sure if the big guy behind me had lifted his hood or even if he still had my gun pointed at me. I refused to turn and look, knowing it would do me no good either way.

There had to be thirty people in the room. The robes they wore were thick enough that I couldn't tell if they were male or female, wolf, vamp, or Pureblood. There were variants in height and weight, but that was the only difference I could make out between one person and the next.

A shadow moved in the far back corner of the room, drawing my eye. Another black-robed figure stepped forward, moving slowly, almost jerkingly.

And then she spoke. "Ah, Lady Death."

I shuddered at the sound of her voice. It was like someone had taken sandpaper to the woman's vocal cords and then pulled them as taut as they would go.

"Countess Baset, I assume." I tried to see into her hood, but she kept her head so low I couldn't make anything out. She moved to stand beside Jonathan's chair. She rested a gloved hand on his shoulder and he flinched away as if she'd pinched him.

That couldn't be good.

"I have searched for you for a long time," Baset said. "You proved to be quite elusive."

"I was on vacation."

Baset laughed. It was worse than listening to Ethan's demon's laugh. At least I knew he'd never been human before. No one alive should ever sound like that.

"But you're here now."

"I am." I tried to stand defiant in the face of the vampires, but my eyes kept going to Jonathan where he trembled in his chair. It made me sick to see him like that. "You can let him go now. He has no part in this."

"He brought you here, didn't he?" She touched his face and his head jerked to the side so fast it was a surprise he didn't break his neck.

"I came because I heard you were looking for me. He just happened to get himself caught before I knew where to find you."

Baset chuckled. "Is he your lover?" she asked. She turned her head just enough so she could look at me. The dim light cast shadows over her face, making it appear a black mask.

"No." My voice caught and I coughed to clear my throat.

"But you want him to be. I can tell. I can smell your desire, can see it in your eyes when you look at him."

I sucked in an angry breath but held back a retort. No sense pissing off the vampire Countess while standing there mostly unarmed.

Countess Baset walked slowly around the chair in that strange, awkward gait of hers. "Sometimes a person comes into your life and they sort of stick. They invade your thoughts, impact your actions, and the next thing you know, they're as much a part of you as your own body."

I swallowed a lump in my throat. I didn't like how the conversation was going at all, especially with Jonathan sitting helpless in front of me.

"Let's get this over with," I said, my voice tight.

Baset went on as if I hadn't spoken, a trait all vampires seemed to share. "And then one day, they are gone. Someone comes along and snuffs them out, leaving you wondering how you'll ever fill the hole they left behind." She stopped just behind Jonathan and looked down at him.

Jonathan shied away from her. He looked beaten down so much, I wondered if he'd ever recover.

"Don't hurt him," I growled.

"Whether I hurt him or not will be entirely up to you," she said. She lifted a hand and trailed a finger down Jonathan's cheek. "If you wish to keep him, all I ask is that you listen to my offer . . . and accept it, of course."

The urge to just say the hell with it and draw my knives was so strong, I found my hands inching toward my belt. I might have drawn if Jonathan hadn't groaned in his seat. The sight of him like that had me near tears.

"What do you want?" I asked.

"Countess Telia was more to me than just a bed warmer," Baset said. "She had a strength about her that made me feel alive." She paced to the side, never straying far from where Jonathan sat. "And that is important to me. Life is precious, especially because it is so easily taken away."

I couldn't hold my tongue any longer. "It's funny listening to a vampire talk about life being precious. I thought you enjoyed killing."

Baset laughed. "If you lived what I have lived, you would feel the same." She took a deep, raspy breath. "I loved Telia for what she did for me . . . and what she did *to* me." I could hear the hunger in her voice. "If I asked her to kill, she killed, no questions asked. She was good at it."

"Not good enough," I said.

"Clearly."

Jonathan shifted in his chair, tried to move farther away from Baset, but there was nowhere for him to go unless he wanted to flop onto the floor. He was terrified of the vampire. I'd never seen him that way before.

"I'm going to give you a choi—" A sudden bout of coughing brought Baset up short. It sounded like she was hacking up more than just a lung. I hoped she would just keel over and die right then and there, and save me the trouble of having to finish her off myself.

Her cough eased and she leaned on the chair for support. I could feel the tension in the room. I don't think even her minions knew whether or not she would survive the outburst.

"Keep that up and I might not have to kill you after all," I said, unable to hide my satisfaction.

Baset jerked upright. She strode toward me, bringing with her the foulest smell I'd ever had the displeasure of breathing. It was like all the bodies in the world had been left out to rot. I took an involuntary step back and brought my hand up to my nose. I gagged and the smell of rot filled my mouth.

"Can you smell it?" she hissed. "I cannot escape it. It's always there, following me wherever I go. When death takes you, it is inevitable."

With deliberate slowness, Baset reached up and pulled back her hood.

The smell was bad enough. Putting it with the face was almost too much.

Baset's eyes were filmed-over white. Her skin hung from her face in sagging clumps, as did her hair; what was left of it anyway. Her eyes were sunken deep into her skull; her cheekbones protruded through the skin. Her lips were shriveled where they didn't have holes in them. Her teeth lay exposed, yellowed and rotten.

It was the face of a corpse left out too long. I didn't need her to take off her robe to know the rest of her body was just as decayed.

I took another step back, wanting only to put distance between us. I felt like throwing up. I tried to say something but only gagged as more of her stench filled my mouth. I could taste the rot on her. The air was heavy with it.

How I hadn't smelled it the moment I'd walked in, I'll

never know. Maybe the scent was somehow limited, a curse of her condition. The horrible stench receded as Baset raised her hood and stepped back. I choked in fresh air and fell to my knees. My legs just wouldn't hold me upright any longer.

"I was beautiful once," she said. "But it didn't matter when my heart was destroyed. The prettiest face cannot stand against the hunger for power." She choked out a laugh. "But my killers didn't know of my skills. They didn't know I'd protected myself against something as inevitable as death."

She walked over to the vamp standing beside Jonathan and ran a hand down his chest. "Henri taught me so much. He brought me back from the dead, and as a reward he has leave to taste of my flesh."

I fought back revulsion as she leaned forward and kissed Henri on the mouth. I could hear the slurping sounds from across the room.

"You can't raise the dead," I managed. I forced myself to my feet, refusing to confront the vampires on my knees.

Baset stepped back from Henri. He licked his lips and made sure I could see that he was chewing on something.

"Necromancy can be accomplished by those with the power. I am living proof that Henri has that power." She paused and gave a dramatic sigh. "But it isn't perfect. The rot still claims the body. This body serves as a vessel, nothing more. I can only keep up with the decay so much. Each year it claims a little more of me, despite my best efforts to keep it at bay."

I considered saying something smartass, but held back. I didn't want her coming back over again. "Why don't you raise Telia, then?" I asked.

Baset stopped moving and I thought maybe I'd gone too far in bringing up her dead lover. When she spoke, she sounded angry. "Her head was removed. No amount of necromancy can return a soul without a head. If she had been shot in the head, then perhaps . . ." She let the thought trail off.

I immediately thought of Thomas. Could he be brought back? Was there a way to keep him from rotting like Countess Baset? I could have him, could fix him.

I angrily pushed the thought away. I could never do that to him. It was too cruel. I wouldn't even want to bring back an enemy this way.

"But all of this is beside the point," Baset said, waving a hand. "My condition worsens, but I am far from dead. I will continue on for many years, centuries even. Perhaps by then, I will find a way to repair the damage done and slow the rot consuming me."

I swallowed. I really didn't want to think of her rotting any more than I had to. "Then what do you want from me?" It was clear she didn't want me dead like I'd originally thought.

"You," Baset said. "I want you to replace my dear Telia, take her place at my side."

The thought of touching Baset in any way, sexual or not, made me gag. I coughed to try to cover it and almost threw up instead. Bile filled my mouth and I swallowed it back with some difficulty.

Baset laughed bitterly. "I will give you a choice. You will not have to fill both of Telia's roles, only one. I will find someone else to fill the other."

Jonathan's head lifted and he looked at me with an intensity that couldn't be ignored. I glanced at him, wincing at the bruises that covered his face. He shook his head almost imperceptibly.

"I would accept you into my bed if you chose to fill that role," Baset said, drawing my attention back to her. "Telia enjoyed tasting me. I believe she liked the taste of dead flesh, much like many of my House do. Perhaps you would enjoy the same."

I tried really hard not to gag.

"But if that is too distressing for you, then all I require of you is to take on the role as my assassin."

"No." I didn't even think about it. "I won't kill for you."

"Then let me see what is under your coat. Your face is pleasing enough to look at, but I would like to know your body more."

The man behind me took a step forward as if to grab me. I quickly stepped aside, really not wanting anyone from Baset's House touching me.

"No way. I'm not getting naked for you either."

"You really have no choice." Baset waved a hand and Henri produced a knife from somewhere in his robes. He looked at me for a long moment before going to work.

Jonathan screamed as the knife bit into his flesh. Henri stood so I could get a good view of what he was doing. He made a sawing motion as he worked at Jonathan's ear, taking his time as if he wanted to savor the werewolf's pain.

"Stop!" I shouted. I nearly rushed forward and tackled Henri, though I knew I'd never get anywhere close before someone shot me. I couldn't stand to see Jonathan hurting because of me.

Baset waved her hand again and Henri stepped back. Jonathan's ear was still attached, but barely. It was looking decidedly ragged where it hung.

"I'll do it," I said. Tears burned my eyes and I couldn't keep them from falling. Jonathan's head hung to his chest. Blood ran down his neck and fell to the floor. I couldn't stand to see him like that, not because of me.

"Do what?"

I took a deep, shuddering breath and closed my eyes to the horrors I'd witnessed. I should have been more careful, should have brought Nathan with me. I doubted it would have made much of a difference, but then maybe we could have fought harder, killed a few more vamps and wolves before being taken.

We could have gone down fighting.

But I hadn't called him. My only choices were to watch Jonathan die, and then most likely die myself, or do whatever Baset wanted. She was right; I really had no choice.

I opened my eyes and stared directly into Baset's hooded face.

"Who do you want me to kill?"

16

Henri started moving forward the moment the words were out of my mouth. I jerked back from his outstretched hand, thinking he was reaching for me, but all he held was a folded piece of paper. I took it from him and glanced down at the name and address written in a neat hand. I didn't recognize the name, but I knew where the address would lead me.

"He is your target," Baset croaked. She seemed to slump within herself, as if our conversation had worn her out. "I'm sure you can figure out where to find him on your own."

I glanced at the slip of paper again and frowned. "Then what's the address here?"

"That is where you will pick up your payment. One of my werewolves will be there with a significant monetary reward for your services once the kill is complete."

I had to fight to keep from balling up the paper and throwing it in Henri's face. I didn't work for money. While I might have been known to grab a wallet or two from a wolf or vamp I killed, it was only so I could pay for Mikael's services, not to mention the bills. Taking Baset's money would make me feel dirtier than I already did.

"I don't need your money," I said.

"But you'll take it," Baset said. "I insist. If we are to both be happy with this arrangement, you will need to be compensated."

I doubted I would ever be happy about our agreement but stopped arguing. I didn't want Henri to start cutting on Jonathan again because I was being bullheaded.

The dead vamp started to say something more but erupted into a fit of coughing instead. I prayed she would drop dead so I could forget about all of this. I hated myself for even considering her offer, let alone going through with it.

The fit passed and Baset slumped even farther. "There is a chance I could have another name for you when you pick up the money. If there is, you will have one week to dispose of your target. If there is not, you are free for the week. You are to return to the address given every Monday at first dark to either collect your payment or receive the next name. If you do not show . . ." She shrugged as if the rest would be obvious.

I was so mad, I was shaking. I had to stare at Jonathan sitting there, helpless, to keep from saying something stupid. It made my heart ache to know I was the reason he was suffering. If I had to suffer the indignity of becoming Countess Baset's assassin to keep him safe, I'd do it.

But that didn't mean I had to like it. As soon as I had Jonathan safely away, I would find a way to break free of her influence, even if it meant I would have to kill her to do so. I'd been planning on doing that anyway.

Baset must have seen something in my face, because she chuckled. "Do not think you can get out of this so easily. Our bargain cannot be broken, not if you care about those around you. If you so much as come near my home again, I will have your loved ones killed. We know where the Den is located." She was silent for a long moment before adding, "I know where you live."

I went cold all over. "How?"

"We have our ways." She glanced at Jonathan as if accusing him, but I had a hard time believing he had told her anything. If he hadn't broken when Count Tremaine had him, then he would have kept quiet now. I had to believe that.

I was pretty sure Baset was bluffing, but I wasn't so sure I could take the chance she wasn't. If she had followed me somehow, could I really risk Ethan's life by turning against her?

I could just move, leave town, go back to Delai and hide in Levi's basement. She couldn't get me there, I was sure of it.

But then everyone I knew would pay for it. Jonathan, Ethan, maybe even Bart and Mikael. Could I really take being responsible for all of their deaths because I was too afraid to face my problems?

I was stuck. There was no way around it. I was going to have to do what she wanted unless I was willing to die here and now, and let Jonathan die with me.

"You won't see me again," Baset said. "I prefer my privacy and would hope you would respect that. Take what I have given, consider it a gift. Your life is worth that."

Jonathan's head lifted and he looked at me. There was so much pain in his eyes, it made me sick. I didn't know why he hadn't shifted, why he'd let them torture him like that. Was someone under Baset's command a sorcerer of some sort? Henri was a necromancer, so it stood to reason he might know other magical arts.

"Your weapons will be returned to you as soon as you leave," Baset said. She turned and walked back to the deep shadows in the back of the room, moving much more hesitantly than she had before.

Henri jerked Jonathan to his feet, causing the werewolf to groan. The vamp nodded for me to turn around, and the guy behind me took me by the arm and led me back to the stairs. If I hadn't been so stunned by what had just transpired, I would have jerked away from him.

As it was, I let him all but drag me down the stairs and to the front door. It wasn't until we reached the door that his touch really started to bother me. I kept thinking of maggots writhing on his flesh even though I knew he wasn't the one who was rotting. I jerked from his grip when I swore I could feel something crawling on me.

He let me go but gave me a little push so I stumbled out the door. He gave me my weapons back, which was surprising since the silver would have been valuable to his Countess. I guess Baset and her minions were hoping it would be a show of good faith in not keeping them.

It was really hard not to shoot Henri and his friend the moment he let Jonathan go. He shoved the injured wolf out the door so hard he would have fallen if I hadn't caught him. The door slammed closed even before we righted ourselves.

I stood there a moment, considering what to do. I'd noticed someone had cleaned up the bodies before we'd come back down, and Baset hadn't mentioned those I'd killed, as if she expected my coming to cause a few deaths.

Of course, I only beheaded one of them. Perhaps she could just raise her other minions again, bullet holes and all.

Jonathan groaned and I turned away from the door with a shudder. It took everything I had not to go right back in and kill as many people as I could before they caught me. Baset was an abomination, and her minions were no better.

We walked back toward Jeremy's car, feet dragging in the rising snow. I kept glancing over my shoulder, fully expecting there to be someone following us. I couldn't believe Baset had let us go. She might think she had me bound, but I was sure I'd eventually find a way out of our arrangement.

Jonathan didn't say a word until I had him seated in the passenger seat and we were heading down the road. His head sort of lolled to the side so he could face me. I'm not sure he could manage much else.

"You shouldn't have come."

"Someone had to save your ass." I went for tough, but I ended up sounding scared.

Jonathan licked his lips. They were dry and cracked, and no matter how much he licked at them, he couldn't form enough spit to moisten them. "You could have let me die."

I didn't dignify that with a response.

Jonathan closed his swollen eyes and I think he fell asleep, because he didn't say anything more the rest of the way to the Den's underground parking garage.

As soon as I stopped the car, his eyes opened. He groaned but managed to get out of the car under his own power. I went over to him and offered my help anyway. It was my fault he was hurting so badly, and I was intent on paying for it in any way I could.

I waved at the cameras hidden around the garage in the hopes someone would see us and come help. Jonathan leaned on my arm, putting his full weight against me as we began the slow, painful walk toward the old library that was now the Luna Cult Den.

No one came out to meet us, so I assumed no one had been manning the monitors when I needed them. There was a good chance Nathan had all the other wolves in the Cult looking for their Denmaster.

Still, it pissed me off. I shouldn't have to do this on my own.

I knew I should call someone, but I didn't have a cell phone. I'd have to see if Jonathan had one somewhere inside so I could call Jeremy and let him know everything was okay. Because the Cult wanted the illusion of privacy, there were no phone lines connected to the old library.

There were still power lines, however, so they at least had electricity. I'm not exactly sure why they thought one was okay and the other not.

I reached for the front door and Jonathan pushed away from me. I let him go, figuring he wouldn't want his Cultists to see him leaning on me when we stepped inside. I waited for him to catch his balance before opening the door and stepping through the glamour of darkness into the light of the Den.

I expected to be confronted by someone as soon as we were through the door, but after a quick glance, I knew we were alone. In fact, I couldn't hear anyone at all in the big building. It was as if everyone had up and vanished the moment their Denmaster had been taken.

"They're in lockdown," Jonathan said as he came in behind me. He sounded relieved. "Nathan must have implemented the protocol." He coughed and blood flecked his lips. "I have to make a call."

He started for the office door, but I intercepted him. "No, not yet. Let's get you cleaned up first. Then you can go around giving orders again."

Jonathan let me lead him up the stairs, through the carved doors, into his sitting room. He took the lead as we headed for the bedroom. I almost stayed outside, but he motioned for me to come in with him. I followed as far as the bed, where I sat down while he went into the bathroom. The shower started up a moment later.

I considered getting up and leaving. I wasn't needed any longer. I'd found Jonathan, gotten him home alive, and that was all I needed to do. He was as safe as he was ever going to get. What did he need me for?

But even as I told myself it was time to go, I remained seated. He'd wanted me to come into the bedroom for a reason. He'd just been abducted and beaten. His ear was hanging on by a thread. While it would heal, he'd still have the scars. He probably didn't want to be alone right then.

There were a few sharp screams from the bathroom that set me on edge. I listened carefully, but there didn't seem to be anything else going on. It was unlikely someone had snuck into the bathroom and assaulted him while I was sitting in the next room.

The shower shut off a few minutes later, and Jonathan came out wearing nothing but a towel. He held his hand close to his chest, and I could tell all his fingers were now pointing in the right direction. I supposed that explained the screams.

He walked into the room, not really looking at anything, and then hesitated when he saw me still sitting here. I couldn't tell if he was happy to see me here or not.

"I thought you would have left by now," he said, walking past me.

I tried to keep my eyes on the floor as he passed, but it was hard. I could see all the old scars, many I'd given him myself. They crisscrossed his chest and back like a chaotic map. His glamour was back up, so at least I didn't have to look at the ruin of his head.

"I figured we should talk about what happened," I said. I heard the towel hit the floor and my neck started hurting. It was taking all my self-control to keep from turning to look.

Jonathan was silent as he got dressed. He padded by on bare feet and went back into the bathroom, which gave me a moment to relax. He returned holding gauze to the ear Henri had been cutting on. The wound was still seeping blood, which for a werewolf meant it was pretty bad.

"What is there to talk about?" he asked, sitting on the bed beside me. He looked much better than he had before going into the bathroom, though he still looked pretty beat-up. I could feel the heat emanating from him, and I hoped it was because he'd taken a hot shower and not that he'd caught something from Baset. Who knew what kind of diseases her rotten body carried?

I could at least look at him now that he was wearing clothes. I shifted on the bed, scooting so I was a little farther from him, disguising it as though I was only moving to face him.

"Why didn't you fight?" I asked. "You could have shifted."

"If I had, they would have killed everyone in the Den. I would rather die than be responsible for their deaths."

"Even after they took you back to the mansion?"

"Even then," he said. "I was hoping they would accidently kill me and be done with it. I didn't want you to come."

"Well, I did."

"You're getting soft." Jonathan managed a smile. He winced and resumed his pained grimace. "Are you going to do what she wants?"

I sighed. "I think I have to."

"You shouldn't have agreed to do anything for her. She'll hold it against you."

"I know."

"What are you going to do?"

Frustration started to boil over in the form of tears. I looked away and hurriedly wiped my hand across my eyes. "I don't know," I said. "I'll do what I have to do to keep the people I care about safe."

The sound of cloth on cloth nearly caused me to leap from the bed as Jonathan moved closer. His hands, gentle and scarred, touched my shoulders lightly before gripping them. He slowly turned me around to face him. The bloody gauze was stuck to his ear.

"Remember, you don't have to do it alone."

I looked into his eyes and knew it to be true.

Before I knew what was happening, Jonathan leaned forward, his lips finding mine.

I didn't budge, didn't react. I was too scared to do anything out of fear of what would happen. If I pulled away, he might take offense. If I leaned into him . . . I didn't even want to think about what would happen.

Jonathan pulled back, eyes searching mine. "You don't have to be afraid," he said. His breath felt warm and inviting on my cheek. His upper lip was bleeding again from the kiss.

I could feel more tears coming and I silently cursed them. My lips started trembling and my hand slid a few inches forward so that it was touching his knee.

"I can't help it," I whispered.

Jonathan's hand slid from my shoulder, lightly trailing up my neck. His fingers played over my cheekbone until his thumb slid under my eye, wiping the tear away.

"Thank you for coming," he said, his voice low. "It means more to me that you of all people came. I . . ." He trailed off and licked the blood from his lips.

My entire world felt like it was being shaken apart. I knew deep down I couldn't have this. As kind and gentle as he was being, I was something different, something dark and terrible. I didn't deserve his kindness.

I stood, brushing his hands away. "I've got to go," I said, hurrying to the door.

"You can always stay."

I turned to look back at him. He was sitting on the edge of the bed, eyes full of hurt. The gauze was starting to fall from his ear, exposing more of the sawed-on ear. No matter how much I wanted to comfort him, to have him comfort me, I knew he was something I could never have.

"I can't," I said. It felt like someone punched me in the gut. "I'm sorry."

I opened the door and all but flew down the stairs and out the front door of the Den.

17

I took my time getting home, not really wanting to face anyone after what I'd just gone through. Morning was just over the horizon, and while I was a mess inside, it didn't mean I wanted to get caught out under the sun's rays.

Jeremy was sipping coffee in the living room when I walked through the door. I almost went upstairs without saying anything to him, but his calm demeanor was unsettling. The last I'd seen him, he'd been a wreck.

"When do you sleep?" I asked, leaning against the wall. I so didn't want him to realize how upset I really was.

He looked up at me and a flare of anger passed over his eyes. He was still pissed about what I'd said earlier, I was sure. I didn't blame him; I'd still be angry too.

"When I can."

"It must be hard on you." I wasn't sure if I meant the staying up or dealing with his missing arm. It just seemed like the right thing to say.

"I get by."

I fumbled for something else to say and then realized I hadn't told him the good news. "I found Jonathan," I said. "He's back at the Den, safe and sound."

His eyes hardened. "I know. He called me."

I felt like the world's biggest bitch. I'd been nothing but cruel to the kid ever since I'd met him.

"Look," I said. "I'm sorry about what I said. I've been pissed off at the world lately, and I've been taking it out on everyone. I appreciate what you've tried to do. Ethan needs someone who can be here for him, and I just haven't been that person."

Jeremy studied me a moment like he was trying to figure out if I was serious or playing some sort of joke. Finally, he dipped his head in acceptance. "Thank you," he said.

I smiled at him. "Get some rest sometime."

"I will." He smiled back, though it was still strained.

I went up to my room feeling a whole hell of a lot better. I was still nowhere close to feeling happy, let alone normal, but at least I'd started to mend one relationship. Jeremy would probably never forgive me for everything I'd done to him, but at least we were making progress.

Ethan was already tucked away in his room by the time I came upstairs. I could hear his snores through his door as I passed. I almost opened the door and peeked in on him like some doting mother worried about her small, helpless child. I wanted him to be safe and I felt like I needed to protect him.

I just patted the door and kept going instead. I might be getting soft like Jonathan had joked, but I wasn't *that* soft.

As soon as I was in my room, I pulled the note with the name and address on it from my coat pocket. I sat down on my bed and stared at it, feeling suddenly lonely. I wanted someone sitting here beside me.

I wanted Jonathan.

His warmth and kindness would get me through this. He'd known exactly what to say, would make sure I didn't do something mind-blowingly stupid. He'd shoulder some of the guilt I'd feel for working for a vampire Countess.

But I was alone and I would deal with this alone. No sense dragging him into this any more than he already was. Even if he asked, I'd tell him no. Jonathan had suffered enough on my behalf. I refused to be responsible for more.

Instead of dwelling on it, I turned my attention to the name written on the page: *Count Strinowski.* I wondered if he was from some other country or if he'd simply taken an exotic-sounding name. Jonathan had told me once that vampire Counts and Countesses took different names when they rose in power, so it wasn't much of a stretch to think this guy had as well.

I ran the name through my memory banks but was coming up blank. If I'd ever heard his name before, he hadn't been important enough for me to remember. There were just too many vamps to remember them all, though I did know most Counts and Countesses.

But if this guy wasn't important enough to remember, why would Countess Baset want him dead? I guess he could be an up-and-comer, someone who'd only recently started making a name for himself. He could also have been one of her vamps who split from her House without her permission.

I hated the fact that I didn't know. I might kill, but I always knew why I was killing. I wasn't even sure this guy was a real vamp. For all I knew, he was just some kid hopped up on drugs who was calling himself a vampire Count to pick up girls.

I tucked the paper back in my coat pocket and tossed the coat onto a chair. I couldn't do anything about it now. The sun was just coming up, so there was no way I was going to be able to leave to get information on the guy. I'd have to wait until evening.

And wait I did. The heavy drapes over the windows kept out the light of the sun, leaving my room nearly pitch-black. I could have turned on a light and read, but the darkness suited my mood. I wasn't feeling nearly as bad as I'd felt before, but I still wasn't feeling happy-go-lucky. I had a feeling it would be a long time before I reached that point again.

It's hard to make it through so many hours of sunlight without going crazy. I didn't even have a TV in my room, which I was starting to think was a mistake. On days like this where I had so much shit flowing through my head, I really could use the distraction.

I did have a few books tucked away that I could read, but that would require turning on the light. While my vampire-enhanced vision was nice, it wasn't so good at picking out tiny words on a page. Besides, I doubted I would be able to follow along with a book right then. I'd never be able to focus.

I settled on alternating between lying on my bed, staring up at the ceiling, and pacing. At around noon, I took a long bath, hoping to soak the bad mood away. I closed my eyes and let the hot water soothe my aching muscles and joints. My back was throbbing where I'd been gouged a few months ago. The stitches were gone, but the scars were definitely still there.

When night finally fell, I was so relieved I almost wept. I hurried out of my room and nearly collided into Ethan as he headed for the bathroom across the hall. The clothes he planned on wearing were wrapped in a tight bundle, tucked under his arm. He'd probably snatched them off the floor, not really caring whether they were dirty or clean.

"Sorry," he mumbled, eyes still heavy with sleep.

"Hey, can you do something for me?" I said, putting as much cheer into my voice as I could. I was going to try to stop grouching at everyone I lived with so their lives were at least bearable when I was around.

"Sure." His eyes lit up with the prospect of something to do. "What do you have in mind?"

"Could you scrounge up a TV from somewhere and get it hooked up in my room? I'm tired of sitting in the dark with nothing to do every day."

He gave me an odd look. I'd never been one for watching television. "Of course," he said. "We don't have one lying around, but I can send Jeremy out later. I'm sure he can pick one up for you."

"Thanks."

Ethan smiled and headed into the bathroom, whistling.

I smiled until the door was closed and then let it drop. I started for the stairs just as Jeremy headed up them. I forced my smile to return and nodded at him.

He stopped, his own smile fading. "What's going on?"

I hesitated. "What do you mean?"

"You're acting strange."

I tried on another smile, not quite sure what he was getting at.

"See," he said. "You're smiling."

I stopped trying. "I'll be back later tonight," I said. "Make sure Ethan stays safe."

Jeremy nodded, his face all seriousness. I frowned at him and he suddenly broke into a huge grin. "That's more like it." He continued on up to his room, chuckling.

I went downstairs, shaking my head. This time, the smile I felt cross my face was real.

I silently thanked Jeremy for that little moment as I went down into the basement for my weapons.

Any and all of my pleasant thoughts bled away as I got ready. I just couldn't be happy when I was going to kill someone for a vampire Countess. This was the sort of thing I'd fought against for years.

I was sulking by the time I had my gear in place and was heading out the door. I still had Jeremy's keys and decided to make the best of them. There was no sense risking my neck on the slick roads with my Honda, especially since I was already distracted.

While I'd resigned myself to having to make the kill, I still didn't know where this Count lived.

But I knew where I could go to find out.

Mikael wasn't all that thrilled to see me again. I don't think I'd ever visited him this many times in such a short span of time before. And I was sure he wasn't happy that I was still coming to him after he'd asked me not to.

He patted the girl he was sitting with on the ass and shooed her away as I approached. I gave him my best winning smile. It only seemed to make him that much more irritated.

"I need information on a name," I said, sitting down across from him. I slapped some money on the table.

He gave me an exasperated look. "We are done," he said, crossing his arms and sitting back. "I have given you all the information I have on Countess Baset. You must do this on your own."

"That's already been taken care of," I said. "This is something else."

Mikael's eyes widened. "You've killed Baset?"

"No," I admitted. "We worked out an agreement."

His mouth slowly unhinged until he was gaping at me. I think it was the first time I'd ever shocked him into silence. He normally knew everything I knew, and then some. The idea that I'd surprised him made me smile another real smile.

"So, about this other name . . ."

Mikael shook his head as if coming out of a trance. "How did you manage it, my sweet? I cannot believe you have dealt with her and survived, yet I detect no lie."

"I think I deserve some secrets of my own, don't you think?"

His eyes narrowed, but he ended up nodding. There was a good chance he'd figure out what was going on anyway. He was good at finding out things.

"Okay," he said. "Who do you require information on this time, so soon after your latest escapades?"

"Count Strinowski. I know absolutely nothing about him. I need to know what he's done and where he lives."

Mikael's brow furrowed. "You do not know what he has done? Why would you ask after a vampire whose crimes you do not know? How did you come by his name?"

"I have my sources," I said, jaw going tight. I so didn't want him to know I was working for Baset. He'd probably figure it out on his own, but I sure as hell wasn't going to tell him myself.

He studied me for a few seconds before sighing. "He is not a good man. Not many vampires are, no?" He laughed. "He is much more in your skill range than Baset was, though I'd love to know how you overcame her."

I bristled a bit at that and motioned for him to continue.

Mikael chuckled wryly to himself. "Not even a hint?"

"No," I said firmly.

He shrugged. "Count Strinowski is only a Count in name, one he has given to himself. He lords over no one but his victims. He is but a step away from rogue, but it is a bad step. He likes torture."

I groaned. Another one of those. "Okay," I said. "Do you know why anyone would want him dead?"

Mikael laughed. "Pick a reason. He claims he is the head of a House, yet he has no werewolves or vampires to call his own. He moves around a lot, so no one can really pin him down. He kills wherever he goes. He tortures anyone he can get his hands on—werewolves, vampires, Purebloods—it does not matter to him."

I nodded. He might have killed one of Baset's wolves. She would want revenge for that. It made perfect sense, though I found it hard to believe she couldn't have taken care of him herself.

"How do I find him?" I asked.

"It is not easy," Mikael warned. "Like I said, he moves around often, never staying in one place more than a week or so. He is very good at hiding, very chameleon-like. Until the bodies start popping up, he is usually invisible."

I didn't like the sound of that. If Mikael didn't know where to find the Count, then I had no other way of tracking him. I didn't know what Baset would do if I failed in this.

"Do you know where he is?" I sounded more desperate than I would have liked.

A smile crept across Mikael's face. "It may be that I've come across information hinting at his current location, yes. It is not confirmed, so I could be wrong."

"But you're never wrong." I felt a smile of my own forming.

Mikael shrugged as if that was granted.

"Where?" I asked.

Mikael gave me an address that would take me quite a ways out of the city proper. In fact, it would take me right past a certain road with a certain little road sign leading to a certain little town. My heart gave a hop at the thought of passing by Delai.

I thanked Mikael and rose. He reached out and touched my hand before I could walk away.

"Is everything really better for you in regard to Countess Baset?" He sounded genuinely concerned.

"Better?" I shook my head. "Not really. But she is no longer hunting me or those I associate with. You're safe."

He nodded and withdrew his hand.

I turned away to catch Bart watching me. We stared at each other for a few heartbeats before he nodded and looked away.

That simple gesture lifted my spirits a little more. Was I finally getting past all the grudges and anger? First

Jeremy, then Mikael, and now Bart. I hoped everything else would fall into place just as easily.

I walked across the room feeling better than I had in a long while. It wasn't as much of a peaceful feeling as I'd had in Delai, but it was something. Now I just had to finish this kill so I could focus on other matters.

I pushed through the doors of The Bloody Stake, mind churning, and walked right into a pair of Adrian Davis's wolves.

18

"Not this again," I groaned. "Don't you have anything better to do than piss me off?"

These two weren't identical twins like the last, but it amounted to the same thing. The woman was a tiny thing, her hair pixie-cut short. Heavy purple eye shadow made her eyes nearly gleam. The knot of scar tissue on her forehead was mostly concealed by makeup, but it was still visible.

The guy was big, but not too big. He was totally forgettable as well. I might have passed by him a thousand times and aside from the scar, I never would have paid him a second glance.

"Adrian wants to see you," the woman said. Her voice was surprisingly deep and I wondered if there was more to her than the obvious.

"So I've heard," I said. I was nervous as hell since we were still in The Bloody Stake parking lot. If they were to attack, there was a good chance Bart would have all our heads. Fighting in Polaris was bad enough. Fighting here was suicidal.

"We aren't to hurt you." The woman's eyes flashed yellow for a split second. "Adrian's orders expressly prohibit it, even if you are responsible for the deaths of the Garretts."

"The twins?"

The man growled, so I took that for an affirmative.

"I didn't kill them." I kept my hands well away from my weapons in case Bart was watching. "They shouldn't have come at me in Mephisto's territory, just like you might not want to start something here. It won't end well for any of us."

I felt bad for what happened to the twins, but there was nothing I could do about it. I wasn't even sure they were both dead. Last I saw of them, one was missing a head, the other unconscious. As far as I knew, Mephisto was keeping the one alive, syphoning information from him.

"We will force you to go if you try to resist us," the man said. His voice wasn't much deeper than the woman's.

I waved a hand dismissively, hoping bravado would make them reconsider confronting me here of all places. "Adrian can wait," I said. "I've got things to do."

The two wolves looked at each other, frowning. Tension flowed between them, and I knew chances were good I wouldn't be able to talk my way out of this.

"You *must* come with us," the woman said. She appeared agitated. It was obvious she wanted a fight, but she wasn't stupid. It was unlikely she'd attack me here against Adrian's orders, but I'd been wrong before.

"It is important you meet with him," the man added, as if that would change my mind.

They were standing between me and Jeremy's car, though I doubted they knew the beat-up station wagon was my ride out of there. I would have to go through them both to get to it.

"I really don't want to have to hurt you," I said. "I'll see Adrian when I have time." I glanced over my shoulder at the bar. So far, it didn't appear anyone had noticed anything through the window, but it was only a matter of time before someone caught wind of the situation.

Actually, that might not be such a bad thing. If Bart were to step outside now, I was pretty sure the wolves would step down. I just had to hope Bart would keep them busy long enough for me to put distance between us so they couldn't follow me.

"No," the male werewolf said. He took a step toward me. "We cannot return without you."

I sighed and moved my hands to my waist. Maybe if I could just incapacitate them, Bart wouldn't hold it against me. The silver wouldn't paralyze them, I knew, but a knife in the gut would slow down even a werewolf.

"If you really thought you were going to be able to bring me in with just the two of you, you were sadly mistaken." Being nice hadn't worked, so I was going for intimidation. I was tired of Adrian thinking he could just send his wolves to collect me whenever he wanted.

The woman smiled. "What makes you think it's just the two of us?"

I turned just as a fully shifted wolf jumped off the roof of the bar. He hit me in the chest and we went down in a tangle of limbs. We rolled a few times and I came out on top. Before he could get a good grip on me with his claws, I leaped off him, hands going to my waist.

Both knives came free and I had one in the air before my coat could settle. It hit the unshifted male wolf in the stomach. He jerked back a few steps and looked down at the blade sticking out of his gut. He reached down, touched the blood running from the wound, and stared at it for a moment before looking up at me.

"You fucking bitch," he growled. "I'm going to kill you."

"You can try."

The female was using a car to shield herself as she

moved around to flank me. She kept her head low so I wouldn't have a target, though I could see her feet beneath the car. I backed up in the hopes of keeping all three wolves in front of me, but when I looked, the shifted wolf was gone.

"Shit," I said. I tried to spin around, but he was already behind me. Huge, hairy arms encircled me, trapping the arm with the knife at my side. I managed to keep one hand free.

The werewolf with the knife in his gut laughed. He pulled the blade free and his laughter turned to a hoarse scream. He looked down at the blade in disgust and stupidly threw it to the ground.

"Get her in the car," he said.

I didn't give the wolf who had me a chance. He wasn't nearly as strong as Baset's man. I jerked my arm free and elbowed him in the muzzle. He howled as something broke. His grip loosened and I easily pulled away.

My fangs pushed through as the thrill of the fight coursed through my body. I drew my sword as I spun away from the were's next lunge. One of his teeth was hanging from his mouth, shattered by my elbow. I kicked him in the back of the knees as he passed and he went down to all fours.

It didn't slow him. He used his momentum to leap on top of a car, spin, and then leap at me in one fluid motion. It looked as if he'd practiced the move a thousand times before.

An explosion rocked the night just as he leaped. The wolf exploded in a mess of blood and guts that rained down over everyone. The force of the blast sent him spinning sideways and he crashed to the ground in a pulped mess.

I immediately dropped to the ground. There was a growl and another boom echoed in the otherwise silent parking lot.

Blood and brains splattered all around me. I covered my head with my hands, though it wouldn't do a whole hell of a lot of good if the gun was turned on me next.

There was a long moment of silence. I stayed down, knowing there was a good chance that if I made any sudden moves, I would lose my head just as the two wolves had. I knew fighting here was a bad idea, and I was terrified I would end up paying for it.

"Get off my property," Bart shouted. I looked up to see he had his gun trained on the female wolf. She was standing a few feet from the car she'd been using for cover. It looked as though she'd been about to come at me from behind when Bart blew her associates apart. "Or you're next."

She snarled at him, but when he firmed his grip on his shotgun, she decided it might not be a wise idea to growl at the guy with the gun. She bared her teeth at me before turning and running away, leaving her dead companions behind.

I watched her go and resisted the urge to yell something after her. I had blood on me and knew Bart wasn't going to let me off the hook, but since he let the female wolf go, I hoped he might do the same for me. I stood slowly and turned around to face him.

He had his gun trained on me, a determined look in his eye. "Tell me why I shouldn't just shoot you now and be done with you."

I put away my sword and knife, making sure to make every movement slow and precise. I didn't what him to think I was planning on doing anything stupid. He was already pissed as it was. Anything I did would only make it worse.

"They jumped me," I said. "I was only defending myself. I didn't kill any of them and didn't want to. I just wanted to scare them off so they'd leave me alone."

His gaze traveled to the bloody knife on the ground. "You bring trouble with you wherever you go, you know that?" he said.

"I know."

Bart stared at me for a long minute, never lowering his aim. "I've let you get away with a lot more than I'd ever allow anyone else to."

"I know," I said again.

"I damn well don't know why." He spat on the ground, grimacing. "One of these days . . ." He shook his head, letting the thought trail off.

He didn't do or say anything for the longest time. I just stood there and waited for him to make up his mind whether he was going to kill me or not.

There was a chance I could reach him and disarm him before he could shoot. But if I were to do that, then I would have to hurt him.

But I was done hurting people who didn't deserve it. I waited for him to make up his mind, my hands held out before me in the hopes he would take me at my word.

Bart heaved a huge sigh and lowered his gun. "Go on," he said. "Try not to get jumped on my property again. I might not be so forgiving the next time."

I let out my breath in a huff and nodded. I walked over to my knife and bent down to retrieve it.

"Leave it," he said. "I could always use a souvenir to remember you by."

I wasn't sure if that was a warning not to come back or if he figured I'd end up dead soon enough. I didn't bother to ask, though I hoped he would let me return to the Stake. It was one of the few places I could go to get away from everything.

I straightened and left the knife where it was. Bart could have it. Since he worked around supes all night, it might come in handy someday.

I slowly walked across the parking lot and got into Jeremy's car. I could feel Bart watching me and it made the back of my head itch. He might have said he was letting me go, but he could change his mind at any moment.

The sad thing was, I couldn't hold it against him. I knew the rules. I should have been more careful. I never should have let the shifted wolf get the jump on me.

I started Jeremy's car and backed slowly out onto the road. I was lucky to be alive and knew that later I would have to thank Bart for not killing me. When I glanced back to check on him, Bart was already gone.

19

As I put the bar behind me, I couldn't help but wonder how Adrian's wolves knew where to find me. I guess I could understand them finding me at The Bloody Stake since Adrian knew I frequented there. He could have had his wolves watching the place for months.

But Polaris? I'd never gone there but once or twice in my entire life, and even then, I only drove through it. How would he have known to keep two of his thugs there waiting for me when I had no reason to go to the mall there? Could it have been a coincidence? Or was it something more?

I looked in the rearview mirror, half-expecting to see a car tailing me, but the road behind me was empty. Someone pulled out of a side street as I passed, but they turned the other way.

The lack of a tail only agitated me more. Someone following me, I could understand. Wolves showing up wherever I went was just a little too convenient to be coincidence. He was tracking me and I really wanted to know how.

I immediately thought of Gregory Hillis. He'd once been a member of the Luna Cult who'd supplied Adrian with information until he was decapitated by the guy he was working for. Could someone else be feeding him information now? It wouldn't surprise me in the slightest if Adrian had someone else on the inside.

My thoughts drifted to Jeremy, but I refused to believe he could be helping Adrian. The kid was too green to defect like that. It wasn't as if he'd known where I was going either. All he could have told Adrian was that I'd returned and then tell him of my comings and goings.

So, if it wasn't Jeremy or someone in the Cult, then how did Adrian know?

I considered calling it a night and heading home to sort things through. I didn't like the idea of anyone knowing what I was doing before I did. The only way Adrian could get his wolves in position, especially at Polaris, was if he knew where I would be and planted them ahead of time. I hadn't been there long enough for him to get his men mobilized in time.

In the end, there was nothing I could do about it right away. I wasn't about to just go home either. I wanted to get this kill done for Baset so I could put it behind me. Once I finished with Count Strinowski, I would hopefully figure out how to break my deal with Baset without getting anyone else killed. I might kill vamps and wolves, but I didn't do it for vampire Countesses.

But Baset wasn't a normal vampire. She'd died and come back. Her body's decay was proof enough of that. How could I kill something that was already dead? If I tried, I might only bring down more misery upon the heads of everyone around me. I couldn't be responsible for that.

I made a turn and slowed as a certain little sign came into view. I pulled off to the side of the road, transfixed by it.

What was I going to do about Delai? Part of me just wanted to turn down the road and forget all about Baset and Strinowski and Adrian and everyone else sticking their noses into my life. I didn't need that kind of stress anymore. Ethan was right when he said all the killing was getting to me and here I was, adding to it. It would be so easy just to put the car in gear and coast into oblivion.

Yet, I couldn't get past the thought that something was wrong with the town, that Ethan's demon might be right about the place. Could I really just forget about everything and let Levi keep doing whatever it was he'd been doing to me?

I couldn't bear the thought of letting the demon do something to me either. I knew Sienna and Eilene weren't bad people, yet I wasn't so sure about Levi anymore. I'd seen what he'd done to Ronnie. What else had he done I didn't know about? Whom else had he hurt?

My stomach started churning and I felt like throwing up. The urge just to drive down the road was so strong, I found myself starting that way.

I stopped just before I made the turn. I closed my eyes and rubbed them with my palms.

"What the hell is wrong with me?" I mumbled. I took a deep breath and swallowed the bile that filled my mouth. I could do this.

I drove past the sign slowly, refusing to look down the road. If I were to look, I knew I wouldn't be able to resist. I would have to know. I would want to see Sienna, make sure she was all right. I'd want to confront Levi, to ask him about what it was he really was doing to me and those around him.

As soon as I was past the road, it felt like something ripped open my guts and tore them from my body through my throat. I slammed on the brakes so hard the entire car jerked and skidded on the road. I was gasping for air, unable to breathe, let alone think.

And then the nausea hit me. I threw open Jeremy's door just in time. I leaned out and heaved. Not much came out since I hadn't eaten much, but it was enough to leave a horrible taste in my mouth. I spit over and over, wishing I had water.

I took a shuddering breath and another wave of nausea hit. I swallowed it back. The bile burned going back down, and it was all I could do to keep from retching.

I closed my eyes as the shakes hit. They were so bad I nearly fell out of car. I grabbed the wheel, held it tightly as wave after wave hit. It was like I was having a mini-seizure, though I was conscious of everything happening to me.

And then, just like that, it passed.

My stomach settled and my head cleared. The bad taste in my mouth was still there and I was a little shaky, but the worst had definitely passed.

I wiped my mouth with the back of my hand and sat back, simply breathing. It took me a good ten minutes before I felt stable enough to drive again.

I had no idea what had just happened, and part of me feared it had something to do with Beligral, yet I was no longer marked. I didn't think he could affect me that way without his mark connecting us.

But if it wasn't him, then what was it?

I considered turning around and going home but nixed the idea immediately. I had to take care of Strinowski now so I didn't have it hanging over my head any longer. I could worry about the implications of my sudden bout later.

It only took a couple more turns before I was on the road that supposedly led to Strinowski's place. The street was mostly deserted, and the snow had started to drift onto the road, obscuring it completely in some places. It would have been hard to drive even on my motorcycle.

The houses appeared empty on either side of the road. Some had caved in, others had broken windows, doors hanging open on busted hinges. One small cottage looked inhabitable. The lights were out, but curtains hung in the windows. They fluttered ever so slightly, as if someone had a fan or a space heater sitting under the window.

Most of the mailboxes were gone, though a few still stood. I could just make out the numbers on them, giving me an indication as to how far down the road I'd have to go to find my mark.

The cluster of houses gave way to farmland long since abandoned. Where the land wasn't flat and ruined, it was hilly. The houses became fewer and farther between. Before long I'd reached a spot where it was impossible to see one house from the next. If someone wanted to hide, the barren stretch was as good a place as any.

I turned off the headlights and hoped I could stick to the road as I got closer. Only the lump of once-plowed snow kept me from ending up in the ditch. Snow crunched under my tires as I worked my way closer to Strinowski's hide-away.

I crested a rise and started a slow descent down the other side. I could just make out a house tucked away behind a barrier of pines. If I hadn't missed my guess, that was my target.

I skidded a few feet down the rise and parked at the side of the road. I shut off the engine and just sat there, listening.

There were no sounds of the night here. It wasn't the peaceful silence I was used to. The quiet here was unsettling. It felt as though there should be more sounds, even if it was just a winter owl hooting in the trees or the sound of a branch breaking as a doe scampered through the trees.

But it was completely and utterly silent, as if the entire area was holding its breath, waiting for something to happen.

The house was dark. Even if a light had been on, I wouldn't have been able to make anything out from where

I sat. The trees were too dense, planted to act as a screen against anyone casually driving by. Whoever had lived here before had valued their privacy.

I got out of the car, leaving the keys in the ignition. I had no idea what I was going to face, and just because Mikael said the guy didn't have anyone under him, didn't mean he was helpless. I might have to make a quick getaway. I wasn't worried about someone stealing Jeremy's car; not out here.

I stood out starkly against the snow as I moved toward the pines. I moved as quickly as I dared, hoping I was as difficult to see from the house as the house was to me.

I got a clear view of the house as soon as I reached the pine barrier. As I'd thought, the place was completely dark. Strinowski was a vampire, so he didn't need light to see by. And since he was hiding, he wouldn't want the light to clue anyone who happened by to know someone was living there.

Then again, he might not be home at all. He could be out, searching for another victim, or simply out for a stroll in the snow. Just because I wanted him to be here didn't mean he would be.

I drew my sword and gun and scanned the grounds. As far as I could tell, there was nothing there. I could see no cameras, no watchdogs of any sort. Just an empty old farmhouse that looked as though it hadn't been occupied in quite a few years.

The windows were almost completely black in the night. He must have put up some heavy drapes to keep out the sun during the day. A farmhouse like this probably had a cellar, but the vamp might not stay down there all the time and would want the extra protection on the other levels.

I prepped myself to move. There was nothing to hide behind the twenty yards from the trees to the house. I'd have to run it and hope Strinowski didn't happen to peek out the window just as I made my move.

I tucked my sword under one arm, checked my gun to make sure it was fully loaded even though I knew it was. I slammed the magazine home, took a deep breath, and started forward.

It was game time.

20

I could smell the house even before I reached it. A deep, thick scent that was almost impossible to breathe in. There was blood, but there was more to it than that. It smelled of dead things, of bodies left to rot. Not even the smell of fresh blood could overpower the smell of death.

A scream came from inside, the first sound I'd heard since parking. It was a woman's scream, one filled with unbearable agony. I couldn't tell if she was a supe or Pure-blood, and honestly, I didn't care. From what Mikael had told me, I knew she was being tortured.

I didn't screw around trying to peek in through the dark windows or sneak into the place. If this guy worked alone, then I wouldn't have to worry about fending off minions. I could focus on simply finding the vamp and ending his torturous ways.

I kicked in the door with such force, one of the hinges tore clean off. The house was so old, it was a wonder it was still standing. As it was, the door slammed hard against the wall, a resounding crash that caused every other sound in the house to cease.

Both my gun and sword were in hand, poised to either fire or strike. While Strinowski might work alone, that didn't mean he wasn't dangerous. A vampire was a vampire, regardless of how many wolves and vamps he has around him. If I wasn't careful, he could kill me before I knew he was there.

The silence caused by my entrance didn't last long. The sound of agonized whimpering came from upstairs.

The front door opened into a small foyer. Traces of blood stained the floor and walls. The living room was just off that, but no one was in there. There was no furniture of any kind, just an empty room.

I started to turn away when I noticed the shades hanging over the windows. I might not have noticed anything was wrong with them, but I'd caught a glimpse of a lump of something on one.

Curiosity took over. I edged toward the blinds while keeping an eye on the stairs. No one had come tearing down them, so I had to hope Strinowski was hiding somewhere up them, waiting for me to find him.

I approached the windows warily. In the dark, it was hard to make out exactly what I was seeing, even with my superior vision. It wasn't until I was almost on them that it all made sense.

The clump turned out to be hair. The stench was horrible, though it wasn't as bad as the general smell of the place that I'd smelled from the outside. The blinds, all of them in the room, and quite possibly in the rest of the house, were made from skin. The side that had once faced inside someone's body was turned toward the window. They left bloody streaks on the glass.

When Mikael had told me the guy tortured people, I hadn't realized how bad it really was. This wasn't just torture; it was pure brutality. How many of these skins were from Purebloods? Were there wolf and vamp skins as well? I wasn't sure I wanted to find out.

I moved away from the nightmarish blinds and headed for the stairs. The woman was still whimpering upstairs, and I just had to hope Strinowski had been the cause of her scream. I hadn't heard a window open or glass break or anything, so I was banking on him still being here.

The stairs creaked despite my best efforts to be quiet. The house was one of those giant farmhouses built back before modern heating. The house was cold, but not the bone-deep chill I would have expected. Chances were good Strinowski had battery-powered heaters somewhere inside or else his victims would freeze to death before he could torture them.

As I went up the stairs, I began to regret kicking in the door. Strinowski was known for being able to hide, to escape anyone who would search for him. All I'd really accomplished by entering as I had was to alert him that someone else was in his house. I could have easily tried the door first to see if it was unlocked. It would have been the smart thing to do.

But it was too late now. If I screwed this up because of my mistake, I knew I'd pay for it later. There was no use beating myself up for it now.

I reached the top of the stairs and scanned the dark hallway. There were only three rooms, two to the left, one to the right. A sliding door on the right-hand wall appeared to be a closet. All the doors were closed, and no light seeped beneath them. I listened, hoping to hear something other than the whimpering coming from the only room to the right.

I started forward, taking each step slowly, eyes scanning from left to right, up and down. I wouldn't let this guy get the jump on me. I had no idea what he was capable of. If he was some sort of shifter, I wanted to be prepared.

The first door I came to was on the left. I pushed it open, bringing my gun up, finger ready to pull the trigger the moment I saw someone. The room was completely empty aside from the thick scent of feces and blood. The tiny bathroom was barely large enough for one person to stand in. There was no curtain in the shower, nothing at all in which the vamp could hide in or behind.

I closed the door to stifle the heavy reek and checked the closet across the hall. Like the bathroom, it was empty. I peered inside just in case before moving down the hall to the last two doors. The one to the right held the whimpering woman. The one to the left was silent.

I could hear the clink of metal on metal coming from the woman's room. It reminded me of the sound a swing would make as its chains clanked in the wind. I started to reach for the door but stopped myself. Would my vamp be in the room with the woman? Or was he banking on me to investigate the room with the sounds first so he could make his move while my back was turned?

I stepped back from the door and turned to the one on the left. I waited, my breath held in the hopes of hearing the vamp breathing on the other side.

There was nothing. I reached out, grasped the doorknob, and pushed the door inward.

A flare of light flashed as soon as the door was open, blinding me. I fired reflexively just as something heavy hit me in the chest. I flew backward and slammed up against the wall, just barely keeping hold of my weapons.

Sharp fangs bit into my shoulder and I cried out. I brought the hilt of my sword down hard on the top of my attacker's head, which was a mistake. The fangs sank deeper from the impact, causing me to cry out.

The fangs withdrew and I caught a glimpse of a mad face before his gaping mouth darted toward my face. I jerked back just in time, smacking my head hard against the wall as his fangs snapped shut just before my nose.

I knew I didn't have much time. This guy was quick, but he was quite clearly crazy. Before he could pull back to launch another attack, I head-butted him. His nose crunched and he screamed. It sounded strangely feminine coming from him, but I didn't have time to worry about that. He staggered back a step, and I used the space to bring my sword around.

It wasn't a clean hit, but it did the job. The blade bit into his side and he slammed hard against the wall. He stood there a moment, shaking as the silver went to work, before finally collapsing.

I took a deep breath and nearly gagged from the stench of blood and sulfur. My attacker was completely naked, his body slick with blood and something else I didn't even want to consider. His back was covered with lashes I assumed were self-inflicted. His eyes were blood-red, sliced from corner of the eye to the ear.

I grimaced as his tongue lolled from his mouth. It was forked and covered with my blood.

"Strinowski?" I said, rolling him onto his back with my foot. He grunted, but that was all he could manage with the silver running through his veins.

I stepped back when I saw him face-on. He had nothing but scar tissue between his legs where he'd removed his sexual organs. He didn't have nipples either, or a belly button. I don't even want to know how he managed the last.

His mouth was modified much like his eyes, cut at the sides, giving him an unnaturally long grimace. His tongue was longer than it should have been, and I wondered if he'd managed to pull it up from his throat somehow.

My eyes passed over him and I wanted to be sick. Just above where his belly button should have been was a long, horizontal slash. The skin flapped at the top, and I so didn't want to see what was inside.

Strinowski stared at me with his blood-filled eyes. I think he was trying to smile, though the cuts on his face made that impossible.

I couldn't stand to look at him anymore. The guy was quite clearly insane, and I was doing both him and everyone he'd ever hurt or planned on hurting a service by killing him.

I had to hack downward to take his head. The floorboards were old, and my silver blade bit into the wood and nearly got stuck. When I jerked it free, blood splattered across my pants and boots. Strinowski's head rolled a few feet before coming to a stop facing the wall.

The whimpering from the other side of the door turned to moans. I walked over to it, just wanting this over with. I pushed the door open, readying myself for another attack, but after one look, I knew the woman was in no condition to hurt me.

Chains from the ceiling and floor kept her suspended in place, hanging in the air with her legs and arms spread as wide as they could go. She was naked and bleeding from seemingly everywhere. As I neared, I knew why.

A bundle of what I took at first to be rags turned out to be her skin. It looked molted and forlorn lying there like a discarded piece of clothing.

The woman looked at me with wild eyes. I had no idea how she was still alive, the damage was so extensive. Her entire face was gone, including her eyelids. All that was left was muscle and bone and gristle. Her teeth stood out without lips to cover them, eyes bulging from skinless sockets.

"Jesus," I said, covering my nose. During her torture, her bowels had repeatedly released. Strinowski hadn't bothered to clean it up. He'd left the stinking pile where it fell.

"Kill me," the girl croaked. I had no idea how old she was, doubted anyone could tell. No one could recognize this as anything remotely human anymore. "Please." She started whimpering.

I blinked a few times, tried to sort everything out in my head. There were sharp knives lying on a table next to the woman. There was also a bottle of pills that contained what I assumed was something that would keep the victim alive and aware during the torture. Beside that was a small flashlight. I guess Strinowski kept it there so his victims could see the damage he was doing to them.

The windows behind the woman were covered with skin, these ones hairy, as if they'd come from an animal. A small space heater hummed under the table. It was so quiet I could barely hear it over her whimpering.

I didn't know what to do. Normally, when I found the victims of vamps, I let them go so they could return to their families. Sometimes the victims didn't survive. Sometimes they were dead even before I arrived.

But this? I'd never seen anything like this before. Even with all the blood, my disgust completely overrode any hunger I might have had. It was just too much of a shock for that part of me to function.

"Kill me!" the woman screamed. She started vibrating on her chains, bloody saliva dripping from her mouth. It was more than just shaking too. She was having a seizure. Her eyes rolled up, though I could still see the iris because there really was nowhere for them to go.

I raised my gun and put her out of her misery. The bullet hit her with a muffled thump and she immediately slumped in her chains. Blood and urine dripped from her as she died.

I turned and staggered out of the room. I had to lean against the wall to catch my breath. I was feeling sick and dizzy, almost unable to think. What had gone on in this house? Why hadn't anyone killed this guy before?

Why hadn't I?

I shuddered and made for the stairs. I wasn't completely sure I'd gotten Strinowski, but I hoped to hell I did. The guy who attacked me could have been one of his victims for all I knew, driven mad by the tortures inflicted upon him.

The smell of death got worse as I stepped into the kitchen and found the cellar door. There was nothing in the kitchen aside from the empty cabinets and sink. I stood in front of the door, wondering if I should go down or not. Now that I knew to listen for it, I could hear the hum of a couple of heaters coming from downstairs.

Finally, I decided I couldn't leave until I knew if anyone was alive down there. I opened the door and immediately the sound of chains clinking reached my ears. I reached for a light switch, but when I flicked it up and down, nothing happened.

Someone started crying and I knew I'd have to investigate in the dark. I could see, but I would have preferred to view the horrors I knew waited for me with a light on.

I went down, gun pointed forward. I wasn't sure what to expect or how many people I'd find, but I had to do it. I prayed it would only be two or three more at the most. Any more than that and it might drive me crazy.

The first man came into view and I froze halfway down the stairs. He was a fully shifted werewolf, though his fur was gone. His skin had a strange, wrinkled look to it, and it took me only a moment to realize that because he was a were, his skin had grown back after being removed.

He snarled at me and thrashed in his chains. I'd seen crazed wolves before, seen them affected by the full moon, seen them hopped up on drugs, yet this was so much worse. Saliva dropped from his muzzle, tinged red. He gnashed his teeth, eyes bugging out of his head.

I shot him without having to think about it. The wolf was completely out of his mind. I didn't even have to think twice to know he'd never be saved.

Someone screamed and I hurried down the last few stairs to get a better look at the room.

Another five people hung from chains all around the cellar. Two were wolves who were just as insane as the first. I dispatched them quickly, knowing it would be pointless to set them free, though I knew Jonathan would have wanted me to.

The next victim was a vampire. She'd been skinned so recently, she was still dripping blood. She stared at me with pain-filled eyes as I raised my gun. I think she smiled just as I pulled the trigger.

The last two appeared to be Purebloods. They were swaying in the back, trying to reach for each other. The man appeared to be in his late twenties, the woman a few years younger. They were crying and looking at me as if they weren't sure if I was there to kill them or save them. It appeared Strinowski had yet to get around to skinning them.

"How many?" I asked, my voice coming out strangled. "Was it just Strinowski?"

The girl burst into tears and didn't answer. The guy was just barely able to hang on.

"I don't know," he said. "I only saw the one."

I moved through the cellar and checked the corners, keeping my eye on the stairs just in case I didn't get everyone. There was nothing down there but the heaters and the chains, which were bolted to the ceiling and floor. There were heavy-looking locks near their ankles and wrists, but I couldn't find a key.

I could have shot the locks off, but chances were good I'd hurt the two Purebloods in the process. The chains had to be strong enough to contain weres and vamps, so it was unlikely I'd be able to break them by brute force.

"Damn it," I said, turning toward the stairs. As much as I didn't want to see the freak show I'd killed in the hallway again, I knew I'd have to go back and look for the key.

The couple started crying out to me as I turned by back and headed upstairs. They screamed and pleaded for me to come back and save them. I did my best to ignore their pleas. There wasn't anything I could do for them until I found the key.

Still, it was hard. I wondered if the girl hanging in the room upstairs had been a friend of theirs, or worse, a sister or mother.

I started in the girl's room, doing my best not to look directly at her. I checked the table, finding it sticky with blood, but a key was nowhere to be found. I grabbed the flashlight as I hurried out.

Next, I moved to the room the vamp had come out of. It was as empty as every other room in the house. Not even a hanger hung in the closet.

I went back out into the hall and stared down at the vamp I prayed was Strinowski. He was naked, but that didn't mean he didn't have places where he could hide the key.

My eyes immediately fell on that pouch of skin on his belly and I groaned. Where else would it be?

I knelt and gingerly lifted the flap of skin, exposing the muscles and organs. At first, all I could see was a mass of blood and guts, and was just about to let the skin fall when I saw the glint of metal.

I retched as I pulled it from his innards. There were at least a dozen keys on the ring, and they kept catching on parts of his body. They were slick with coagulated blood and gore by the time I pulled them free.

I grabbed the vamp's head and took it with me as I headed back down into the cellar. I needed to know for sure I had Strinowski and not one of his other victims.

I turned on the flashlight as I approached the scared Purebloods. I held the head up for the couple to see.

"Is this him?"

They both burst into tears, nodding and thanking me over and over. I tossed the head aside and used the bloody keys to unlock their chains. I left them there to huddle together on the floor, leaving the flashlight with them.

I all but ran to Jeremy's car, so sick I nearly threw up twice before I was safely behind the wheel. It wasn't so much the blood. I'd seen more than enough blood in my time. It was the sheer brutality of the killings that had my stomach doing flips.

It took me a couple tries to get the car started and when I did, I tore out of there like Strinowski himself was after me.

I regretted leaving the couple behind, knowing it would be hard for them to find a way home. They were naked and I hadn't seen a scrap of clothing lying around anywhere.

But at least I'd given them a chance, something they might not have had if I'd taken them with me. With as screwed up as I was, I didn't trust myself not to attack them on the way home. It was better this way.

It had to be.

The car coughed and shook as I pressed down on the gas, intent on getting home as fast as I could.

I didn't even notice the road sign as I shot past Delai.

21

There comes a point when you figure that things can't get any worse and you do something you probably shouldn't. The world seems to conspire against you, and you just decide that you might as well dive in headfirst rather than take the cautious approach.

I'd reached that point by the time I got home, still splattered with werewolf blood and brains, not to mention whatever slime that had covered Strinowski.

Jeremy was standing in the kitchen. He jumped when I threw open the door and stalked past him. He watched me go without a word, mouth slightly agape, eyes as wide as they'd go.

I headed straight for the stairs that led to Ethan's lab without paying him much more than a glance. If I'd been in a better mood, I might have thought his reaction funny. Instead, it just irritated me all the more.

The lab door was firmly locked and I punched it once before pressing the intercom button. "Ethan," I snapped. "Get up here."

I had to wait only a few seconds before the door opened. Ethan was bathed in sweat and looked as though he hadn't really slept. His hair was tousled like usual, his shirt stained with something that looked like ash.

He looked me up and down and gulped. "You've got blood on you."

I glanced down at myself and shrugged. "That happens when people piss me off," I said. Normally, I would have changed first thing after coming home from a kill, but I was so pissed, it hadn't even crossed my mind.

And it wasn't what I'd seen at Strinowski's place that had me in such a foul mood. I'd seen death before, had seen some pretty sick things, so that wasn't anything new. Sure, the sight of Strinowski's victims had shaken me up, but that was something I'd eventually get over.

No, my biggest issue was that Countess Baset had wanted me to kill him. I would have killed Strinowski on my own if I'd known about him, but having a vampire tell me to do it made the act seem vile somehow. I wasn't given a choice.

I hated having my choices taken away from me.

"Is he down there?" I asked.

"Um." Ethan glanced over his shoulder, giving me all the answer I needed.

I stepped toward the door and Ethan moved to block my way. I could have forced him out of the doorway, but I might have hurt him in doing so. I was tired of hurting my friends.

That didn't mean I wouldn't threaten them.

"Ethan," I said, putting as much warning into my voice as I could. "Move."

"You're free," he said. "You don't want to do this."

"I'll decide what I want and don't want to do. I'm in no mood to piss around, so get the fuck out of my way."

Ethan held his ground. "Kat," he said. His voice was trembling and he was clearly terrified, yet he still blocked my path, something he wouldn't have done a few months ago. "If you go down there, he'll trick you into another mark. Do you really want that?"

"I have to know," I said. "I'm tired of not knowing,

tired of people lying to me, controlling me. If what the demon says is true, I *have* to know."

Ethan looked uncertain and then slumped. He knew I was going down there with or without him. "Okay," he said, stepping aside.

I brushed past him and went down the stairs. Heat blasted into me, taking my breath away for a split second before I was able to recover. My eyes watered and my skin felt like blistering, but I stood against it, refused to let my discomfort show.

"Ah, my sweet Lady Death," Beligral said. He was lazing in his chair, one leg tossed over the arm casually. "Come to see me again, I see."

"What is this going to take?"

He raised an eyebrow. "What is it you are referring to?" He gave me a wicked smile.

"You fucking well know what I want," I snarled. "What is it going to take for you to show me what Levi is and what he's doing to those people?"

Beligral's smile turned satisfied. "You'll have to come into the circle with me."

"And?"

"And you'll have to promise that once you see, you'll come back to me. A small price to pay for the truth, don't you think?"

I looked at the circle and then back to the demon. I really didn't want to get in there with him. I had no idea what he was capable of. Were his powers diminished here? Or was he as strong as ever, even trapped inside the circle?

"I don't want to be toyed with," I said. "If you are lying to me . . ."

The demon laughed. It grated on my nerves to the point I wanted to draw my gun and shoot him just to make the sound stop. I didn't know if a bullet would break the circle or not. I didn't plan on finding out either.

"As I've said before, when have I ever lied to you? Think back. I've been nothing but honest with you ever since the first time we met. I've given you everything you've ever wanted that was within my power to give. Even before you knew I existed, I was helping you become the killer you are today. Don't you think I've earned some of your trust by now?"

I so didn't need to be thinking about how the demon had helped make my weapons. I could almost feel them burn through my clothes. They'd been at least partly crafted by him, if not completely. I had no idea what role Ethan played in their creation, if any at all. And as far as I knew, the silver used to craft them had come from the demon realm as well.

What kind of person did that make me in using them?

"Ethan," I said, glancing back. He was standing at the foot of the stairs, watching the conversation with dismay. "Dismiss him. I'm going in there."

"Kat, please . . ."

"Do it."

Beligral smiled as Ethan dismissed him. As soon as the demon was gone, I stepped over the chalk outline and silver circle, and waited for Ethan to set everything again.

He didn't speak as he worked. He didn't even look at me. I knew what I was doing was dangerous, but I had no choice. I couldn't keep going on like I had been. This was the only thing I could do and stay sane.

It was that last trip past Delai that had done it. I'd felt so sick and the urge to drive down that road had been so strong, I knew it couldn't be natural. Something was going on there. I couldn't just ignore it.

As soon as the circle was set, Ethan looked at me. "Are you sure?" he whispered. He looked terrified. I had to admit, I was terrified too.

"Yeah," I said.

He started summoning his demon.

Inside the circle, the heat was almost unbearable. As soon as the candles stopped flickering and froze, it was like standing in the middle of a bonfire. The light blazed around me to form the pentagram and as it faded, Beligral stepped out from the tear between realms. My eyes were burning too much to watch.

He stared at me as if he expected me to try to run, but I held my ground. I knew if I were to break the circle, he'd be free. I was stuck in there with him until Ethan dismissed him.

"You should have left your weapons outside," the demon said. He sighed as he walked a slow circle around me.

"They make me feel better," I said, following him with my eyes.

He reached out toward me and I jerked away. He tsked. "I'll have to touch you if you want me to do this."

I ground my teeth, but straightened, giving him one sharp nod. God, I hated this.

He didn't touch my bare flesh, which was a relief. He went for the hilt of my sword. He didn't draw it, but instead caressed the hilt as if it was precious to him.

"It can feel my nearness," he said. "It wants to go home." He bared his yellowed, pointed teeth. "I'm surprised you were able to take them with you to Delai."

"Get on with it," I said. "It's almost morning."

Beligral glanced toward the wall, though there were no windows down this far. "Is it?" he said. "There is no night or day where I come from. It would be perfect for you. There's no sun to burn you. Just shadows and fire and things of such magnificence I can hardly describe them." He looked wistful.

My mouth went dry. I wasn't sure if it was from the heat or what he was implying.

"Forget it," I said. "I'm not going home with you. Just get this over with already."

The demon smiled as he chuckled. "So feisty."

I really wanted to punch him. Sometimes I wondered if the demon was all talk. I'd never actually seen him do anything. Even his marks appeared on their own without him actually making a move. And when he tried to save Thomas, he hadn't appeared to do anything at all but look at him. As far as I knew, he hadn't. It sure as hell hadn't saved my brother.

"What now?" I asked, frustrated. I just wanted this over with.

"Now? I need you to agree to my terms."

"I already did."

"Humor me." He bared his teeth.

I growled and clenched my fists. Was he making this hard on me solely for his amusement? "Fine," I said. "You do this and make it so I can see who or what Levi is and what's going on in Delai, and I'll come back and see you."

"And you won't just walk in and call it done. You'll spend time with me, listen to what I have to say. You never know, you may learn something. You might even find a way out of your current . . . condition." He smiled.

"Kat . . ." Ethan said from outside the circle.

I ignored him. "Whatever. Can we just get this over with?"

"Then it is done."

Searing pain exploded from behind my ear. I gritted my teeth, refused to show how much it hurt in front of the demon. He would take too much pleasure in it.

"You are so much stronger than I'd ever hoped," Beligral said as the pain subsided. "You've made me proud for so long, it almost feels as if you're my own child."

I reached up and touched the mark. Had I done the right thing? It sure as hell didn't feel like it.

"I'm not."

Beligral shrugged. "We'll see."

I could have stood there and argued with him all day, but to do so meant to stand in his presence for far longer than was healthy.

"Okay," I said, trying really hard not to grind my teeth. "I've made my promise. Now do whatever it is you're going to do so I can get the fuck out of here."

The demon's face went blank. We stared at each other, seemingly locked in some sort of battle, though I had no idea what kind of battle we were fighting. Did he want me to kneel, to beg? He was out of luck if he thought I was going to do anything that would show subservience to him.

A small smile quirked the edges of his mouth. "So strong," he said again as he raised his hand. I managed not to flinch as he reached for me. He poked me gently in the middle of the forehead.

It felt like a nuclear bomb went off inside my skull. Pain like nothing I'd ever felt before became the only thing I knew. I was blinded, struck deaf. I was screaming, thrashing, but I couldn't feel anything but the pain in my head, couldn't hear a sound. My eyes felt like they were melting in my skull.

I couldn't even think. It felt like I was dying, but then again, dying wouldn't hurt so much.

I have no idea how long the pain lasted. I might have even blacked out, because the next thing I knew, I could hear the sound of my own ragged screams as my hearing returned. Something scrambled around me and hands grabbed me by the arms. I thrashed even more, intent on killing anything that touched me, certain it was the demon come to drag me through the portal, where I'd burn every night in the fires of his hell.

"Kat!" The voice sounded far away but kept me from lashing out more. My vision cleared, and instead of the face of the demon, I was looking into Ethan's frightened eyes.

I looked frantically around, terrified I'd see the demon bearing down on me. Much to my relief, only Ethan and I were in the circle.

Beligral was gone.

22

I thought I'd suffered through some pretty bad days before, but the day following Beligral's "gift" was one of the worst of my life. I spent most of the time lying in bed, alternating between sweating and shuddering uncontrollably. I couldn't get warm, couldn't cool off. I took at least three baths, each lasting only a few minutes before the water became either too hot or too cold.

Ethan came in and out of the room every so often to check on me. I was naked nearly the entire time, which usually had him sputtering and blushing until he looked as though he'd suffered sunstroke, but this time, he hardly appeared to notice.

At first, I was panicked he had broken the circle in his haste to see to me, but Ethan assured me the demon had been sent back home before he broke the circle. It took him a few tries to get me to believe him. I was so sure I'd screwed up and set the demon loose in my thrashing, I just couldn't seem to wrap my head around everything being okay.

Not that it was, mind you. I couldn't talk without my teeth chattering or mumbling like I was hallucinating. Half the time, I wasn't sure if I was or not. My vision kept swimming in and out, and my ears rang almost nonstop.

I was terrified the demon had done something permanently damaging to me. I wasn't sure what he might have done, I just knew it couldn't be good. I was already screwed up enough without having a demon in my head as well.

It might have made me feel better if this Sight he was supposed to have given me made the world around me look different. As far as I could tell, everything was the same other than the pounding in my head and my fluctuating internal temperature.

It wasn't until near dark that my body started calming down. I was able to get dressed, though my hands shook as I pulled on my leathers. My mouth felt like I'd been sucking on cotton balls for the last six hours, and no matter how much water I drank, I just couldn't seem to make the feeling go away.

I was afraid my hunger would erupt and I'd attack someone unintentionally, but at least that part of me still seemed under control. Ethan brought me a slice of buttered toast before finally collapsing in his room from exhaustion. I ate it slowly, hoping it wouldn't come right back up.

When night finally fell, I made my way out of my room and headed downstairs. Jeremy was waiting for me with a beer and a slice of turkey. For whatever reason, the two men must have figured I'd be hungry after my experience. I had to admit, I was ravenous. Other than blood and beer, I hadn't eaten anything for days.

I downed the meat in just a few bites and chased it down with the beer. It did little to sate my hunger. The food sat heavy in my stomach, but at least I did feel marginally better than I had before.

"You okay?" the young wolf said, moving casually across the room without overtly trying to appear as if he was putting space between us.

"Some," I said. I chugged the rest of my beer, hoping it would rid me of the cottonmouth.

"Ethan was worried he screwed up."

That made me a little angry. Ethan shouldn't take on any of the blame for my actions. "It wasn't his idea. He did what I told him to do."

"That doesn't mean he doesn't feel guilty about it. If it wasn't for him, you wouldn't have been put in this situation to begin with."

I turned an unhappy glare on the wolf. He cringed a little under my gaze but didn't back down. While losing his arm seemed to have made him grow up a bit, he was still just a scared kid. I'd definitely been too hard on the guy. He'd gone through more than what a lot of other people had in his short life.

I looked away and tossed the empty bottle in the trash. I could apologize to him later. Right then, I didn't have it in me. He'd understand.

I left him standing in the dining room as I went down to grab fresh weapons. I had things to do and I planned on getting as many of them done tonight as I could. No sense waiting around. I had no idea how long the Sight was supposed to last, so Delai had to be high on my list.

But I was scared. I didn't know what to expect. I was afraid at what I'd find when I got there, terrified at what I'd do afterward. I wanted to know what Levi was, and yet at the same time, I didn't. Finding out he was some sort of monster would take all those months I'd spent with him and turn them into something dark, something sinister. I wasn't sure I wanted to do that.

Still, I had to know.

Of course, I had something else I needed to do first. Baset's man might be waiting for me. Even though I'd killed Strinowski the night before, I had a feeling she would know he was dead. I didn't want to avoid going to the pickup spot and have her take it the wrong way. I mean, it *was* Monday and she'd wanted me to go there every Monday. I'd much rather play it safe than to have Baset show up on my doorstep looking for me.

Jeremy didn't say anything as I mounted the stairs and headed out to the garage. He didn't have to. I could see the concern in his eyes and wondered where it came from. The guy used to be terrified of me. Now he acted like we were friends in an awkward, "don't show it if you don't have to" sort of way.

His concern did lift my spirits, however. It meant everything wouldn't be lost if I found out Levi was something evil. I still had a place I could go, people I could trust. I might not like the idea that most of those people were werewolves, but at least I wasn't alone anymore.

How I never thought of it that way before was beyond me. Maybe Levi *had* done something to me. Maybe my own prejudices had gotten in the way. Just because Jonathan and Jeremy were wolves didn't mean we had to be enemies.

I checked the address where I was to meet Baset's man before heading out into the garage. The place was pretty public, but not so much that it would be dangerous for me to be seen. I doubted anyone there would know me by sight.

More snow had fallen during the day, so I took Jeremy's car. It appeared he'd taken it out sometime and gotten gas, probably while I'd been half unconscious in my room. He'd returned the keys to my coat pocket where I'd left them, which I hoped meant he didn't mind me taking it out again.

I pulled out of the garage, silently thanking Jeremy for not holding my prickly attitude against me.

I drove, growing more and more nervous about the pickup. It felt dirty working for cash like this, but what was I to do? I needed money to pay Mikael, and Ethan had to pay the bills, so why not take it?

Then again, what if Baset was just using me and her men would jump me the moment I arrived? Just because it was a public place didn't mean they wouldn't try something. I didn't know what kind of situation I was walking into here, and that really bothered me. I had no reason to trust her, which made it all the worse.

I'd killed her lover and assassin. She would want revenge; though forcing me to work for her was revenge enough in my mind. I wondered what else she would end up wanting from me later down the road if I didn't take care of her before then.

I turned onto the street that would lead to the pickup site. The streetlights were bright, illuminating anyone and anything that would dare walk under them. A few pedestrians walked huddled together, eyes scanning all around them. Shops were lit up, places that sold things that anyone could enjoy, regardless of monster status.

I drove past them, clunking along in Jeremy's junk heap. A few other cars patrolled the roads, but nothing that would worry me. It felt kind of peaceful here, though I knew that down some of the alleys and inside some of the buildings, dark and bloody things were happening.

I pulled up outside the building where the meeting was to take place and stared at it. It stood five stories high, most of the windows still intact. A chain lay broken on the ground in front of the door, which was closed firmly. There was graffiti on the walls, everything from gang signs to lovers' initials scrawled in flowing scripts.

"Great," I said, shutting off the engine. The place was obviously abandoned. I'd hoped I'd meet Baset's man outside somewhere under the lights, but it looked as though I was expected to go inside.

I sat there for a few minutes waiting anyway. Maybe he'd grow impatient and come out to meet me. I knew they wouldn't recognize the car, but perhaps whoever was inside would see me through the window. Dark, abandoned buildings did little to bolster my confidence.

Someone banged on the back of the car and I jumped. Two teens ran by, laughing. One stuck his tongue out at me before they both vanished around the corner.

Anger flared, but this time I was angry at myself. I was too jumpy. Baset wanted to use me. She wouldn't send her men to kill me. I was just being paranoid.

I got out of the car and slammed the door a little harder than I had to.

The snow had been cleared from the sidewalk, though I had to walk through it to get there from the road. I stomped my boots clean and looked around for anyone who might be watching. Other than a group of kids standing outside a gas station, no one seemed to have noticed my arrival. The kids were watching me out of curiosity more than anything, and I pushed them from my mind.

As I neared the front door, I saw a few scattered cigarette butts and empty wrappers. The building was more than likely a common place for kids to stand around and smoke and pass the night away, whether they were Pure-blooded or not. The building sat between a convenience store and what appeared to be a small apartment complex. It looked out of place sitting between their well-maintained fronts.

I stepped up to the door and knocked. It rang hollowly through the empty building. I waited for a good minute before trying again.

There was no answer.

I touched the doorknob and gave it an exploratory turn. It moved easily in my hand and I pushed it open the rest of the way. The chain at my feet looked to have been broken, and by my untrained eye, it looked recent.

The door squealed as it opened into the dark building. The smell of blood assaulted me as a gush of fetid air whooshed outward. I choked on it and took a step back, fear thrumming through my body. I knew that smell, knew what it meant.

Someone was dead inside.

I didn't want to draw my weapons out on the street, but I didn't want to go in without them either. I pulled my Glock from its shoulder holster and kept it hidden in the flaps of my coat as I stepped inside.

The smell of blood was stronger in the dark room. It took my eyes a moment to adjust to the gloom. I stood just inside the door until I could see well enough to move in without being blinded.

The front room was large and empty of everything but a few scattered boxes that looked to have been abandoned. They were sagging, as if they'd gotten wet at some point, and most of them were torn, exposing scraps of cloth.

I scanned the room carefully before moving on to the first open doorway across the room. As I stepped through, the smell of blood just about knocked me from my feet.

The body was lying a few feet into the room. He'd started to shift but hadn't gone much more than a sprout of fur on his face and arms. He was lying on his back, hands crossed over his chest. If it wasn't for the blood, he might have been simply sleeping.

I stepped closer and got a good view of the gash on his throat. He'd been slit from ear to ear and had obviously bled out. Blood had pooled all around him and had run toward the far wall where the floor sloped gently downward.

Something glinted on his forehead from light seeping in from a window. I reached down, careful not to touch the wolf any more than I had to, and picked it up.

It was a golden cross.

I shot to my feet, dropping the cross to the ground where it clattered loudly in the silent building. I had my gun at the ready, turned left and right, searching for the killer, though I knew it was likely they were long gone.

There was only one group I knew who killed supes

like this. They'd nearly killed me before, and I so didn't want a repeat of the experience.

I held my breath and listened carefully. These people were Purebloods, so they weren't as quiet as a vamp or wolf might be. If I paid close enough attention, I was sure I'd hear them if they were still here.

The only sounds came from outside. A burst of laughter nearby caused me to jump and I nearly shot the wall. It took me a moment to realize I was facing the alleyway, and that someone had probably strolled down it, oblivious to the dead body only a few feet away.

I swallowed with some difficulty and looked for my payment. There was no briefcase or envelope anywhere beside the body, and I wasn't about to rifle through his pockets. The money wasn't important to me anyway. I was more worried about what Baset would think when she found out her man was dead. I was sure it was him, though I had no way of confirming it.

Without waiting a moment longer, I hurried back to Jeremy's car. The kids outside the gas station were gone, replaced by a big guy in a trucker's hat. He was smoking and staring across the road. His eyes fell on me as I all but ran out of the building. He gave me a wide smile, but it faded quickly when he saw my gun. He snuffed out his cigarette on the wall and hurried away.

My heart was pounding as I got into the car. Everyone seemed to be a likely suspect. Could those kids have done it? The trucker? I had no way of knowing.

I started the car up, certain I would feel the bite of the syringe at any moment. One little pinch and I'd be done for.

The night had suddenly become a whole hell of a lot more dangerous.

The Left Hand was here.

23

I almost couldn't see to drive. The Left Hand, a group of Purebloods who stalked the night injecting silver, blood thinners, and some other unknown ingredient into were and vamp veins, were in Columbus. I'd felt the bite of the syringe before. I'd seen the serrated knife the woman had planned on cutting my throat with. She might have been crazy, spouting off religious nonsense, but I couldn't deny the fact that she'd been dangerous.

And now there were more of them here.

I couldn't help but wonder if I was responsible. I'd killed the woman we'd captured, tore her throat out with my bare hands when she antagonized me at the worst possible moment. Had the others come looking for her? Have I condemned the city to their slaughter?

Of course I knew they were going to show up eventually. Davin, the vampire the Luna Cult was holding in their basement, had told me this day would come when I'd last talked to him. He'd lived it before, had barely escaped with his life. It wasn't because of me they were here. They'd planned it all along.

Still, I couldn't help but feel responsible. Maybe if I'd had better control of my rage, things would have turned out differently somehow.

I considered heading for the Luna Cult Den. Jonathan would need to know about this. He could warn his wolves to be more careful, to be on the lookout for anyone with a crazed look in their eye, wielding a syringe, stalking the streets in search of weres and vamps.

I knew it wouldn't be that obvious, but I couldn't get the idea out of my head. Maybe they all weren't as crazy as the woman who'd nearly killed me, but it was hard to picture anything but the mad grin she had on her face as she knelt above me with that knife in her hand.

I shuddered and nearly drove off the side of the road. My eyes were burning and I rubbed at them with the back of my hand. We were so fucking screwed if they were all as crazy as she'd been. You can't reason with insane.

As much as I wanted to flee back to the Den to tell Jonathan what I'd found, I kept on a straight path toward Delai. I didn't know how long the demon's Sight would last, nor did I want to face the Denmaster and explain to him what was coming.

I was afraid. There was no denying it. Never before had someone snuck up on me as easily as that Left Hand woman had. She'd made me weak, an easy kill. If it hadn't been for Adrian, I would have died that night.

I prayed the demon was wrong about Levi. I could use his help in dealing with The Left Hand. He'd know what to do, would know how to handle them. He could keep me safe, keep those I cared about alive.

Somehow, I knew it wouldn't be that easy.

My stomach started churning as I neared Delai. I fought hard to forget about The Left Hand and tried to focus on my other troubles.

Baset. What if she thought I killed her man? While I wasn't sure if he'd been sent there to pay me or kill me, that didn't mean she wouldn't seek retribution for his death. She'd gone after Jonathan to get at me before.

What else would she do to punish me? Whom else would she hurt?

The closer I got to Delai, the more torn I became. I really wanted to turn around and head back to the Den. I couldn't leave Jonathan in the dark like this.

Yet, I felt I'd passed the point of no return. I felt drawn to the little town, felt sick and elated at the same time. I didn't just want to go back, I *needed* to go back.

The sign came into view and I slowed to a stop. I stared at it, wondered if I was doing the right thing in coming there at all. What would I do if the Sight didn't show me anything out of place? Would I be able to leave again? Or would I stay, hide in Levi's basement until all my troubles passed?

My stomach clenched and I just about threw up on the steering wheel. My head swam and I had to close my eyes to keep from getting dizzy.

I had to go. There was no other way.

I eased down on the gas and turned onto the road. As soon as I passed the sign, the sickness passed and I felt something brush against me. For an instant, I felt calm, composed, but the feeling was fleeting. My tension increased tenfold, and it was all I could do to keep my jaw from clenching.

As much as I wanted to rush into town and demand to know the truth, I kept my pace slow, afraid of what I *would* find when I got there. If the demon's Sight wore off before I reached Levi, I would simply ask him to explain himself. I was sure with a little reason, he'd open up to me. He'd always been straightforward with me before.

I could trust Levi. He was a friend, someone who only wanted to do what was right. Why in the world had I ever believed a demon would tell me the truth?

I slammed on the brakes so hard I just about threw myself through the windshield. My head hurt, seemed to pulse in time with a beat I couldn't feel or hear. I closed my eyes, tried to repulse the strange feeling washing over me. The pulse fluttered and faded.

Why in the hell had I been thinking of Levi in such a positive light? I'd felt suddenly at home again, completely relaxed and content to stay there forever. It felt . . . wrong.

I opened my eyes again and immediately saw the lights.

I wasn't sure what they were or how to describe them. Bands of colored light crisscrossed the sky, floated there like ribbons made from a single strand of a rainbow. They seemed to come from everywhere, arched across the sky, all heading in the same direction.

How I'd never seen them before, I'd never know. I should have seen those lights the moment I turned onto the road, yet it wasn't until I'd pushed away the strange influence that they'd become visible.

I put the car in Park and got out. Looking up, I noticed a red band floated from where I stood toward the others, joining the greens, the whites, the oranges. I didn't know what the different colors meant and I didn't care. My mouth and throat went completely dry, and the rage I'd fought so hard to suppress for so long surged up from my gut to consume me.

Levi had done this. I didn't know how, didn't know why, but this was his fault.

I threw myself back into Jeremy's car and tore down the road. The snow here was light, just a dusting, which was completely opposite of what it was like a few miles back. There should have been drifts in the road, and yet there was hardly more than a token dusting of snow.

I hit the town in full-blown rage. Every single person I passed had a band of color coming from their heads. They moved around, seemingly oblivious to what was happening to them.

The entire town seemed to turn toward me as one. Every eye looked my way, appeared to look straight through me. I knew that because of the light, Levi would know I was here. It made sense in a strange way. He'd always known when I'd arrived in town before. This was probably why.

A fog rolled through my head and I slowed. Maybe those bands were there to help these people. They could be the way Levi connected with them, helped them overcome whatever dark secret they harbored. Just because it was strange didn't mean it was evil.

I shook my head and the fog slipped away. I could feel it trying to invade again. I put down mental defenses, refused to let whatever it was cloud my head again. It wanted me to love the town, wanted me to melt back in with the populace like I'd never left. I never had to fear for my life again if I'd only give up the fight.

If it wasn't for the bands of color, I might have relented. It would be so easy just to give in and let Levi take over. I'd done it before and I'm not sure I'd ever been happier.

But I knew it was a lie. These feelings weren't my own. I knew I'd never be able to fight off Levi's influence normally, but somehow, the Sight was shielding me, keeping me from succumbing to his will.

Even though I'd seen the colors, even though I knew the source, I really wanted to believe I was wrong, that the colors wouldn't lead me to Levi, wouldn't condemn him as something other than the big, friendly man I'd known before. I didn't want to have to hurt him, even if he was hurting these people. It wasn't fair.

Levi's house came into view and I slowed down. The house was almost glowing from the colored lights streaming in from the citizens of Delai. The bands entered the house from every direction, went right through the walls, through the roof. I wasn't sure if it was Levi himself or something else they were drawn to. I wasn't sure if it really mattered.

I parked across the street and just stared at the house.

I kept the engine running, not sure I wanted to get out. Just because I'd fought off the influence from a distance didn't mean I could do it when I was face-to-face with the man himself.

I growled and knuckled my temple. I needed to forget the fear. I could do this. Levi might try to keep me from leaving, but he couldn't truly stop me. I'd gotten out before without his consent and I could do it again. I had my weapons with me this time. Whatever he was, I was pretty sure a bullet would stop him. I just hoped it wouldn't come to that.

The door opened and Sienna's curious face poked out. She looked across the street at me, squinted in the dark. She must have glanced out the window and saw the car idling there. I had a feeling strange cars weren't common in town.

I thought about just driving away. I could leave, could get out before Levi knew for sure I was sitting outside his house. I wasn't naïve enough to think he didn't know I was in town, but he might not know exactly where I was.

I might have done it if I hadn't seen the faint glow trailing from Sienna's head.

I couldn't leave her here like that. She deserved so much more.

I opened the car door, leaving the engine running in case I needed to make a hasty retreat. I stepped out, letting my coat fall around me, hiding the weapons I didn't want her to see.

Sienna's face immediately lit up. She leaped from the doorway and ran through the yard, grinning ear to ear. She threw her arms around me and all but wept into my coat.

"You're back!" she sobbed, hugging me as hard as she could. "I'm so happy to see you. I was afraid you wouldn't come back."

I put my arms around the girl, hugging her back. Tears

slipped from my eyes and I didn't care. No matter what kind of monster Levi might be, I knew Sienna was something different. She was an innocent. He was hurting an innocent.

I tensed, any good feelings of seeing Sienna gone. Those damn glowing trails drew my eye and I knew I couldn't let it go. I had to put an end to this, and I had to do it now.

Sienna stepped back as if she'd felt me stiffen. She gave me a worried look. "What's wrong?"

I didn't know how to answer. The girl knew something was happening in town. Both her and her mother had always acted afraid. Did they know what Levi was? Did they know what he was doing to them? Or was it just a feeling they had after spending so much time with him?

"Is your dad inside?" I asked. I was ready to do battle.

Sienna immediately looked terrified, further confirming my suspicions. She glanced back at the house and then nodded. "He's upstairs with Mom," she said. She swallowed and clutched at my hand as if she was afraid I'd leave her behind again.

"I need to get you out of here," I said. "Get in the car and I'll take you somewhere safe."

"What? Why?" she said, sounding both frightened and anxious.

"Something is going on here and I don't think it's safe for either of us to stay."

Sienna's gaze traveled from my face to the hilt of my sword. When she hugged me, she'd pushed my coat back. I don't think she'd noticed the weapon until right then.

"Are you going to kill him?" She surprised me by sounding hopeful.

I looked into her eyes. She was terrified of something and I think I knew what that something was. I couldn't condemn her to this life any longer.

"Do you want me to?"

She glanced back at the house before meeting my gaze. She lowered her voice to a whisper. "You've got to help us," she said. "Please help my mom. He won't let her die."

"Sienna!" Levi's voice rang loudly in the night.

The girl immediately backed away, fleeing back to her yard like she was afraid he would kill her if she lingered. I watched her go, wishing I would have just packed her away and driven off before Levi realized she was gone.

I raised my eyes to face the man who was responsible for everything that was happening in the town.

But it wasn't a man standing there.

All the colors in the sky crashed down on his head, illuminating him so that he seemed to glow.

Hell, maybe he glowed naturally. It was hard to tell with as bright as he was.

Levi stepped down from the walk. He was dressed in white from head to foot. White wings fluttered out behind him. His hands were empty, but I knew they were more dangerous than any weapon I'd ever wielded.

His glare was intense. His face was unlined, unmarred by time. He looked hard, as if a sledgehammer would bounce right off him. Gone was the kind face, the friendly demeanor. I somehow doubted it had ever really been there. It had all been a lie, a glamour made to trick me into believing he was something normal when he so clearly wasn't.

I looked into his eyes, saw how deep and pale they were. It was as if he could stare straight into my soul and dissect me from the inside, could sort through my every thought, could see what I saw when I looked upon him.

No, Levi wasn't a man.

He was an angel.

24

I hid the surprise as best as I could. "Levi," I said. I kept my hands near my weapons, though I seriously doubted they would do any good against him.

He ushered Sienna back in the house, eyes always on me. The girl didn't want to go, but go she did. She scurried away, crying again. I thought I saw movement just inside the door as she entered the house. The door closed before I could catch a glimpse of who it was. I hoped Eilene was okay.

As soon as his adopted daughter was gone, Levi turned his full attention on to me. "You've returned." His voice sounded flat. I wasn't sure if he was happy to see me or if he was planning on gutting me right then and there.

"I had some things to take care of," I said, doing my best not to let my fear show. "I thought I'd stop by for a little visit, see how the family was getting along. . . . Is everyone okay?"

It was hard not to stare at his wings, at his altered features. Everything about him was different, yet I knew it was Levi. I wondered how I never saw through the glamour before.

Did he know I could see through it now? I couldn't tell by his voice or appearance at all.

Levi looked around as if making sure no one was around and listening. He checked the house windows twice before he started walking toward me. He seemed almost to float with every step, as if his feet never actually touched the ground.

"You had us all scared," he said. "Sienna cried for hours when you left." His voice was still flat, emotionless. I'm guessing he was trying to sound disappointed, but the Sight appeared to cut through anything he tried to do that wasn't natural. "I was worried about you."

He stopped a few feet away and I breathed a sigh of relief. Just standing in Levi's presence was awe-inspiring enough. I didn't want him any closer or else it might weigh me down. It was nearly as bad as standing around Beligral, though the demon always kept his human glamour up. How bad would he be if he were ever to drop it so I could see him for what he really was?

I wasn't sure I ever wanted to find out.

"I still have some things to do," I said. "I just wanted to see Sienna and make sure she was okay." I reached for the car door, wanting to get out of there. I could always get the girl later, once I had some backup.

"STOP!"

I cried out and dropped to my knees, hands going reflexively to my ears. Levi's voice tore right through me, set my teeth to vibrating. I was surprised when I pulled my hands away that they weren't covered in blood. It had felt like something had ruptured in my head.

I looked up to find Levi towering over me. His wings were spread, his face a mask of anger. I knew he could smite me down with a word if that was what he wanted. I couldn't stand against something like that.

"I can smell him on you," he said. "I can *feel* his mark where it writhes on your flesh."

The mark behind my ear flared up. I cried out in pain and the agony stopped almost immediately. I'm not sure if Levi had caused it to hurt or if Beligral had done it, and honestly, I didn't care.

"You have walked with the darkness and let it consume you. You are twice marked now. I couldn't save you even if I still wanted to."

I forced my way to my feet despite the fact my legs were shaky. I would not take this on my knees. If Levi was going to kill me, he was going to have to fight for that right like everyone else. I had no illusions that I could kill the angel, but I sure as hell would try.

"Why?" I asked. "Why are you doing this to these people? This isn't a real place, is it?" I made a sweeping gesture with my arms. "This town isn't really here."

I don't know how I knew, but I was positive Delai wasn't what it appeared to be. Beligral's Sight didn't show me, though it might have aided in my understanding.

Levi smiled. It was as cruel of an expression as anything I'd ever seen.

"I help people here," he said. "Those that wish for help, that truly wish to be saved, receive it. Those that do not . . ." He shrugged. "They leave."

"I seriously doubt that."

His expression turned neutral. "You know nothing about me or what I do. I was so close to curing you, to separating you from your demonic blood. And now . . . now you are nothing to me." He spat. "You cannot be saved."

"You weren't helping me." I took a step toward him despite the fact I knew he could crush me. He was taller now, so I had to look up to stare into his eyes. "You were turning me into one of your zombies. The people here aren't people anymore. They're just empty shells. I've known it all along. It just took me a while to realize it."

Levi met my stare for a few seconds before looking away, indifferent. "They are no longer the creatures they once were," he said. His eyes met mine again, and the intensity of his glare forced me back a step. "I've cured them of their taint. I am fixing what has been unleashed here one demon at a time. You cannot fault me for that."

I laughed. "Then why hide what you are if you are so confident you are doing the right thing?"

Levi's eyes widened for a heartbeat before he resumed his neutral stare. He looked deep into my eyes, seemed to be looking for something. Apparently, he found it.

"I see," he said with a sigh. "You accept the gifts of a demon over what I have to offer. I knew you were damned. I didn't realize how much of a hold it had on you until now."

"You are no better than he is," I said. "Don't pretend you are."

Levi waved a hand dismissively and started to walk away. "Leave," he said. "You are no longer wanted here."

"Not without Sienna," I said, drawing my sword. I doubted I could take him, but I sure as hell was going to give it all I had. I owed it to the girl to at least try to save her.

All it took was a wave of his hand and I was slammed up against Jeremy's car. The air was pressed from my lungs, expelled in a huff. It felt like a vise was slowly squeezing the very life out of me. My sword fell from my hand and clattered to the ground. I dangled there, my feet inches from the pavement, trapped by a force I couldn't see.

Levi turned to face me, anger blazing in his eyes. It was like an actual fire, burning deep within his sockets.

He wasn't a beautiful vision, the kind of thing read about in books. He wasn't the angel spoken of by those in prayer. He was a destructive force, a demon in his own right. He cared nothing for me or the other Purebloods or supes he might harm. He only wanted to get his way and would stop at nothing to get it, even if it meant killing everyone in the process.

"Your blood sickens me," he said. "It taints the air I breathe. I only wanted to help you. I thought you wanted it, thought you were ready. I let you into my home, my realm, in the hopes I could pull you away from the darkness that consumes you."

He grunted and shook his head. "Go back to your home, go back to the monsters to kill and maim, because that is all you know how to do."

The invisible vise squeezed harder. Blood dripped from my nose. I could taste more of it in my mouth. My eyes felt just about ready to pop from my head.

"But things like you never truly go away, do they?" He took a step toward me. One of my ribs groaned in protest. "You'll keep trying to come back. You'll think you're doing the right thing when all you'll really be doing is ruining the good work I've done here. I cannot let you destroy what I've worked so hard to accomplish."

Another step and the rib didn't just groan this time. It broke with an agonizing snap.

"Dad!" Sienna called out from the house. The door was standing wide open. I could just make her out through the haze in my head.

The vise was suddenly gone and I fell to the ground. I sucked in a painful breath and starting coughing. My lips were flecked with blood. My eyes burned so badly, I was afraid I was bleeding from them as well.

"What is it, sweetie?" Levi said. I glanced up, thinking I'd see the big, hairy man again, but he still looked like an angel to me. Even his voice sounded flat, emotionless, though I knew that's not what Sienna heard.

"Don't hurt her," she said. "Please, let her go home."

Levi stopped in front of his adopted daughter, putting himself between her and me. "Why would I hurt her?" he said. He put a hand on her shoulder and she flinched as if she was afraid he might hit her.

I wondered what kind of monster he thought she was.

As far as I could tell, she was just a Pureblooded girl, trapped in this place like so many others. If Levi thought he was curing her, then what was he curing her from?

Not that it mattered, really. I knew I'd have to save her somehow. I just wasn't sure how I'd ever manage it.

Movement by the door caught my eye. Eilene stood there, bathrobe pulled tight against her shoulders. She gave me a sad, resigned look that said more than words that she wished I'd never returned. I wanted to call out to her, but as soon as she saw me looking, she turned and walked back into the house.

Sienna said something I couldn't hear past the ringing in my head. She looked so scared, I wanted to get up and just shoot the bastard in the back of the head. I doubted my bullets would do a damn bit of good, but it sure as hell would feel good, giving me that one last glint of enjoyment before he squashed me like a bug.

"Go back inside," Levi said. "We're just talking. Kat will be leaving shortly."

Sienna glanced past him at me. It was obvious we hadn't just been talking, but she nodded anyway. I'd do anything in the world to save her and I hoped she knew that. I might be no match for her adopted father, but somehow, I'd do it.

"I'll come back for you," I mouthed, hoping she would be able to read my lips.

She seemed to understand. She gave me a curt nod before running back to the house.

Levi stared after her before giving a heavy sigh. He turned back to me and stalked toward where I lay. I fully expected the pressure to return, but it didn't. He just knelt beside me and shook his head. He knew I couldn't hurt him. He had nothing to be afraid of.

"You are lucky," he said. "Against my better judgment,

I will let you live." He reached out and I cringed. It only made him laugh. "Let me help you up."

"I can do it myself." I spit a glob of blood at his feet.

Levi stared at me, and for a moment, he looked genuinely sad before shrugging and standing. "Suit yourself."

I used the car to help me work my way back to my feet. There was a huge dent in the driver's side door. My sword was lying a few feet away. I walked over to it. It hurt like hell to bend over to pick it up.

"I want you to get in your car and drive," Levi said. "I want you to go straight down the road and out of Delai and never return. I will have eyes on you. If you so much as hesitate, I'll know and I will come for you."

I so wanted to bury my blade right between his eyes, but instead I sheathed the sword and staggered over to the car door.

"If you are thinking of trying to take my girl from me, you can stop right now. She is mine. If you insist on hounding me, I will make sure there is nothing left for you to save."

My teeth ached from clenching my jaw to keep from saying something stupid. He was threatening a girl he was supposed to care for and it pissed me off to no end. What kind of creature was he?

"I'll leave," I said, putting as much venom in my voice as I could. "But I *will* be back. Remember that. Someday, when you think you are safe, I'll be there."

I was hoping for disdain, but instead I got a smile. "No, you won't."

And with that, Levi turned and walked back to the house.

I watched him go, wanting to fight him with every fiber of my being. I didn't care that he was an angel. I didn't care that I'd probably die in the process. I just wanted to shoot him, to stab him, to make him regret ever threatening Sienna in that way.

But I didn't do anything. I knew I was being weak, but I was also being smart. I needed more than my demon-forged weapons, my demon-tainted blood.

What I needed was the demon himself.

I squeezed my eyes shut, hating myself. Leave it to me to side with a demon over an angel. If Sienna hadn't been involved, who knew what I would have done.

I fumbled with the car door, my fingers not quite working right. The metal handle was warped, making it that much harder to grip. I managed to get the door open, though it popped and groaned with every inch. I slid into the driver's seat and slammed the door closed.

Or at least I tried to. The door popped right back open and I felt like screaming. I reached out and yanked it closed with all my might; this time it stuck.

The station wagon was still running, so all I had to do was put it in gear and turn around. I could see a face in the upstairs window, watching me. I hoped it was Sienna and I silently promised her I wouldn't let her suffer any longer than I had to.

I drove away from the house, vowing to return. No matter what Levi thought he could do to me, I could do so much worse. He might be an angel, but I had a demon on my side.

My stomach flipped. What was I becoming? I might as well give in to my monster now and forget any pretenses of trying to do what was right.

All eyes watched my passing as I made my way through town. I refused to look at them, knowing Levi would know and would take pleasure in it. It felt so much like running away. I felt sick to my stomach, wanted to just crawl into a hole and die.

Right then, I needed someone to tell me everything

would be all right, that they'd do whatever it took to help me. I couldn't do this alone anymore.

The last stretch of the road was empty, but I didn't slow down. I drove right past the sign, hoping I was doing the right thing in leaving without Sienna. I glanced back once, but there was nothing more to see.

25

The Luna Cult parking garage felt colder than usual as I parked Jeremy's beat-up car in one of the spaces. I really just wanted to go home, to curl up into a little ball and let the pain and misery pass. But with what had just happened with Levi, as well as the discovery of the body that meant The Left Hand was in town, I needed to see Jonathan.

My ribs hurt horribly and I couldn't stop shivering as I made my way through the snow toward the old library. I pulled my coat as tight as I could without making my ribs ache any more than they already were and hunched my shoulders against the bitterly cold wind.

I felt horribly alone out there, walking in the dark. I could see lights from the part of the campus that still functioned, but they were distant, barely worth noting. Debris poked out of the snow where someone lost a shoe or a branch had fallen. There were no howls this night, no animals crying out. Everyone and everything was safely tucked away in their homes.

Or so it seemed to me at the time.

I was so wrapped up in my own misery, I was nearly to the front steps before I noticed the lights. The entire Den was lit up. I stared at it in awe, wondering why the glamour had dropped. Had something happened to Jonathan while I was gone?

My heart rate picked up, but before I could do something stupid like go charging in screaming his name, I realized it must still be the Sight working. It was allowing me to see through this glamour just as it had helped with Levi's.

I stepped back so I could get a better view of the Den without Jonathan's magic concealing it. It looked far better with the lights on, though they hadn't done much to the outside. Why bother when no one would ever see what truly lay beneath the glamour. Faded graffiti marred much of the lower portion of the wall. A few bricks were busted, but otherwise the place didn't look half bad.

I shook my head as I trudged up the stairs. How powerful was Jonathan, really? If he could conceal all those lights, keep the glamour up indefinitely, did that make him stronger than he tried to appear? Or were glamours really that easy to maintain? Perhaps it was time I asked him.

I had a fleeting thought of asking Jonathan's help with extracting Sienna and Eilene, but squashed it immediately. I had barely been able to shrug off Levi's influence, and even then, I had help from the demon's magic, so what would happen if I took the wolves there? Would Levi gain control of them somehow? I really didn't want to find out.

I paused just outside the doors to the Den and peered in through the glass. Pablo and a few other Cultists were sitting near the stairwell, a card table set up between them. They were all wearing their robes and were engrossed in their game, so they hadn't seen me yet.

No one was coming down the stairs to let me in either. I'd seen guards haul a man away who'd wandered onto their property before, knew they had cameras hidden all around the green, yet no one even bothered to come out to show me in.

And for some reason, that pissed me off.

I pushed open the door and stepped through. It was strange entering the Den and not being blinded by the sudden light. It was actually quite refreshing, and I hoped the demon's Sight would last more than a few days. It could really come in handy.

"You," Pablo said, rising. His crescent moon tattoo seemed to pulse in the middle of his forehead as he glared at me. The big Mexican had never liked me, and I was pretty sure he never would.

"Yep, me." I looked around casually just to irritate him. "Where's Jonathan?" While I might be a wreck inside and my ribs hurt like hell, I didn't want to show weakness in front of Pablo or the other Cultists. I didn't know who might be able to take advantage of it some way. Hell, if someone was reporting to Adrian, I definitely didn't want them to tell him I'd nearly been crushed.

Pablo continued to glare at me, refusing to tell me a thing. Thankfully, one of the female Cultists behind him spoke up.

"He's upstairs in his rooms," she said, her bald head gleaming in the light. "We can send someone for him if you want."

"No," I said. "I know the way."

Pablo opened his mouth to protest, but I pushed past him and climbed the stairs before he could utter a word. I think he might have fought me before, but after being scolded by his Denmaster a few times about harassing me, he seemed to have finally gotten the message. I was a part of this Den whether he liked it or not.

I could feel his hateful eyes on my back as I headed upstairs. I grinned at him and gave a little wave as I reached the top, solely for the purpose of agitating him more.

As soon as I was out of sight, I leaned against the wall and took a few deep breaths. Good God, I hurt. Levi had nearly crushed me with a thought. I was just glad he'd decided to make me suffer rather than squishing me all at once. I might hurt, but at least I was alive.

Breathing was painful and it took me a few minutes to catch my breath. Once I was sure I could move without wincing, I straightened my shoulders and walked the last few yards to the gilded doors that led to Jonathan's sitting room. While I knew there were other rooms upstairs, I was sure he would be there.

I considered knocking, but decided to hell with it and opened the door myself. There were no guards posted outside tonight, which made me feel a little better. Having wolves standing on either side of the door meant things weren't good at the Den. It appeared they no longer feared that Baset would come in and abduct anyone for a while.

Jonathan was seated on the couch and started to rise as the door opened. He eased back down when he saw me and set a glass of wine on the table in front of him. He marked his place in a book and set it aside.

"I didn't expect to see you tonight," he said.

It took me a moment to formulate an answer to that. I stared at him, at the slope of his head, at the scarred flesh where I'd taken part of his skull back before I knew who he was. It was unsettling to see him without his glamour, though I was pretty sure it was still up.

"We need to talk," I said once I could speak. I would have liked to remain standing, but I hurt too damn much. Just the act of supporting my body's weight was wearing me out. I strode across the room, doing my best to keep the pain off my face. I sat down in a chair across from Jonathan, probably a bit slower than I should have.

"You're hurt." He frowned and nodded to a Cultist who was standing by the wet bar. The Cultist gave his Denmaster a quick nod and hurried out of the room.

"It'll pass," I said.

Jonathan's frown deepened. "What happened?"

I winced as I tried to relax. Breathing was harder while

I was sitting. I prodded my rib where it was broken. It hurt like a bitch, but I was pretty sure it would heal okay. I hoped it was merely cracked rather than a full-on fracture. The latter would take too long to heal.

I opened my mouth to tell him about The Left Hand, but all that came out was a sob.

I didn't know where it had come from. I'd been certain I'd be able to do this; that I'd just walk in, tell him how it was, and then ease my painful way back to Jeremy's car where I'd drive home and collapse in bed for a few days.

But for whatever reason, I just broke. Jonathan was up and off the couch in an instant. He knelt in front of me, put a hand on my arm, and forced me to look him in the eye. He studied me, his face full of concern.

"Are you okay?" he asked.

I started to nod but shook my head instead.

"Tell me what happened."

I didn't know where to start. The Left Hand was bad enough, but now with Levi and Delai thrown on top of it all, I wasn't sure what was important anymore. I hated myself for not being able to save Sienna when I had the chance. The girl didn't deserve to suffer, and I'd left her there to do just that.

Of course, I wasn't sure how much she was really suffering. She was unhappy, sure, but I don't think Levi was hurting her. Then again, mental abuse is still abuse. She was terrified of the man. I couldn't let it keep happening.

I opened my mouth a few times but gave up trying to say anything. What could I say? Telling him about Delai was out. He already knew about Baset, though he knew nothing of Strinowski. There was The Left Hand, and I'd also made a scene in Polaris, so there was Count Mephisto to consider.

"Start from the beginning," Jonathan urged. His hand was running up and down my arm. It sent tingles throughout my body and helped distract me from my misery.

"I found a body," I said, deciding The Left Hand was the most immediate threat to him. The rest was my problem.

"What kind of body?"

I had to laugh at that, though there was no humor in it. My ribs protested and I stopped abruptly.

"The dead kind," I said.

Jonathan gave me a wan smile, though the concern never left his eyes.

I took too deep a breath and nearly screamed. The pain shot through me so fast and hard, I just about blacked out. I was thankful it would be better by morning. Being a vampire did have its perks sometimes, even if I often hated it. Still, if I'd been a normal Pureblood, I wouldn't have gotten myself in this mess to begin with.

"It was a werewolf," I said. "He was laid out, placed as if for someone to find."

"Okay?" Jonathan's brow furrowed.

"His throat was slit and he bled out." I stared at him meaningfully.

It took him a moment, but realization dawned. "Completely drained?"

I nodded.

His hand stopped moving on my arm. I noticed his other hand was resting on my knee. I never even realized he'd put it there until that very moment. I shifted in my seat so it fell away.

"There was a cross placed on his forehead. He was left lying in his own blood. It had to have been The Left Hand."

Jonathan stood and started pacing. "Are you sure? It could have been someone else."

"As sure as I can be," I said. "You saw how they work. There was no sign of a struggle. Whoever did it had to have snuck up on the wolf, injected him, and then slit his throat. He'd managed to start his shift, so I'm guessing he must have heard something just before his attacker struck."

Jonathan was nodding, a distracted look on his face.

"And this wasn't a small guy either. He would have fought a whole hell of a lot harder if he'd been able. It had to have been them."

He didn't say anything.

"We should talk to Davin," I said. I made my slow way to my feet, wincing with every inch. "He might know something else about them that might prove useful."

Jonathan froze. He was looking away from me so I couldn't read his expression.

"What?" I asked.

"We can't ask him."

I frowned. "Why not?"

Jonathan sighed and turned to face me. I didn't like the look on his face. "Because he's not here anymore."

"Okay," I said, nonplussed. "Then where is he?"

Jonathan's frown joined my own. He ran a hand through his hair, on the side that actually had hair. "I don't know."

"You don't know?" My voice rose as a flash of anger shot through me. The pain in my ribs flared up, but I didn't care. "How can you not know? You had him locked up in your fucking basement."

"We did," Jonathan said, heat in his voice. "But we honored the deal you struck. We took him out to see the moon as promised."

My anger bled away at that. I'd all but forced Jonathan to agree to it, hadn't really given him a choice. "And he escaped?"

"With help." Jonathan sighed. "I can't be sure, but I have a feeling Adrian had something to do with it."

Adrian.

I turned and kicked the chair I'd been sitting in. It

jumped a little and my ribs hurt even worse, but it kept me from shooting someone.

"How in the hell could he have managed that?"

"I don't know," he said. "I was told it happened fast."

"Wait," I said, turning an angry glare on him. "You weren't there?"

"I had more important things to worry about at the time," he snapped. "Nathan and a few Cultists took him outside so he could see the moon. They were jumped." He held up a hand as I was about to say something else. "No one was hurt. They were restrained by men with hoods, most likely other werewolves due to their strength, though it could have been vampires as well. We just don't know for sure."

I shook my head. "How?"

"How what?" Jonathan said. "How did they manage it? By superior numbers and stealth. How did they know when we would be taking him out?" He shrugged. "That is the question I can't answer."

I was so pissed I didn't know what to say. I never liked the idea of keeping a vamp locked up in the basement, but I didn't want him running free either. He knew my face, knew who I was. It was just another threat running loose I'd have to eventually deal with.

"Fuck," I finally managed. At least this time I refrained from kicking anything.

"Exactly," Jonathan said.

"What are we going to do?"

He spread his hands. "We go on as we normally would. We can't do anything about Davin's loss now. If Adrian had a hand in it, then so be it. If it was a vampire House, then I will need to learn how they knew we had him and when we were taking him out."

I chewed on my lip, uncertain. I'd been counting on

Davin for information on The Left Hand. They were going to be a problem sooner rather than later, I was sure.

"We know this group is made up of Purebloods," Jonathan went on. "They hunt vampires and werewolves. Our goal will still be to find them and stop them before they kill someone dear to us."

"But how? We don't know who they are, where they are hiding. They're supposed to be good at this stuff, remember?"

"We wait until they make a mistake."

If they ever did.

I shook my head and leaned against the wall. Pain and exhaustion sapped the anger out of me.

"There is little we can do now," Jonathan said. "I'll make sure to alert the Cult about them. We'll watch for any indication as to who or where they are. We can do little else."

"I know," I said. I raised my hands to my head. I felt dirty from head to foot and I had blood on me. "I need to go home and clean up," I said. "I'll figure out what to do later." I started for the door.

"You can shower here," Jonathan said.

I stopped walking. Good sense told me I should keep going, that I should just walk right out the door and go home and shower in my own room. There was nothing else I could do at the Den. I couldn't bring up Delai. I couldn't do anything about The Left Hand. Or Baset. Or Mephisto.

But I didn't want to leave. If I went home, I'd have to face reality. I'd have to go down, talk to Beligral, and tell him he was right. I didn't want to admit it, but the goddamn demon had been telling the truth. I could almost see his satisfied grin. The mark was just about throbbing with it.

I turned around and looked at Jonathan. He stood across the room, hands held respectfully behind his back.

He looked good, even with his marred features. All I wanted to do was to sit and have him hold me so I'd stop hurting so much.

"Okay," I said at a whisper.

Jonathan crossed the room, took me by the hand, and led me into his bedroom, past the bed, and into his private bathroom.

Dear God, what was I getting myself into?

26

My coat came off first, falling to the bathroom floor in a heap. Jonathan went to a closet for a washcloth and wet it down for me. He started dabbing at my face, though I wasn't actually cut. The dried blood had come from my mouth and a little from my nose, but he was careful anyway.

"Is it bad?" he asked, indicating my ribs where I kept my arm pressed tight.

I shook my head.

The washcloth felt almost gritty against my skin, like sandpaper rubbed a little fine. The water was warm, soothing, and the soap he used smelled of spring.

I closed my eyes and let him take care of me. It felt good not to have to do it myself. I was so tired of having to do everything on my own. Just sitting back and letting someone else do all the work was like bliss, something I should have done a long time ago.

Jonathan put the washcloth down and gently touched my face. "At least you weren't cut here." His voice was heavy, deep. His eyes traveled to my ribs. "Can I see it?"

I nodded again. The world felt far away, like I wasn't even in my body anymore. I was vaguely aware of his hands as he worked at my shoulder holster and removed it. Then his hands slid down to the bottom of my shirt. He started to lift, but my arms were in the way. I tried to lift them to help.

And that's when the pain ripped through the daze. I hissed in a sharp breath and jerked away from him.

"I'll get it," I said through gritted teeth. I wasn't sure how I was going to manage it myself without causing more pain, but I wasn't going to let him baby me forever.

I turned my back on him. Some semblance of sense was returning and I realized I couldn't be stupid. Just because he was being kind to me didn't mean I needed to let my guard down. The last time I ended up topless in the Den, things came up missing.

"My gun," I said, thinking back to that night. I turned around with my shirt still firmly covering by breasts. "I left a gun here."

Jonathan's brow furrowed. "When?"

"Months ago. Do you still have it?"

Any moment that might have been building died. Jonathan frowned, looking both hurt and confused.

"No," he said. "I didn't know you left one here. Where was it?"

"I think I left it beside your bed." A flush crept up my neck when I thought of the bed and how close we had come to doing something that day. It might not have been *that* close for anyone else, but for me, it was a huge leap.

"I'll look for it while you shower," Jonathan said. Yep, he definitely sounded hurt. "Maybe it got kicked under the bed." He walked out of the bathroom, back stiff. He closed the door softly behind him without looking back.

I almost called for him to come back. It was lonely in the bathroom by myself. I'd spent so many lonely days and nights in my own room, I didn't want to spend another elsewhere. It would be so easy just to call for him, to make sure I never spent another day alone . . .

Biting my lip, I peeled off my shirt. My skin was

bruised where my rib had cracked, but it was already fading. By next evening, the bone would be healed enough for me to go about my night like always, and the bruise would be completely gone.

I started to unbuckle my belt but paused to lock the bathroom door.

Okay, so part of me wanted Jonathan's company, wanted him to wrap his arms around me and tell me he'd take care of everything, but the more sensible part of me knew that it would never work. He was a werewolf. I was a vampire. There was no way to mix those two things and come out with something good. It was a disaster waiting to happen.

I stripped down and quickly stepped into the shower. I didn't want to be naked in the Den for very long. Who knew who might walk in, who might have a key. It would be just my luck to step out of the shower to have Pablo standing there, eyeing me up and down. Just because he hated me didn't mean he wouldn't ogle me if given the chance.

I jacked the heat up as high as I could stand it to burn away any desires I might have. I couldn't believe I'd even put myself in this situation at all. I should have been smarter, should have rejected his invitation.

Jonathan's showerhead shot water at me like it was coming out of a gun. It pounded my face, stung where it met flesh. I whimpered in pain as it battered my ribs, yet it also felt good in a way. I needed the pain to prove I was alive.

By the time I was done, my skin was pink where it wasn't black and purple. I looked down at my clothes and hated the idea of putting them back on. I always preferred fresh clothing after a shower. There was no way I was going to wear anything Jonathan offered me, however, so I reluctantly got dressed.

The bedroom was empty when I emerged. I hesitated

before crossing the room into the sitting room. I expected Jonathan to be waiting for me there, but he wasn't anywhere in sight.

Someone else was.

"Nathan," I said, feeling all sorts of self-conscious. There was no way to hide the fact that I'd just taken a shower in Jonathan's bathroom. My hair was still wet and I was sure I smelled of Jonathan's soap. Who knew what Nathan thought we'd been doing before my shower.

The big wolf just stood there, staring at me. I couldn't read his face, couldn't tell if he was angry or confused. He could have been the happiest guy on the planet and I wouldn't have been able to tell just by looking at him.

Since he was obviously not going to say anything and was solely interested in a staring contest, I stared right back, daring him to say something accusatory.

The seconds stretched by and I started to get an itch on the back of my neck. It felt like he was trying to lure me into some sort of trap, that someone would sneak up behind me while Nathan and I stared at each other. It was a struggle not to glance behind me to check.

"You rem—" Nathan cut off and shook his head angrily. His hair had started to grow out from the buzz cut he'd sported before. It was still short, but now he could actually do something with it.

I had to admit, it did a lot to improve his severe looks. He might even be able to pull off handsome if he'd stop being such a prick.

"Where's Jonathan?" I asked, just wanting to be out of there. I wasn't going to stand there staring at him forever.

"He's looking for someone," Nathan said. I waited for him to add something, a name, a reason why, when he'd return, but all I got was that stare of his.

"Okay," I said. "Well, then, tell him thanks for the shower and I'll let him know how things turn out."

I took a step toward the gilded doors that would lead

me into the Den proper and out of here. Nathan was standing in the way and didn't show the slightest inclination that he was going to move.

"I want to leave," I said, putting a warning in my voice.

Nathan blinked slowly. He still didn't move.

"Is there something you wanted? I'm not going to screw around with you all night. I have things to do." I really just wanted to shoot him and step over him. It would serve him right, though I knew Jonathan wouldn't be happy with me if I shot his second in command.

"I believe Jonathan has intentions for you to stay for the day," Nathan said. "Unless you would like to burn on the way home, that is. If the sun does not bother you, feel free to go."

The sitting room had a few windows, but they were heavily draped. I felt weak like I did when the sun was up, though that could be from my confrontation with Levi as well. The only way to know for sure was to look.

"It's still dark," Nathan said as I started for the windows. "But it won't be for long. You'd never make it home."

"I'll be in a car."

Nathan snorted. "With windows all around you."

I scowled. "I'm not staying here."

Nathan stepped aside. "Then go. I won't stop you."

I wanted to spit something back at him, but I didn't have anything to say. It had been a long night and it could easily be near morning. I really didn't want to risk getting caught out under the sun, even for a few seconds.

I walked the rest of the way to the window and parted the drapes anyway. The sky was still dark, but the horizon was lightening. Nathan was right; I'd never make it home.

"Damn it," I said, turning back to the big wolf. "I guess I'm staying."

"It'll make him happy."

Something in his voice irked me and I stalked toward

him. "Do you have a problem with me staying here?" I was itching for a fight and Nathan seemed to be the perfect target for my ire. He might be strong, but he couldn't crush my ribs with a thought. I could handle strong.

"I have a problem with the way you are leading the Denmaster along."

I froze in midstride. "What?"

Nathan sneered at me. "He believes it will only take time and you will soften toward him. I don't think so. I believe you are using him to get what you want. Once you've finished with him, you'll discard him, if you don't kill him first."

"Who the fuck are you to judge me?" I said, resuming my angry stride toward him. "I'm only here because . . ." I trailed off, my step slowing. Why the hell *was* I still there?

I glowered at Nathan as if it was all his fault. I might have come to warn Jonathan about The Left Hand, yet something else had kept me here. I could have turned around and walked right out after I'd said my piece. I could already be home, relaxing in my room, waiting for my ribs to heal.

And yet, I'd stayed.

Why?

There were only a few feet remaining between us. Nathan covered it in one large stride. He was mere inches from me. He was much taller, much broader than I was. I was forced to look up to see his face.

And what I saw there confused the hell out of me.

I'd expected him to still be angry. After his accusations, he could easily have come at me angrily, spat threats into my face. The Nathan I knew wasn't afraid of confrontation, had no problem expressing himself.

But that's not what I saw. Sure, his mouth was pulled down in what I took to be a grimace and he was standing so close I could smell him. He smelled of cinnamon and something heavier, sweat maybe.

It was his eyes that threw me completely off. There was no anger in them. He looked confused and lost. There was a strange kindness behind his gaze, something I'd never seen from him before.

I took a step back, unsure what to think. I struggled to come up with something to say, but what was I supposed to say to that look? I think I'd much rather have him scowling at me than looking at me like he was.

Without saying a word, Nathan lifted his hand and gently touched my cheek. His thumb traced my cheekbone before I could jerk back.

Sudden pain filled his eyes, and he turned and stormed out of the room, leaving me completely dumbfounded.

What in the hell just happened?

Before I could consider the implications of Nathan's strange behavior, Jonathan returned. He had my gun in his hand.

"It was picked up and taken to where I keep the few wea—" Jonathan slowed and stopped just inside the door. A concerned look crossed his face and he looked around the room as if he expected someone or something to be there. "What happened?"

I turned my dazed stare to him. I licked my lips, tried to shake the confusion out of my head. "Nothing," I said. "Just feeling kind of woozy is all."

I reached out and took the gun, checking to make sure it was still loaded before slipping it into my coat.

"The sun will be up shortly," Jonathan said, still looking at me warily. "You can take my room. It is proofed against the sun. You will be safe there."

I wondered why his bedroom would be sunlight proof. A werewolf didn't need to worry about it like a vampire.

Was I the first he'd ever invited over? Or had there been others?

"Thanks," I said, pushing the thought away. I really didn't want to know.

"There's a set of women's clothing in a chest by the wall. You can find something to sleep in there if you want. There are also clothes you can wear home if you would like to change."

"I don't sleep," I said. And add the whole keeping women's clothes thing to my list of things I didn't want to know about.

Jonathan smiled in what I took as a slightly annoyed way. "Or at least there is something to wear so you are more comfortable as you wait for the night. Feel free to come out here as well. The sun cannot reach you as long as you keep the drapes and blinds closed. There are books there." He indicated a small line of bookshelves in the back of the room. "You can read any you like."

I nodded. I felt sick to my stomach and I wasn't sure why. Was it the thought of staying at the Den? Was it how Nathan had treated me? I wasn't sure.

"I'll leave you, then," he said. His eyes lingered on mine as if he hoped I would ask him to stay.

I kept my lips firmly sealed. I knew if I opened them, I'd say something I'd regret later.

Jonathan nodded once before leaving. I let out a pent-up breath, wincing as my ribs groaned.

I watched the closed door a moment longer, half wishing Jonathan would come back in, half hoping I'd somehow be transported all the way home so I wouldn't have to go through this any longer. When it was clear neither was going to happen, I turned around and went into Jonathan's bedroom to wait out the long day ahead.

27

I somehow made it through the day without going crazy. I kept my dirty clothes on, steadfastly refusing to look in the chest by the wall, knowing if I did, I'd start asking questions. I sat in a chair in the bedroom, more or less sulking, when I wasn't pacing.

More than once, I considered going out and grabbing a book from the sitting room, but I had a strange fear that if I did, someone would come in and catch me in the act. It was totally irrational, I know. I just couldn't get the idea out of my head that I was somewhere I shouldn't be.

So I stayed, bored out of my mind.

At least no one bothered me all day. I knew there were probably guards stationed outside the sitting room doors, which suited me fine. They would keep anyone away, though it did irk me a little that they might be there for *my* protection . . . if they were even there at all.

The hours sludged by and the moment I felt it was evening, I was up and heading for the door. I risked a peek out the window to make sure and much to my satisfaction, I saw twilight had already come and gone.

A startled Cultist gasped at me as I threw open the sitting room doors. He staggered back, looking as though he thought I might hurt him. He was just a kid, head freshly shorn. I didn't recognize him at all.

I barely paid him any mind as I headed for the stairs. The guy had probably been my guard for the last few hours. Seeing how small and frightened he was, it made me feel a little better. I was pretty sure Jonathan had only put him there just to make sure no one bothered me.

I hurried down the stairs and made for the front door as quickly as I could. I didn't want to see Jonathan or Nathan. I just wanted to get home without having to talk about anything that had gone on recently.

Neither wolf was in sight and I nearly laughed. Pablo peered at me from a side room. He wasn't wearing his robe, which was kind of odd. Instead, he had on a white T-shirt, pajama bottoms, and bunny slippers.

I almost stopped to stare at him. Never in a million years would I have thought Pablo of all people would wear something like that, but really, I'd never taken the time to get to know the man. Just because he was an ass to me didn't mean he was that way all the time.

I kept walking and he let me pass without a word. I glanced back toward the stairs to see if he was still watching me as I opened the front door, but he was already gone.

I stepped out into the night with a sigh. It felt like I was running away again. Jonathan would probably be hurt when he found out I'd bolted. Then again, he seemed to understand me relatively well and would know I didn't like feeling as though someone was taking care of me. Hell, he probably expected me to be gone before he roused for the night anyway.

I kept my shoulders hunched as I walked toward the parking garage. It was bitingly cold, and the slightest breeze stung my cheeks. Winter was in full throttle. And winters here could be pretty rough.

My extra gun sat heavily in my coat pocket and I kept

fingering it like a long-lost lover. It was a wonder I didn't accidentally pull the trigger and shoot myself in the leg. I was surprised the bullets were still there, that someone hadn't taken the gun and hidden it. My best guess is that whoever found it had no idea what it was loaded with and just put it away with the rest of Jonathan's weapons.

It did make me wonder what kind of weapons the Denmaster kept stored away. I'd never seen him carry anything, and from what I understood, no one in the Cult was supposed to have weapons. When we went into a fight, the Cult weres went in with only claws and teeth. Did he keep the stash for emergency situations only? Or were they simply the weapons he confiscated from his Cultists?

I didn't know, though it was an intriguing question. I might have to ask him sometime. Those weapons might be useful someday.

The Luna Cult garage was empty as I entered. I went straight down toward where I'd parked, not even pausing to look for the cameras. If Jonathan didn't know I was gone yet, he sure as hell did now.

As I neared where I'd parked Jeremy's car, I grew concerned. The old beat-up piece of shit was gone. In its place was a black car, new by the look of it. I approached warily, wondering if Jeremy had someone pick him up and bring him to his car, or if it was such an eyesore Jonathan finally had it towed away.

A piece of paper had been slipped under the windshield wiper and I pulled it free. I looked around, wondering if whoever had put it there was watching me. I wasn't even sure the note was for me or if it was left for someone else. I could always put it back again if it wasn't mine.

There was a note written on the page in an elegant hand.

Kat,

The car is for Jeremy. Tell him his assistance has been much appreciated.

Jonathan

I tucked the note in my pocket with a grunt of admiration. Jonathan did seem to care about those under him, whether they were wolves or not. If you had asked me a year or so ago if a werewolf could be this caring, I would have laughed in your face.

I tested the door handle. It opened easily and I found the keys lying on the front seat. I picked them up, weighed them in my hand thoughtfully, and then slid inside and started the car.

It purred to life and I couldn't help but smile. I could really use a car like this for myself when the snow was at its worst. I wondered if Jonathan would give me one if I asked.

I pulled out of the garage and hit the road going a bit too fast. It felt good to be able to drive something that could reach fifty without exploding. It was almost exhilarating, though I did miss having the wind blow through my hair, the feel of the motorcycle beneath me. A car just wasn't the same.

I hadn't gone too far when I realized my eyes were no longer burning from what the demon had done to me. I didn't know if that meant the Sight was gone or if I'd become accustomed to it. I should have turned and looked back at the Den when I'd left.

The good news was my rib seemed to have healed most of the way. It was still sore, but it wouldn't hinder me in a fight. Only a direct hit on it would cause it to flare up. I'd just have to be a little more careful is all.

I made it home and parked the car in the garage. I pulled the note from my pocket and dropped it on the seat. I closed the door and walked into the house, knowing I'd probably have to go see Ethan's demon now. I wanted the mark gone, but the thought of confronting him again so soon had me squirming.

I didn't get much more than a step into the kitchen when Ethan came tearing in from the living room.

"Where were you?" he asked, sounding frantic. He looked awful, as if he hadn't slept since I'd left.

"Out," I said, shrugging off my coat. I still had the car keys in my hand and I tossed them to Jeremy, who was standing just inside the dining room. He caught them easily. "From Jonathan," I said. "Go on out and look."

Jeremy eyed me suspiciously a moment before walking past me and out the door. I could hear his gasp even from inside.

"Kat," Ethan said, "I thought you got killed or something." There was something in his voice that told me it was more than that. I had a feeling I knew what he had really been thinking.

"I didn't," I said. "And I didn't run away either. It was a long night and I got stuck at the Luna Cult Den. I didn't mean to. If you had a phone, I would have called."

"Jeremy does."

Oh yeah. I'd forgotten about his cell. "Well, I'm here now," I said, feeling stupid. It would have been so easy to have told Jonathan to call Jeremy and tell him where I was. I'd been so upset I'd completely forgotten I'd been planning on doing just that.

Ethan ran his hands through his already mussed hair. He didn't look all that happy with me. I didn't blame him, though I was pretty sure it was less about his fear of me leaving and more to do with where I'd been.

Maybe he wasn't so buddy-buddy with the wolves after all.

I considered explaining to him that nothing had happened, that Jonathan and I were merely acquaintances—I wasn't ready to use the word *friends* just yet—but decided to do so would probably make me sound guilty. He already thought Jonathan and I had something going, and I didn't want to reinforce the idea in his head. Or in mine, for that matter.

"I need to talk to your demon," I said, deciding to just drop the whole thing.

"Uh, is that really such a good idea?" Ethan looked worried.

"Why wouldn't it be?"

He chewed on his lip. "Well, for one, interacting with a demon can turn into an addiction. I'm starting to think you're already addicted as it is. I don't want it to get as bad for you as it is for me."

"It's not an addiction when you're marked and forced to do it," I said. "I don't really *want* to see him, but I do want to get this over with as soon as possible. Let's just do this so I can put this mess behind me."

"Kat . . ."

"Ethan," I warned, "just summon the damn thing so I can get this mark removed."

He slumped and then nodded as he headed for the stairs.

"I'll be down in a minute," I said, then went upstairs to change my clothes. I didn't want to confront the demon wearing my dirty, bloody clothes again.

I switched one set of leathers for another and then hurried downstairs to exchange my weapons for a fresh set. Jeremy had yet to come inside, so I imagined he was still drooling over his new wheels.

As soon as I had my weapons ready, I went down the stairs into Ethan's lab. The demon was already seated and waiting.

My eyes burned from the heat, forcing me to squint at him. He looked the same as always, so I assumed the Sight was truly gone. What a shame. I kind of wished it would have been permanent. It really could have come in handy.

"Well?" He smiled knowingly. "How did it go?"

"He's an angel," I said. Ethan choked on his own spit over by the workbench.

"Of a sort," the demon said.

"What's that supposed to mean?"

"It means he may appear that way to you, but there is nothing angelic about him. Angels and demons, we are from the same plane and are more alike than different."

I might have argued that point before, but after having Levi's power nearly crush me, I had a feeling the demon might be right.

"Okay, so how do I kill him?"

Beligral laughed. "Kill him? You cannot."

"I'm not going to sit around and let him continue to torture those people. Tell me how to get rid of him."

"That is entirely different than killing," the demon said. "I may be able to help you there . . . for a price."

Ethan made a disparaging sound.

I ignored him. I couldn't let Levi hurt Sienna any more than he already had.

"What do you want?"

Beligral took a deep breath and made a show of stretching his legs. "For the information I possess, all I require is for you to promise to return."

"Done."

"And . . ." he said with a smile. "I would like you to listen to an offer I have for you. I may have something you want more than anything. There is a chance I could provide it for you if you are willing to accept the cost."

I hesitated. There had to be a catch in his little offer somewhere.

"What offer?" I asked warily.

The demon waved his hand. "I will get to that the next time we talk. No sense discussing it now. It wouldn't do to tell you. The curiosity should be enough to bring you back without me having to remind you." He smiled.

I glanced at Ethan. He didn't even bother shaking his head this time. He gave me a pleading look, though it appeared his heart wasn't in it. He knew I was going to do this whether he wanted me to or not.

I knew I should have taken his silent advice. It would have been the smart thing to do. While it might take time, I was sure I'd find a way to stop Levi.

But time was something I was sure I didn't have. How long before Levi hurt someone else? How long could I let him continue without trying to stop him?

"Fine," I said. "Tell me how to get rid of him."

Beligral smiled and pain shot through my head, right behind my ear. My hand went up reflexively and I felt the skin raise where the new mark replaced the old.

"Di'leviathan *is* an angel," he said as soon as the pain subsided. "But he isn't an angel your religious types would recognize these days. He was never a crusader for good. He was born in my realm, and there he should have stayed."

"That's fine," I said. "I don't care what he is or where he came from. I just want to get rid of him."

"But it is because of what he is and where he came from that you should already know how to be rid of him. It should be obvious."

I frowned. "What do you mean?"

Beligral gave a frustrated sigh. "And here I thought you were observant."

I refrained from comment and waited impatiently for him to go on.

"He is like me," the demon said, rolling his eyes as if my stubborn silence annoyed him. "He cannot come and go as he pleases. He is not of this world and unless freed, he would not be able to stay."

"So someone has freed him."

"I did not say that." Beligral shook his head. "If he had been freed, he would not be where he is today. Think of that town as his circle. He is trapped there, unable to leave, though his influence can reach those outside his prison."

"But I've been there," I said. "If it is his circle, then wouldn't my arrival have broken it?"

"Don't think of it as a real circle." He sighed. "Delai is not a real place, so, therefore, the circle likewise is not real."

"It sure as hell felt real to me."

"It would," the demon said. "But before you went there for the first time, had you ever heard of the place, ever seen it on a map?" He spread his hands. "*All roads lead to Delai.* It is more than just a saying to those of us who know of it."

The heat surged as Beligral spoke. Sweat dampened my entire body.

"So he was summoned, then? How do I send him back to wherever he belongs?"

"If you find the summoner, you find the means of removing him. It is unlikely the summoner can send him back, so you must kill them instead. Di'leviathan will no longer have an anchor to keep his reality intact. It should collapse."

"And what of the people inside?"

Beligral shrugged. "It depends on how much of a hold he has on them. It may kill them all. They could be sucked into the nether, torn to shreds. Or they may end up completely unharmed but for the damage Di'leviathan already has done. I do not know."

I tried to think. Who could possibly have summoned the angel? No one I'd seen in Delai seemed the type.

"But you will have a problem," Beligral said before I could think it through.

I forced myself to look at him. He looked gravely serious. His insidious smile was gone, as was any hint that he was enjoying himself.

"Okay," I said. "What's the problem?"

"You won't be able to go back there."

"Watch me."

Beligral shook his head sadly. "If it was as simple as walking down the road, many others would have stumbled upon it. Tell me, how many travelers have you ever seen within the town? One? Two? Or were you the only outsider?"

I frowned. I'd noticed before how it always seemed like no one new ever came to town. As far as I knew, I was the last person to pay Delai a visit. After a few months among them, I'd started to recognize most of the faces. I couldn't name a single time when I'd seen someone new.

"All roads may lead to Delai, but it is the person's will to change that gets them there. You no longer wish his help and he no longer wishes to have you. Di'leviathan will not allow you entrance."

"I know where the road is. He can't keep me out."

Beligral gave me a patronizing smile. "The road was there because you expected it to be. If you had wanted, the road could have materialized at the end of your driveway or in your backyard. As long as you believed it would be there, it was."

"That doesn't make sense."

"It doesn't have to. It is a magical place, created and maintained by the will of an angel. Do you really think your worldly rules apply?"

I refused to believe him. I couldn't afford to. If what he said was true, then there was no way I could save Sienna.

"I'm leaving," I said. "And when I come back, Levi will be gone." I refused to use the name the demon kept calling him by.

"You can try," Beligral said with a shrug. "But let me say in advance that I told you so."

I turned and stormed out of the lab, irritated beyond belief. The demon was trying to stop me for some reason. Was he afraid that if I confronted Levi, I would learn something important about dealing with his type? Was he afraid if I managed to get rid of the angel, I'd figure out how to get rid of him as well?

It didn't matter. I was going to Delai. Levi needed to be stopped.

I didn't wait for Ethan to dismiss the demon. He knew where I was going and knew I wouldn't wait to take action.

Jeremy was sitting in the living room and I asked him for his keys. He reluctantly gave them up and watched me with a forlorn expression as I headed for the garage.

Nothing was going to stop me. Tonight I was going to send an angel back to the hell that spawned it.

28

The car idled as I stared at the empty space where the sign should have been. I just couldn't wrap my head around the idea that the road was gone.

But it was. I was staring right at the spot where I knew it to be, and yet there was nothing. There was no sign, no road, nothing.

Beligral had been right. I was never going to be allowed back in.

I refused to believe it. An entire town just didn't just up and vanish, whether it was real or not. I no longer had the Sight, so there was always a chance Levi had disguised the road, hid it underneath a glamour. All I had to do was head toward town and I'd surely find my way there. It only made sense.

I shut off the engine and started walking. Miles of empty land stretched ahead. There were hardly any trees. Delai had sat in what was once an old strip-mining location. Snow covered the tough grass beneath. No one would ever want to live out here.

"Sienna?" I called, hoping she might be able to hear me. There was no answer.

"Levi!"

A deer startled from some brush and ran off toward the distant trees. Nothing else moved.

I'm not sure how long I walked, searching for any hint that the town was still there. I knew it was gone, knew I was wasting my time, yet I kept looking, growing more and more frustrated with every step. By the time I gave up and was heading back to the car, I was in a full-blown rage, shivering from both the cold and my anger.

How could Levi have done this to me? How could Delai *not* be there? I didn't want to believe the demon had been telling the truth, yet here I was, looking at a dead landscape that had never held a sleepy little town where the monsters were kept at bay.

I threw myself back into Jeremy's new car and slammed the door so hard the entire car rocked to the side. I had no idea what I was going to do. I could try to force Beligral to tell me how to get back, but deep down, I knew the demon could not help me.

Then what the fuck was I going to do?

I started driving. I had nowhere to go, no place I could run to. The town I'd grown to love was gone. All I'd wanted to do was be done with Baset and Beligral before heading back. Now I was even farther into both their grips and there wasn't a damn thing I could do about it.

I slowed, an idea creeping into my head. I didn't want to go home and face Ethan. I didn't want to go to the Den and see Jonathan, didn't want to confront Nathan about what had happened in the sitting room.

No, none of that would make me feel better. Those were problems I couldn't deal with, not in my state.

But there *was* a problem I could take care of right then.

I turned the car around and headed for a stretch of road that would lead me to a victim I knew deserved all the pain I could dish out. I might not be able to do anything about Levi and Delai just yet, but there was another I would happily dispatch in his place.

Adrian had been asking to see me. It was about time I gave him his wish.

It took a good thirty minutes before I turned onto the road that led to Count Tremaine's old mansion. After I'd helped the Cult take care of the vampire Count, Adrian had moved in, claiming the place for his own. Why I hadn't finished him off long before now, I'd never know. I should have killed him more than once already. Only Jonathan's request had kept me from doing it before.

But tonight would be different. I didn't care what Jonathan thought. I was done screwing around, letting people get away with things I would have killed others for. Adrian was just too damn dangerous to be allowed to live.

It wasn't going to be as satisfying as rescuing Sienna and Eilene from Levi's grasp, but it would have to do for now. I swore to myself I'd find a way to save the women and send the angel back to where he belonged. It just wasn't going to happen tonight, no matter how much I wanted it to.

The old ballpark came into view and I drove Jeremy's car off the road to park behind the backstop. No one would be able to see the car from the road, which I hoped would give me more time before Adrian knew something was up. The tire tracks would be obvious, but not every driver paid close enough attention to the side of the road.

I got out of the car and quietly closed the door. There was always a chance Adrian already knew I was coming. I was dealing with an old, paranoid wolf here. He probably had eyes everywhere, not to mention the fact that he seemed to always know where I was going to be anyway.

But that didn't mean I was going to take any chances. If there was even the slightest possibility he was oblivious to my arrival, then I would take it.

I kept low to the ground as I crossed the road and melted into darkness cast by the snow-covered trees. Within minutes, I was leaning against a familiar old oak, looking down on Adrian's mansion.

It looked the same as it always had, minus the vampire lackeys everywhere. The pond in the front yard looked well cared for, but frozen. Soft lights illuminated the ice, causing it to glow appealingly in the night.

Lights were on outside of the house, creating no real shadows to hide in. There were a few lights on inside, though it wouldn't matter if the place was completely dark either. I was pretty sure every member of Adrian's House was probably a werewolf by now. He'd taken on former Luna Cult members who didn't approve of Jonathan's refusal to turn them into the monsters they worshipped, so he'd done it himself, earning quite the following.

Adrian had no qualms about turning those loyal to him. He probably thought of it as a reward. He was building a werewolf army right under my nose. He needed to be stopped.

I scanned the grounds, searching for any indication that someone was watching. The snow in the back looked undisturbed, and a few old tire tracks in the driveway said that someone had either left or returned a while ago.

I thought furiously. I needed to find a way in. I had a feeling sneaking in through the laundry room window wouldn't work this time around. It was winter, for one, so the windows wouldn't be open this time. Breaking in would only alert the wolves I was coming.

There was really only one way I could do this. Adrian wanted me alive. He wouldn't let his wolves kill me. I didn't need to sneak in at all.

I stepped away from the trees and drew my Glock and sword. The katana shone in the moonlight sifting through the clouds. There was a light snow coming down, but not enough to impede my vision in the slightest.

I started walking toward the mansion.

I strode tall and proud, ready to fire the moment anyone poked their head out. I knew I was wading into the lion's den. Adrian might not want me dead, but that didn't mean he wouldn't hurt me. I just had to be faster than his wolves, catch them off guard and it would be over with even before it started.

I reached the side of the mansion and worked my way around the front. There were a few cars in the driveway, but they were all covered with snow. Tracks leading away from the house told me some of his wolves had shifted and probably gone out for a hunt. I just hoped Adrian wasn't one of them.

I didn't bother checking the front door. I kicked it in with all my might. It slammed hard against the wall and the wood splintered at the lock. I brought my gun up as I stepped inside. I swept it from side to side and checked the stairs leading up to the second floor.

Something moved to my right and I swung my aim around and fired. My bullet took the unshifted wolf in the middle of the forehead. He died before he could utter a sound. Not that he needed to. The report of my gun would be enough to alert Adrian that all was not well within his house.

I started walking, gun trained ahead of me. I held my sword at the ready, remembering how Baset's men had caught me unprepared. I would not let that happen here.

Another blur of motion sped by to my left. I fired before my eyes could even adjust. The bullet hit the door frame and someone cried out from the other side, more from surprise than from pain.

I stared at the entryway, daring whoever was there to move. There was a long stretch of silence that made me nervous. The mansion was huge. There was no telling how many wolves were hiding inside. If they came at me all at once, I was going to be in for some serious trouble.

"Lady Death." The trembling voice came from the other side of the wall, just to the left of where I'd splintered the door frame. I considered trying to shoot through it, but knew it was futile. My bullets moved too slowly for that.

I didn't recognize the voice, nor did I bother to respond. I waited, listening for the sound of anyone who thought they might sneak up on me.

"Packleader Adrian wants to see you," the wolf shouted from his hiding place. "He's waiting for you in the ballroom."

I hesitated. I didn't like the idea of one of Adrian's men behind me when I went to confront him. The wolf might be lying for all I knew and would come at me the moment my back was turned.

Three quick strides took me to the doorway and I spun with my gun up, finger on the trigger, ready to put an end to the wolf.

The room was empty. Whoever had spoken must have beat a hasty retreat through the door across the room the moment his message was delivered.

Smart man.

I turned back toward the ballroom doors. I could just see them at the end of the hall. Those doors were a symbol of the nightmare I'd suffered here at the hands of Count Tremaine. It was the place where Jonathan had learned his Denmaster was dead; it was the place where I'd been captured.

It was also the place where Count Tremaine had met his end. It would be a fitting place for Adrian's demise.

The doors were heavy and I was forced to put my gun away so I could open them. As soon as I got them open a few inches, I drew my gun and used my shoulder to open them the rest of the way.

Two wolves stood just inside, facing me. I fired two quick shots, taking each in the chest. They dropped to the ground, either dead or severely wounded. I didn't care which as long as they were out of my way.

"Please stop shooting my men." Adrian spoke from the dais at the far end of the room. There wasn't a thronelike chair like there had been when Count Tremaine had lounged here. Adrian must have had it removed, which was fine by me. He stood with his hands behind his back, frowning at me in irritation.

I immediately turned my gun on him. "Then I'll settle on shooting you."

His face was impassive as he stared down the barrel of my gun.

"If you think you can kill me with that weapon, then shoot. I will not move."

I didn't need him to ask twice. I fired three times in rapid succession. Adrian held true to his word and didn't even flinch as the bullets bounced away, mere inches from hitting him.

"Fuck," I growled. I looked around, searching for whatever or whoever had stopped the bullets, but we were alone in the ballroom.

"I would just stay there if I were you," Adrian said. "There really does not need to be more bloodshed."

"Tough shit," I said, taking a step forward. While the gun might not work, the sword sure as hell would. I just needed to get close to him. "Nice trick," I said in the hopes of distracting him. "How'd you manage it?"

Adrian didn't smile, didn't show any reaction at all. He pretty much ignored my question, choosing to lead the conversation himself.

"I've been asking for you to meet with me for a long time now. And when you finally do arrive, you come in shooting my wolves without provocation. That isn't very polite."

"No one ever said I was polite." I glanced behind me to check to make sure no one was trying to get the drop on me. The hall was still empty. "And I don't call having your wolves try to forcefully haul me off as asking," I said, turning back to him.

He shrugged, indifferent as always. "They did what they thought they had to do. You do not cooperate as often as I would like."

He glanced to the side toward where the rings had once been. The wall was still pockmarked from where the werewolves had broken free on the night of the full moon.

As soon as his eyes left mine, I raised my gun and fired once at his head. The bullet bounced harmlessly away.

This time he did flinch. His eyes flashed in anger as he turned back to me.

I shrugged. "Had to try."

The anger vanished as if he'd pulled a shutter down over his emotions. "I have a proposal for you," he said, his voice flat.

"Not this again," I growled. "Haven't we gone over this before? Don't you ever give up?"

"No," he said simply.

"Well, neither do I." I took a step toward him.

"I don't want to have to force you into anything, but I will. I would much rather you make the decision on your own."

"Come down off there and try to force me," I said, grip tightening on both my weapons.

Adrian laughed. It was a horrible thing to watch. The sound was void of humor, seemed to fall dead from his lips like he was only going through the motions of laughter. His face remained entirely impassive. It was like trying to watch some sort of machine feign emotion. It was downright creepy.

"Fine," I said. "I'll just come up there."

I made it all of two steps before there was a click from

the dais under Adrian's feet. I had a moment to think, *Oh shit,* and the front of the dais dropped, revealing a line of what looked vaguely like small cannons. Before I could even think to move, they fired.

I fully expected to be hit by some sort of projectile, but instead, a silver-white dust sprayed out, hitting me in the face. It coated my body, filled my nose and mouth, burned my eyes.

Everything seized. I fell to the floor almost instantly, eyes burning, lungs locked. My grip on my weapons loosened and they clattered away as my hands spasmed.

"Silver dust," Adrian said from the dais. He jumped down and started walking my way. "You gave me the idea, though I find the stuff utterly intolerable."

Rough hands lifted me easily from the floor. My eyelids were squeezed shut from all the silver dust I'd gotten into them, but I didn't need to see to know it was Adrian who had picked me up.

He carried me out of the ballroom. I tried to fight the paralysis, tried to squirm out of his grip, but it was no use. I was completely at his mercy.

It wasn't until he descended the stairs and opened a door that I knew where he was taking me. I tried to scream, tried to fight, but I couldn't so much as twitch a finger.

We descended into the basement, down to the cells where my life had nearly ended almost a year ago.

29

A bulb flickered above me, sending out erratic bursts of light that seemed to match the small twitches in my head as the silver worked its way through my system. Chains held me down despite the fact I couldn't have moved even if I tried. The table under me was cold, hard.

A thick metal band held my head in place. I could just make out the cells out of the corner of my eye. I was outside them, which would have been a relief if I hadn't been strapped to a table with a crazy werewolf somewhere out of sight.

I was just happy I could open my eyes. I'd blacked out for a few moments when he'd carried me to the basement, the overload of silver sending my brain on a short vacation. I came to already strapped to the table, feeling dreadfully alone.

I took a deep breath, closed my eyes, and tried to settle my nerves. Getting worked up would do me no good. I needed to take stock of my surroundings, see exactly what kind of situation I was in, before I could come up with an escape plan.

Opening my eyes, I focused on the light. It was a bare bulb hanging from the ceiling. A dangling cord hung right above my face, though I'd never be able to reach it lying down. I looked to my right, using only my eyes, and I could see the cell bars. They all appeared to be empty. By the smell, Adrian hadn't cleaned them out, but at least he didn't have anyone down here.

My gaze shifted to the cells to my left. There were a few bars missing to one of the cells, and it took me a moment to realize it was my old prison. Adrian had removed some of the silver bars. I was assuming that was where he got the silver dust.

"Everything will be fine." Adrian's voice came from somewhere deeper in the basement. A chair creaked as he stood, and I could hear his heavy tread as he moved. There was a clink of glass on glass and then the slosh of a liquid.

Try as I might, I couldn't see him. I couldn't move my head at all, meaning as long as he stayed where he was, I would have no idea what he was doing. All I knew for sure was that whatever he was planning couldn't be good.

I listened, but Adrian's movements were the only sounds I could make out. If there were any other wolves down here, they were being awfully quiet. It was more than likely we were alone together.

A shudder ran through me and I closed my eyes. They still burned from the silver dust, probably would until I washed them out with water. I still had some of it in my nose and I wished I could just sneeze it out. If the stuff stayed there, it would take days, if not weeks, before I would be able to move properly.

Another clink of a glass brought my eyes open. I strained to see what Adrian was doing, but it was impossible. The fact that I couldn't see him just about drove me crazy. I whimpered, a sound barely audible in my paralyzed state.

This was a man, a beast, who had wanted me to become his mate. I was now completely under his power, unable to move a single muscle to stop him if he decided to take advantage of the situation. There was nothing I could do. I was trapped. He could take his time with me, do whatever he pleased, and I would feel every damn second of it without being able to do anything but watch it happen.

Bile rose in my throat and I frantically swallowed it back. It didn't want to go and I nearly choked on it. I managed a weak cough and some of it bubbled into my mouth before slipping back down my throat.

"You don't need to get so worked up," Adrian said. "Everything will be fine."

The sound of his voice made me want to scream. I fought against myself, tried to get my muscles to cooperate. A finger twitched, but that was all.

"Things could have been easier for you." He sounded completely indifferent, as if he didn't care how he got me, as long as he did. "You could have come to me, arms open, and I would have taken you in. We could have done much together."

I groaned something that was supposed to be a curse.

"But these things take time. I understand why you cannot bring yourself to trust me yet. Your mind has been tainted by others, turned against me before we could be properly introduced."

Another clink was followed by a heavy sigh. What was he doing back there?

I became aware that my coat was missing. He'd taken my shoulder holster and belt off as well. He probably had them back there with him, if he wasn't wearing them. If I made a move, he could easily stab me with one of my own weapons to put me down again. I was defenseless.

I thought frantically. Adrian wanted something from me, so it was unlikely he would kill me. He might rape me, might torture me, but he wouldn't kill me.

I wasn't sure if that was such a good thing. If he were to touch me like that, I would want to die. I couldn't live with myself. If he didn't kill me when it was over, then I'd be sure to find a way to do it myself.

"All those things were in my past. They are but mere memories of a life I once had. Nothing I've done has been harmful to you. I'm sure you see that by now."

I wasn't so sure where he'd gotten that idea, but I was in no position to argue. I tried to move my finger again in the hopes of gaining some strength by it. Nothing happened.

"I really did try to let you come to me on your own. I hoped you would see past the lies and would realize how much I could benefit you." He sighed again, which was a lot more emotion than I usually heard out of him. "I may not like how this will be done, but I *will* get what I want."

My blood ran cold. I knew right then and there he wasn't going to kill me. There was absolutely no doubt about it. He already thought of me as some sort of prize. He would take me however he wanted and what could I do about it?

But my clothes were still on. If he was so intent on making me his mate, he would have stripped me down before strapping me to the table. He could have already taken what he thought was his, but he hadn't.

I held on to that slim shred of hope, prayed I would find a way out of this before things went too far. Just because he hadn't torn my clothes off yet, didn't mean he wasn't planning to do so later.

"I want much from you. Some, I will take by force. Others, I will let you come to me. I still need a mate, but I will not stoop so low as to force myself upon you. You will come to me eventually. There is no doubt in my mind that we will reach that point. For now, I must be content with having your loyalty."

I started to breathe a sigh of relief, but Adrian walked into view carrying a syringe and the breath caught in my throat. He waved the syringe into my field of vision before setting it aside.

I went into full-fledged panic mode. I didn't have to see it to know what was inside the syringe. I'd thought back to when we'd captured The Left Hand woman months ago that Adrian might have taken some of her things for his own use.

Now I knew for sure. He already had me paralyzed, but now he was going to inject me with something that would keep me completely at his mercy.

But that didn't make sense. Why would he need it since I was already as immobile as I was going to get?

My mind flickered to the serrated blade the woman had been about to use to cut my throat and I whimpered. He could cut me and bleed me out if he so desired. Was it some sort of threat? Was he going to make me pledge my loyalty to him or he would kill me?

"I've learned much while you've been missing," he said. "There are things I never knew were possible until recently."

I managed to clench my jaw. My tongue moved slightly in my mouth. If I wasn't careful, I could block off my airway and start choking on my own spit. My mouth was dry now, but it wouldn't stay that way forever.

"I've always assumed I would have to convince you that I'm the greater good. I had no idea how I would go about it because you are, let's admit it, quite stubborn."

I blew out my nose, hoping to dislodge some of the silver dust. It tickled and I fought the urge to sneeze. I needed to get out of here but had no idea how I would ever manage it.

"But that won't be necessary anymore. I do wish for you to trust me, and I will do what it takes to make sure that happens. I won't give up on you. You will eventually be mine and we will rule this House, will tear down the vampire empire one Count at a time."

I struggled harder against the silver keeping me down. My brother had overcome the effects of silver a lot quicker than he should have the day he died. I didn't know if the demon had anything to do with it and I didn't care. I had to break free of my paralysis. If I didn't, I knew something terrible was going to happen.

I kept seeing the syringe in my mind's eye. My heart was hammering in my chest, my head pounded. Adrian had set the thing down near me. I couldn't see a table or anything nearby, so it was likely he placed it on the table with me. If I could just move my arm, get just enough of a grip on it so I could stab him with it, I had a chance.

But no matter how hard I fought, I just couldn't get my body to obey. A twitch of a finger was hardly enough to get excited about.

"I cannot do what I wish alone," Adrian went on, oblivious to my futile attempts at movement. "Even just the two of us would struggle. I needed another, and who better to recruit than the man who told me how to accomplish what I wished?"

As if on cue, the basement door opened. Light footsteps warned me that someone else was coming down the stairs. The stride was weak, faulting, as if they were having a hard time walking.

I wracked my brain, tried to figure out who Adrian could possibly mean. His men had been in Mephisto's territory. Had he somehow managed to ally himself with the Count?

"Lady Death." A face peered down at me and a groan escaped my lips. His face was thin, almost to the point of emaciation. It was a skull, eyes sunken deep, skin pulled tight, straggly, dirty hair hung in his face.

No, it wasn't Mephisto or Baset or any other vampire Count.

It was Davin.

He smiled at me, exposing his missing incisors. He poked his tongue through one of the holes and waggled it at me.

"The Oath is a strange thing," Adrian said. He moved beside me, but I couldn't stop staring at Davin. The vampire looked healthier than the last time I had seen him, but that wasn't saying much. He still looked like shit, and there seemed to be a madness to his eye that hadn't been there before.

Davin glanced up at Adrian and then moved away. It was then that what Adrian had said hit me.

The Oath—the magic bond between vampire and werewolf. It only worked one way and one way only. A vamp could bind a wolf, but that was all.

Had Adrian sworn the Oath to Davin for some reason? I remembered how he had told me he would swear to me, though I'd never even considered taking him up on the offer. It would have helped keep him from directly harming me, but it wasn't as strong as some vamp Counts thought. Just ask Count Tremaine how the Oath had turned out for him.

I tried to remember if a wolf could be sworn to more than one vampire. As far as I knew, it wasn't possible. It didn't make sense for him to swear to Davin, especially if he still had his sights set on me.

My entire left leg twitched. A surge of hope ran through me, but it died quickly as Adrian spoke.

"I see you are regaining control," he said. He lifted the syringe and held it up to where I could see it. "It is marvelous stuff, but like your silver dust, I do not like to use it. If I knew I could trust you not to fight, I wouldn't bother, but we both know that is unlikely. I cannot have you thrashing about during the ritual."

My heart just about stopped. What ritual?

"There is no need for you to worry," he said. "I want you to trust me, and for that to happen, I must prove to you I deserve that trust. I will do nothing to harm you in any way."

I growled at him. I thought I caught a flicker of a smile flash across Adrian's face, but it was gone in an instant, if it was ever there at all.

"If you do not believe me when we are through, I invite you to return and test it. I assure you, Davin has tested this himself, and he is quite incapable of harming me."

My mind raced. What was he talking about?

"The Oath," he said, as if reading my mind. "We've always been told it works only one way, that a were can only be bound to his vampire master, forcing us to be servants to those who would abuse us."

Davin took over, leaning over me with that mad grin on his face. "For a long time it might have been true," he said. "But there is a reason I was so valuable to the Counts who took me in. I know things, can discover much that others thought impossible."

He cackled. Saliva dripped from between his teeth and he sucked it back with relish. "The Oath can be changed. I can force the binding the other way and it is so very easy." His eyes flashed in delight. "Many have tried before, but they didn't have my spark. No one else can do this, of that I can assure you."

My stomach dropped. I wanted to shake my head in denial, but I was trapped there, forced to look up into Davin's sickly face. He might be a madman, but he was still smart in his own way.

And that made him dangerous.

I knew it was impossible, but listening to the certainty in both men's voices, I was afraid I was wrong. The Oath was supposed to work only one way. Not even Davin could change the laws of magic.

Could he?

"You will not be able to harm me," Adrian said. He

sounded satisfied, which frightened me more. There usually was never any emotion in his voice.

"And while you might be able to make my life hell, you won't. If you go after my weres, after Davin, I will be forced to bring in those you care about. If you leave me and mine alone, I will let Jonathan and the Luna Cult live. I will not add them to my ranks. I will not go after your other friends."

I couldn't help but think that this was where having friends got me. Everyone was using Jonathan against me, whether we were friends or not.

A tear slid from the corner of my eye. I managed a strangled, "Fuck you," but it took all the effort I had to squeeze that little bit out.

Adrian's voice didn't change in the slightest as he continued. "As much as I would love to take that as an offer, I will not. You will eventually come to see things my way and the prospect will not be so . . . sickening for you. I will wait for that day."

He took a deep breath and looked through the glass of the syringe. "This will not only keep you down throughout the process, but it will knock you out. I cannot risk having you find a way to interrupt the ritual. I regret having to do this, but it is necessary for both our sakes."

The syringe dropped below eye level and I felt a pinch in my arm. Heat swarmed through my body, leaving me breathless.

"Thankfully, I do not need you awake for this," Adrian said. "Swearing the Oath is a magic process, involving blood, as you well know. No words are needed, though they are often spoken." He rested a hand on my cheek. It was rough and calloused. "I will speak them for you."

I tried to jerk away from his touch, but even the thought made me tired. Black dots swam in and out of my vision, and my stomach flipped a few times.

"When you wake, we will be bound." He leaned close, whispered in my ear. "And you will discover I have given you another gift, one so valuable you will know how much I desire you." His lips brushed my earlobe.

I screamed inside, thrashed in my mental cage. My lips barely moved; no sound was uttered from my throat.

The light flickered above me, once, twice, and on the third, my consciousness flared out, leaving me easy prey to the monsters all around me.

30

Pain brought me screaming awake. My hand immediately went to my throat. I could feel the slice of the blade as it bit into my skin, could almost hear the mad laughter of the woman as she left me to bleed out.

My fingers were wet, but not from blood. The pain wasn't coming from my throat at all.

I reached down and felt the hilt of a knife sticking out of my thigh. I groaned as I grasped it and yanked hard. It came free with some difficulty, and it was all I could do to keep from screaming again. Blood oozed down my leg, onto the soft snow beneath me.

I started shivering, confused. Where the hell was I?

I looked around, trying to get my bearings. There were trees all around me, familiar trees. It took only a quick glance to realize I was in the woods near my house.

It hurt to swallow as I took that in. Adrian had brought me most of the way home. That meant he had to know where I lived. After all this time thinking I was being careful, he'd discovered where I lived. That meant not only does the Cult know, but now Adrian and most likely Baset, if she was to be believed.

A weight at my chest told me my shoulder holster was back in place. I checked the gun and found it to be still loaded. I hadn't counted my shots from earlier, so I wasn't sure if all the bullets were there or if Adrian had taken some for himself. My belt was back around my waist and my coat lay on the ground. I'd been using it as a pillow.

I stood and shook my coat off before throwing it over my shoulders. My leg throbbed and my head swam, forcing me to lean up against a tree for a few seconds before I could start walking. There was blood on the ground from where I'd bled, but it wasn't much. I couldn't have been there long.

I turned the knife over in my hand and it finally sank in what I was holding. I stared at it incomprehensively for a moment, unsure I was willing to believe what I saw.

The blade had my blood on it, but I could still see the silver beneath.

And it had been in my leg.

And you will discover I have given you another gift . . .

I dropped the knife as if it had burned me. I checked my belt and sure enough, one of my knives was missing.

This couldn't be right. Adrian and his wolves were immune to silver. He wouldn't have given that to me.

Or would he?

I drew my other knife and looked it over. It was definitely mine, not some fake. I drew it down my palm, cutting deep into the flesh.

It hurt like hell, but I didn't collapse from silver poisoning.

I was immune.

I didn't know how long I stood there, just staring at the blood oozing from the cut. I couldn't believe what I was seeing. I knew the knife was mine, knew it was pure demon-forged silver. There was no doubt in my mind that he hadn't exchanged my weapons.

"Holy shit," I said. Out of all the things I expected from him, this was the least likely. He'd just made me immune to silver. While that might not help in my everyday hunts, it would help me against those vamps who didn't care about their own laws and used the illegal metal, not to mention those that would use my own weapons against me.

I sheathed my knife and picked up the one I had dropped. My blood still stained the blade, so I wiped it clean in the snow before sheathing it.

Numbly, I started walking. I trudged up the hill, using the trees for support. Each step hurt. I was still weak from the injection, and my head felt like someone had hit it with a hammer a few thousand times.

But I was alive. Adrian had kept his word in that regard. I could vaguely feel him behind me even now, miles and miles away. We were bound. I knew it without having to test it. I was sworn to him, and there wasn't a damn thing I could do about it.

I sagged against a tree as the realization set in. I was bound to Adrian. The Oath had worked without me being conscious for it.

But that wasn't the worst of it. I was sure I would find a way out of the Oath eventually. I just needed to find a way for Adrian to die without me being the one to shoot him.

I couldn't use Jonathan. If I told him what Adrian had done, he would surely go after him, he and Nathan both. And what then? It was unlikely the few wolves Jonathan had at his disposal would be enough to overcome Adrian and his weres.

I groaned. Now I wasn't just bound to Baset, but Adrian as well. My life wasn't my own anymore. They each had control over a part of me, had me in a situation where I was powerless against them.

I started walking again. I was leaving a trail of blood on the snow from the wound on my leg. Tearing out the knife had reopened the gash. It wouldn't be hard for someone to follow the trail to the house.

But it really wouldn't matter. If they didn't follow the blood, they could follow my footprints. There was nothing I could do about it if someone was tailing me.

I sighed and kept plowing ahead, just wanting to be home. Ethan would be there, would try to make things better. I needed to assure him I was staying for good this time, that I wasn't going to run off without him ever again.

Of course, thinking of Ethan made me think of his demon—another monster I was bound to. Hell, I was in so deep now, I might as well go all in and see if he could help me with the vamps and wolves trying to take control of my life.

It looked like all the lights in the house were on as I broke into the clearing. Without the trees for support, I nearly fell twice on my way to the back door. I could hardly breathe, but I don't think it had anything to do with my injuries.

I nearly broke down before I made it inside. I collapsed against the glass door and ran my finger down the fingerprint reader, my entire body quivering from both the cold pelting me from the outside and the cold growing from within.

Before I could get the door open, Jeremy opened it from the inside. I fell into him, tears streaming down my face.

He just managed to catch me, using his one good arm to keep me propped up. Someone else closed the door behind us as he led me into the living room.

"She's home," he said as he dumped me onto the couch. I think he tried to be careful, but with only one arm, lowering someone down who was in no condition to help had to be awkward.

"Kat." The voice seemed to come from a long way off.

It took me a moment to realize it wasn't Jeremy or Ethan. "Are you okay?"

I started to nod but shook my head instead. "I don't know," I said. My throat hurt and I winced with every word.

Jonathan was sitting on the edge of the couch. He brushed the hair out of my face. "Water," he said.

Jeremy bolted from the room, and a moment later the faucet started up in the kitchen.

I took a shuddering breath and buried my face in my hands. What was I going to do? All my enemies weren't trying to kill me anymore, they were trying to take me under their control, to force me to do their bidding. They threatened my friends if I didn't comply. How was I to deal with that and not blame myself?

Give me personal threats any day. I could handle those. But when you started bringing those I cared about into the equation, things got complicated.

I hated complicated.

Jeremy returned with the water and pressed the glass into my hand. I drank it down, eyes watering as it burned its way down my throat. He took the glass as soon as I was done.

"Where's Ethan?" I asked, looking around. Jeremy and Jonathan were the only ones in the room.

"Downstairs," Jonathan said. "Nathan is with him."

Momentary panic caused me to rise, but Jonathan pushed me gently back down. "They are in front of the fire, keeping warm. We didn't want to crowd you." He glanced down. "Are you hurt?" He touched my leg.

I hissed in pain and jerked back. "I'm fine," I said. "It'll heal."

Jonathan nodded and just sat there, letting me collect my thoughts.

It wasn't an easy task. I kept thinking of Adrian, of the Oath. Then Baset would cross my mind, quickly followed by Levi and Beligral. My life had become a mess in such a short amount of time.

"Ethan received a message," Jonathan said after a little while.

I looked at him. Concern was written all over his face. "What message?"

"He didn't know what to think about it, so he had Jeremy call me. It's why we are here."

My mouth went dry again as Jonathan handed me a slip of paper. I took it from him with a trembling hand.

You have done well. Will's death is not on your hands. We are searching for the culprit now and may have a name for you soon. We will expect to see you on the designated night.

Henri.

I stared at the flowing writing. Baset didn't blame me for her man's death, which was a relief, I supposed. But the fact that the message had reached me here meant she hadn't been bluffing when she said she knew where I lived.

"Who's Henri?" Jonathan said as I looked up from the slip of paper.

For a moment, I was confused. He'd met Henri, had heard me strike a deal with Countess Baset. How could he not know?

And then it hit me. He was protecting me. He hadn't told anyone else what had happened that day. Jeremy didn't know I'd promised to be Baset's assassin. Nathan might not even know. Jonathan was giving me a chance to explain myself in front of Jeremy, allowing me to decide what to tell him.

"Someone I once knew," I said. "It's no longer a problem." I bared my teeth in what I hoped to be a deadly smile.

Jonathan touched my hand and squeezed. I flinched back and forced myself off the couch. I couldn't stand the thought of someone touching me.

"I need to shower," I said. "Tell Nathan everything's okay and he can go. I don't need him here."

Jonathan nodded.

I limped toward the stairs but stopped halfway there. I glanced back to Jeremy. "I'll get your car tomorrow," I said. "I had to leave it behind." I didn't want him going out in search of it. I really didn't want anyone knowing where I'd been. That would lead to questions, questions I didn't want to answer.

Without waiting for a reply, I headed for my bedroom. I didn't like lying to him, not after how much the young wolf had tried to help me, but I felt I had no choice. To get him involved with my troubles would only cause him more pain. One lost arm was enough.

I paused just inside the bedroom. A plasma television hung from the wall, facing my bed. The remote sat on my nightstand. There was a big red bow wrapped around the TV and a smaller one on the remote.

I burst into tears, closing the door quickly so no one would hear me. I wasn't sure if I was happy or miserable. I think I was a little of both.

I stripped and went to the bathroom to run a shower, blinded by my tears. It would be a long time before I would be able to look into Ethan's face without feeling guilty. He was always so good to me and I'd run from him, left him behind.

I hated myself. I stepped into the shower and let the hot water scour me. The chill from the snow was gone, but the ice in my gut remained. No amount of heat would ever make it thaw. I just hoped it would get better with time.

It didn't.

I struggled through the next few days, unsure whether

or not some disaster would come knocking on my door. I kept expecting to hear that someone I knew had died, or would open the front door to find Adrian or Countess Baset standing there.

I stayed home, afraid that if I left, I'd cause something to happen. I didn't even have to leave to get Jeremy's car. Jonathan found it parked just outside Luna Cult territory. None of the cameras caught who had left it there. Even though I knew it had to have been Adrian or one of his wolves, I didn't tell anyone else. They could keep wondering for all I cared.

Jonathan stopped by once during the week but didn't stay long. I wasn't in much of a mood to talk to him, or to anyone else for that matter. Ethan was concerned but did well to keep to himself.

As the weekend neared its end, I found myself nearly bouncing from the walls in agitation. I spent that Sunday night staring at the wall of my bedroom, dreading the following evening.

I didn't tell anyone where I was going when Monday finally rolled around. I left at first dark, slipping out before Jeremy or Ethan had even roused themselves.

A thaw had melted most of the snow, so I was able to ride my Honda out to the abandoned building where I was to meet Baset's man. I circled the block twice before deciding it seemed safe enough, though I wouldn't know until I actually went inside.

I parked out front, but before I could make it to the door, Henri stepped out from the alleyway.

He didn't say anything. He simply walked over to me, handed me an envelope, and turned and walked away. There was enough cash there to keep me funded for quite a long time.

I breathed easier as I mounted my Honda and put distance between me and the vampire. There was no name with the money and quite frankly, I was surprised he had even paid me. I was assuming The Left Hand had stolen the last payment and that Baset wouldn't be willing to pay me again.

Still, the money sat heavy in my coat. It would help make sure there was food in the house and that Mikael would get paid for his information, yet I really didn't want it. It was blood money. There was no way around it. I'd killed someone for the cash, and even though the vamp deserved it, I still didn't like it.

On the way home, I drove past the empty landscape where the road to Delai had once been. I idled there and watched the horizon, hoping to catch some glimpse of a fire, of a light that would let me know that someone was there.

After a while I gave up. I had a feeling that no matter how many times I drove by, the road would never be there again. Delai was lost to me, and there wasn't a damn thing I could do about it.

The rest of the ride home was filled with bitterness. I had half a mind to turn around and storm Adrian's mansion again, just to see what would happen. Just because the Oath prevented me from hurting the big wolf himself, it didn't stop me from hurting his underlings.

But then I would put my friends at risk. I wasn't sure how quickly Adrian would act on his promise to retaliate, though I was pretty sure the bastard would eventually get around to it. He had me right where he wanted me.

At least for now. I would find a way out from under his thumb eventually. The same went for Countess Baset. It would just take time.

While there was little I could do about Baset, Adrian, Levi, or even Count Mephisto, if he decided to inject himself into my life as well, there was one thing I'd been putting off ever since I'd returned.

Before heading home, I made a stop at a flower shop that stayed open for those of us who walked the night. I carried my purchase in through the garage and found Ethan and Jeremy sitting in the living room talking.

They glanced up at me as I entered and a flood of warmth passed over me. While I might not have wanted Jeremy to stay at first, I'd come to like the kid. He could have the spare bedroom for as long as he wanted it. I kind of hoped he decided to stay permanently. Ethan could use the company.

I took a deep breath. Out of all the things I'd tried to do over the last few weeks, this was going to be the hardest.

"Where is he?" I asked.

It only took a moment for Ethan to understand what I was talking about. He grew somber as he stood.

I followed him out the back door. He paused just outside, looked worriedly at the wide-open world, before finally walking through the backyard. He glanced over his shoulder to make sure I was following and gave me a shaky smile.

He might be terrified of the outdoors, but in important matters, he always found a way to suppress his fear. It was a strength I envied.

Jeremy followed us out. He stayed a few feet back, head down, as if he knew what was going on. Hell, he might. Who knew how much he knew of what had happened all those months ago.

We reached the edge of the woods and went in only a few feet before Ethan stopped beneath a huge pine. A stone rested on the ground a few feet away. There were no words on it, no indication that it was anything more than a large stone. I wouldn't even have noticed it if Ethan hadn't pointed it out. It looked natural there, like it had always been in that very spot.

I didn't need him to tell me that this was the place. I walked alone over to the stone and knelt to the frozen ground. My throat constricted and I almost got up, unable to do what I so desperately needed to do.

Instead, I laid in front of the stone the single red rose I'd purchased. The flower would wilt from the cold, but that was okay. Everything died eventually. It was perfect in its own way.

I pressed my hand against the stone. It was icy to the touch. The ground in front of it was still bare of grass. It hadn't had time to grow before the cold had set in.

"I'm sorry," I whispered. "I promise to do better from now on."

The wind rustled the trees above my head. It blew across my face, swept the tears away before they could freeze on my cheeks. The air breathed new life in me. It felt good on my skin. I didn't care how cold it was. I was already as cold inside as I was ever going to get.

Fresh snow started to fall. The brief respite from winter had come and gone.

I bent and kissed the stone before standing. My coat billowed out behind me as a strong gust of wind passed through the trees.

Without another word, I turned and walked back to the house, leaving Thomas's grave to be covered by the fresh falling snow.

GREAT BOOKS,
GREAT SAVINGS!
When You Visit Our Website:
www.kensingtonbooks.com
You Can Save Money Off The Retail Price
Of Any Book You Purchase!
• All Your Favorite Kensington Authors
• New Releases & Timeless Classics
• Overnight Shipping Available
• eBooks Available For Many Titles
• All Major Credit Cards Accepted
Visit Us Today To Start Saving!
www.kensingtonbooks.com